Excerpt from Chapter Six:

John's heart grieved for Willy's blindness. Compassion for Willy swept over John as he planted his face on the carpet. Soon, his gut ached so hard he couldn't breathe. Then everything went blank. John felt light as a feather. He floated toward the ceiling, and he looked down at his body, collapsed on the floor of his bedroom.
"Whoa!" John gawked at his motionless body. "I'm dead? That's not supposed to happen when you let the Holy Spirit intercede through you for a friend."
John then found himself floating fifty feet above his home with a view of the whole town as though hang gliding but frozen in time.

Journeys into Suprafuge
By D. Henry Roome

Journeys into Suprafuge Copyright © 2024 by D. Henry Roome. Except as provided by the Copyright Act no part of this publication may be reproduced, stored in a retrieval system, or transmitted in any form or by any means without the prior written permission of the publisher.

Most Scripture verses quoted or paraphrased in this story are taken from the New King James Version® (NKJV) Copyright © 1982 by Thomas Nelson. Used by permission. All rights reserved.by Thomas Nelson Publishers. A few Scriptures are quoted from the King James Version of the Bible (KJV) and one English Standard Version (ESV) verse is quoted.

This novel is a work of fiction. Presidential candidates, renowned scientists, epidemiologists, and doctors are only mentioned peripherally and are referenced to reflect the author's opinion, and statements about them do not represent statements of fact. US Representatives, Senators, and various business moguls have fictitious names to emphasize that the story is fiction and represents the author's opinion. All other names, characters, places, businesses, industries, and incidents are likewise the product of the author's imagination or used fictitiously. All the characters that participate in the plot line of the story are fictional, and any similarity between people living or dead is purely coincidental.

Acknowledgments

The Lord may have put this novel on my heart and inspired the writing, but my wife, Barbara Roome, had to suffer many lonely evenings without her husband as he hyper-focused on completing it quickly. Thank you, Sweetheart, for your loving patience these last five months and for your encouragement and wise advice as I worked on the novel.

A special thanks to Julie Hansell for her generous help in editing this novel. She went way beyond what was expected of her—fact-checking, developmental and copy editing, steering me in the right direction, and working faster than I expected.

The people in my life who have inspired my prayer life are too numerous to mention. Many of the places in the novel might feel familiar to some of my friends because the town I call Bluffview in the story has identical features to my hometown. Many features are different. Most dissimilarities were made to help the flow of the story and prevent possible offenses. I trust the similarities to my hometown made the story more enjoyable for my friends and more realistic for those who don't know me.

Suprafuge definition:

1. the power available to Christians through intercession to overrule or dismantle the schemes of men and the devil
2. the position of power obtained by sitting in heavenly places with Christ, the position of authority over events and conditions on earth (see Ephesian 2:5-6)
(Etymology) inspired by the Holy Spirit in the thoughts of D. Henry Roome and set as a contrast to the subterfuge of the evil one.

Chapter One

"Relax, Bill." John Greenberg motioned with his hands for Bill to sit in a stuffed armchair in front of his desk.

"It's an existential threat to humanity!" Bill's eyes bulged as he remained standing.

John nodded thoughtfully. Although he'd known Bill as a friend for 25 years, his anxiety had to be unbearable for him to drive five miles once a month to an Edward Jones downtown office and seek comfort from his investment advisor. His fear never had anything to do with investments. Recently, Bill's panic attacks had become weekly. Undoubtedly, the Sunday School classes John taught Bill as a youth made Bill feel comfortable laying out his anxiety.

"What does Philippians 4:6-7 say?" John used an appropriate Scripture to divert Bill's attention away from the cause of his anxiety.

"We're seconds away from a nuclear holocaust. Why are you quizzing me on Bible verses?" Bill rocked back and forth on his feet.

John calmly put his hands on Bill's shoulders. "Getting anxious about Russia nuking us won't stop the war in Ukraine."

"It's your Christian duty to warn all your clients and friends." Bill squatted and perched on the seat of the armchair in front of John's desk.

John walked behind his desk and sat on his swivel rocker. "Bill, was the sun shining this morning?"

Bill gawked at John with an open mouth.

"Today was your scheduled day for trash pickup. Did they pick your trash up?"

"Yeah. Why do you ask?"

"God takes care of you. Philippians 4:6-7. What does it say?"

Bill took a breath and exhaled sharply. "Be anxious for nothing, but in everything by prayer and supplication, with thanksgiving, let your requests be made known to God."[1]

"And the verse after that?" John beckoned Bill to respond by fanning himself with his right hand.

Bill sat back, and his eyes traced an unseen arc in the air. ". . .the peace of God, which surpasses all understanding, will guard your hearts and minds through Christ Jesus."

"Is the Lord no longer in control?"

"You always wave your hands and act upbeat. Underneath that boldness, you've gotta be worried. If we don't do anything, we're as guilty as those who don't teach their kids to respect guns, God, and human life!" Bill took a deep breath and scooted to the edge of his chair. "Then their kids shoot up their classmates."

"How can you stop the war?"

Bill slid back from the edge of the chair and wagged his head. "We can stop sending them weapons."

"How will you make our country do that?" John studied Bill's expression. He wished the Holy Spirit could zip him overseas like Philip the Evangelist was transported in Acts. Then maybe he could spook their corrupt leaders and scare them into signing a peace agreement.

Bill's shoulders slumped.

John smiled, grateful that Bill's large account had performed well and hopeful that his anxiety was winding down. "Did you want to adjust your investments?"

---

[1] Philippians 4:6-7

Bill asked, "How do you think the war will affect my investments?"

"I've been an investment advisor for almost thirty years. I've seen that the stock market suffers when uncertainty looms over the country. The booming market tells us all is relatively well in the world."

"Ha!" Bill scoffed. "Yeah, that's because arms merchants are raking in the dough. Should we be happy and prosperous with that?"

"Perhaps you would like to invest in companies that manufacture weapons?"

"What! Are you crazy?"

"No, you could show up at their stockholder meetings and give them a piece of your mind."

Bill scrunched up his nose. "No thank you."

John sensed his suggestion had the desired effect of further deflating Bill's worries. The issue with Ukraine seemed too complicated for John. Several of his clients considered the appeasement of Russia to be the sure path to World War III. For them, pulling the plug on support to Ukraine could have just the opposite effect Bill desired.

John paused a minute for Bill to suggest something. "The market hasn't changed. Shall we keep your investments where they are?"

Bill's gaze darted back and forth between John and the floor. "Humph! I suppose you're right."

John hoped Bill would give up worrying about the war for longer than the last time he visited. He barely persuaded Bill to keep most of his money invested in stocks as a better hedge against inflation than gold. Like Bill, John looked forward to an early retirement, and he figured gold wouldn't keep up with inflation.

As Bill stood to leave, he asked John about his clients who believed in sending weapons to Ukraine. He wondered whether those clients also believed in Critical Race Theory and vaccine mandates.

John shrugged. "I don't know." Inwardly, John shook his head. Even in Minnesota in a town with less than 16,000 residents, the political polarization among his clients and Christian friends baffled him. Some of them, like Bill, insisted he couldn't remain noncommittal.

John thanked Bill for coming into the office and watched him put on his winter coat and trudge out into the blustery, late autumn weather. John chuckled. Bill was an odd one.

John looked for a middle ground on most issues. Recently, he thought a good middle-ground solution for the next President would be RFK Jr. Then he discovered that friends on the extreme Right and the far Left hated that solution. They hoped everybody would ignore him because they feared Kennedy would steal votes from their candidate.

John mulled over the divisiveness of the current culture in America as he packed up his briefcase and left the office. He had quoted Bible verses to Bill. We had to do more than recite words if we hoped to stop the destructive polarization in America. Something deep inside him longed to pray effectively enough to prevent the inevitable rioting in the streets that would occur after the elections. The nation needed God to transform the hearts of Christians supernaturally, so they prayed, moved, and talked more like Jesus.

John's face and neck felt suddenly warm as he considered the numerous distractions that weakened his faith. Without faith, the Bible said, it was impossible to please God or to receive answers to prayers. John chuckled. If Christians could pass through closed doors like Jesus did after His resurrection, then we would rescue our country from moral chaos.

John's arms and hands went limp, causing him to almost drop his briefcase. He cringed at the shallowness of his Christianity. He should strengthen his faith, but that proved challenging in the day-to-day challenges of modern life.

John smiled as he drove the last block to his home. God had helped him navigate the political tides in the past, so he could continue to leave politics and politicians in God's hands. Christians were supposed to focus on their families, and he embraced that wholeheartedly.

As he parked his car next to his 1980s vintage bungalow home, John relished the thought of giving his wife and children a kiss, hug, or pat on the back. When he entered the kitchen, he came up from behind his wife, Leah, and squeezed her around her waist as she put frozen vegetables into a pan on the stove.

"How is my sweetheart?" John asked as he kissed the back of her neck.

Leah scrunched her neck. "Busy. Something has Rachael down at the mouth. See if you can figure out what's bothering her."

Our greatest ability as humans is not to change the world, but to change ourselves.

Mahatma Gandhi

Chapter Two

John walked into the living room and found his daughter on the sofa.

"Hey, Partner, why so glum?" John settled on the sofa next to his daughter Rachael. Usually when he called her *Partner*, it elicited a little smile. Today, she shrugged so slightly that it looked like her shoulders barely twitched. Whatever troubled his eleven-year-old daughter apparently deflated her normally spunky spirit.

"Want to talk about it?" John waited for a few minutes, but when she remained like a statue, he rose to leave.

"I'm available to talk when you are ready to shake off this blue funk you're in." John bent over and kissed Rachael's lilac-scented forehead. He straightened slowly, studying her face before walking toward the kitchen.

"It's not fair," Rachael said to his back as he reached the kitchen door.

John returned and sat next to his daughter.

"Jack changed his name to Jackie, and now he can play on the girls' basketball team." Rachael folded her arms across her chest and clenched her jaw.

John waited for her to unload at her own pace.

"He or *she*," Rachael said, emphasizing the feminine pronoun with obvious disgust, "could train with teams and coaches for boys his whole life. Then he comes over to the girls' team and beats me out for first-string forward. How is that right?"

John took a deep breath and patted her knee. "Whoa! That's totally unfair!"

John looked at his daughter, waiting to see if she perked up. When she remained still, he continued. "Wouldn't it be awesome if you and I practiced until you were good enough to beat Jackie out of the forward position?"

Rachael smirked with half of her mouth and continued to stare straight ahead.

"How do the rest of the girls on the team feel about Jackie?" John leaned forward and turned his head so he could see her reaction better.

"They're all mad at Jackie, too. Except for Amanda. She's thrilled that I'm not the first-string forward." Rachael frowned and refolded her arms across her chest.

"What position does Amanda play?"

"She's the other forward."

"Hey, let's practice together every evening until you're good enough to beat out Amanda. Yeah! Wouldn't that be sweet?" John nudged her arm with his elbow.

Rachael shoved his elbow away. "But Jackie stole my position. He or *she* would have made the first string on the boys' team. Now, the boy's team doesn't have the best player possible on the court, and the girl's team has a forward that nobody will pass to."

"Boy, that stinks!" John hesitated. What could he say to encourage Rachael and give her a better attitude?

"You can't blame the team, either. Jackie is a ball hog. Whenever *she* gets the ball, she bulls her way to the basket and shoots."

John reckoned Jackie had a reason for being a ball hog if nobody passed to her. He didn't have a solution for this knotty problem his daughter faced. "Wow! You've got some choices before you. You can ask your friends on the team to pass the ball to Jackie so your team does better. You can ask them to pass her the ball extra hard so she fumbles it, which makes her look bad. Or you can try out for a different position."

Rachael glared at him out of the corners of her eyes.

John thought she might want to try out for a different sport, but he nixed suggesting that. He wanted to turn this father-daughter talk into a topic of prayer. However, he figured Rachael needed a little levity to get her in the mood. "Maybe I should watch your team practice, and I could boo whenever Jackie gets the ball."

Rachael raised a troubled eyebrow at him.

"I could ask the parents of all the other girls to come and boo with me." He nudged her arm with his elbow, and she smiled briefly. "Now, wouldn't that be something? We could chant 'We want Rachael, we want Rachael,' and when your coach put you in, we'd all cheer like crazy!"

"Daa. . . aad!" Rachael complained good-naturedly at his ridiculous idea.

John suggested they pray over her problem. God didn't want her to have a bad attitude because somebody played better than her and took her position in basketball. John did most of the praying as he asked the Lord to help Rachael and her friends and to give them wisdom on what to do. Rachael prayed for God and the coach to do the right thing.

After praying with Rachael, John headed to the kitchen to ask Leah if she knew anything about Rachael's controversy. On top of all the polarization in politics, he had to help his children deal with the confusion surrounding the transgender issue. While he always sought a balanced and compassionate stance, gender fluidity made little sense to him. He figured transgender ideology defied logic because it had no basis in scientific fact and lay outside the domain of empirical evidence. The trans activist had a peculiar faith in what it meant to be male or female. They also believed those distinctions might not even exist at all but in some personalized conception. As odd or contradictory as their beliefs were, John didn't hold that against them. Everybody had a right to practice their chosen faith. However, didn't promoting one's faith in public schools violate the separation of church and state? Where did they get the right to do that?

He had put off talking to his wife and investigating this for too long. His daughter had been impacted by it. Schoolchildren must feel confused by the beliefs of trans activists. To ply them with doubts during puberty while they groped to fit in with peers seemed diabolical.

When John opened the door to the kitchen, the comforting aroma of pork chops sizzling on the stove greeted him. While Leah stirred a pan of veggies, he asked her whether Rachael had mentioned Jackie.

Leah turned to John and grimaced. "Oh, that's right, I forgot. Rachael complained about Jackie stealing her position on the basketball team."

Leah turned back to the stove and flipped the pork chops. "We didn't talk any further about it because as soon as the kids came home from school I asked David to help me. An app I downloaded on my laptop caused me fits, and he figured it out for me."

"Well, did she mention that Jackie was trans?"

"No!"

"According to Rachael, she was good enough to make the boys' team, but now that she's on the girls' team, none of the girls will pass the ball to her, which doesn't make for a good outcome for either Jackie or the team." John considered asking Leah if they should ask Rachael to lead in getting the team to change their attitude toward Jackie. Leah's angry narrowed eyebrows told him that would not be well received.

"Rachael worked so hard on her basketball skills," Leah sputtered, "and now she's being cheated!"

"What would you have us do? Talk to her coach and give her a piece of our mind? I don't think that would go over well with Rachael."

Leah waved a serving spoon at John and scowled."We have to do something. If we call on the phone, we might find a fair solution, and we can tell the coach to keep Rachael from knowing we called."

"I'm not sure that would be wise. Let's pray about it."

"Yes! Let's pray about it after dinner. I want to dish up dinner now."

Praying later suited John fine. In the process of praying, he hoped he and his wife would discover the proper attitude a Christian should have. Leah took a harsh view of trans kids and adopted the thinking of her ultra-conservative friends. John desired for both of their children to think independently and to have a tender heart toward the lost and confused. He prayed Leah would encourage Rachael to talk to Jesus about the proper attitude to have.

After dinner, John asked Rachael and David to clean up the dinner mess so their mom and dad could pray. Rachael complained and recited all the homework assignments she had due the next week. David reminded her of seven or eight favors she owed him and her parents. When she continued to whine, David grabbed her hair. She let out an ear-piercing scream.

Rachael punched David in the gut, and David put her in a headlock. Rachael stomped on his feet. Both kids yelled and protested to their parents.

John walked over and pinched a pressure point at the back of their necks. When they cried for him to stop, he made them promise to stop fighting and clean the dinner mess without saying another word.

\#   \#   \#

John and Leah sat in the spare bedroom, which they used as an office, and discussed Rachael's reaction to Jackie taking her place as forward.

"Her problem isn't a bad attitude toward a trans girl," Leah said. "She thinks she's being cheated, and she's right. You said so yourself."

"I said that she shouldn't get an attitude because she got beat out of her position." John extended open hands toward her like asking to hold a baby. "Rachael's reaction to Jackie hides the real issue. She's playing sports to develop character, grow physically stronger, learn sportsmanship, and have fun. Besides, if she complains, how is she going to show Jackie Christ's love?"

Leah rolled her eyes. "Oh, sure, you expect an eleven-year-old to swallow those trite answers when she is being treated unfairly."

"No, but I expect her mother to have God's perspective. If you modeled a Christ-like attitude for her, she might learn to overcome an injustice and grow spiritually."

"Fine!" Leah said. "Let's pray and ask God to show us how we should handle this matter." She closed her eyes and bowed her head.

John locked his eyes on her. She wanted to dismiss the issue and him with a perfunctory prayer. He supposed he couldn't fault her for being impatient with the school. Though he freely admitted to being too hasty, he wanted to change that bad habit. How could they know and love God better if they didn't take time to wait for Him to communicate with them?

Since neither one of them had the tenacity to untangle the transgender issue, they wouldn't make any further progress tonight, so he bowed his head while she prayed and rattled off what she wanted God to do. He followed her prayer with a prayer of his own, though doubted their conversation with each other or with God accomplished much. At least, transgenderism wasn't a crucial problem for them.

> *A pack of jackasses led by a lion is superior to*
> *a pack of lions led by a jackass.*
> George Washington

Chapter Three

That night, when they crawled into bed, Leah suggested they pray about the transgender kids in school during the prayer team's weekly meeting on Saturday. John grunted his approval half-heartedly. Later, as he lay in bed waiting to drift off to sleep, he fell in love with the idea of having the prayer team look at issues outside their usual personal concerns. Typically, their prayers focused on a distant aunt with cancer, a grandfather in a nursing home who fell for the hundredth time, replacing the worn carpet in the church, finding a new youth pastor, etc.

In the morning, John rose early so he could eat breakfast with David and Rachael. He compared the kid's breakfast hour to a cage of starving monkeys at the zoo. Controlled mayhem. Children ran to the kitchen table and grabbed a bite of food, ran around to look for homework assignments, ran back for another bite of food, ran to comb their hair, searched for missing articles of clothing, ran back for another bite, and fed the cat, birds, and fish. Usually he waited to eat until after they left and enjoyed a more peaceful breakfast with Leah. This morning, though, John wanted to see whether he could brighten Rachael's attitude toward Jackie.

Rachael stopped at the kitchen table long enough to chew on a piece of toast. John asked her how she felt about Jackie this morning. She nodded with her mouth full. After she swallowed, she jabbered as she left that the whole thing didn't bother her that much anymore. John next heard her yell from where she stood in the laundry area asking if anyone had seen her yellow hair band.

David toasted a Brown Sugar, Cinnamon Pop-Tart, and the aroma motivated John to put one in the toaster to enjoy with his coffee. He asked David how gymnastics practice went. David's answer: "Fine."

"No problems, huh?" John waited until David looked at him. "Your coach called. Would you like to have another coach to help you on the rings?"

"Yeah, Dad, that'd be great."

A few minutes later, Rachael sat at the table and wolfed down scrambled eggs. John considered asking her how the girls on her team felt about Jackie, but he saw she had to be out the door to catch the bus now. He decided to ask her when she came home. John walked upstairs to their office to read his Bible and talk to the Lord about the day ahead.

Leah called him after she had prepared his usual oatmeal and boiled egg. They ate a leisurely breakfast and discussed their plans for the day. Leah's work as a receptionist at Edina Realty had been reduced to less than 15 hours a week during the winter months, so she planned to work part-time at Joann Fabrics during the Holiday season.

John told her about a phone call he had received from David's gymnastics coach. The freshmen needed tips from someone who had competitive experience with the rings. Evidently, David bragged his dad had competed in gymnastics in college, so the coach asked John if he'd help the freshmen three afternoons a week. John's first practice with David's gymnastics team would be that afternoon.

# # #

After John arrived at his downtown Edward Jones office, he asked his receptionist to reschedule his appointments so he could finish by 2:30 PM. He wanted to make sure he arrived on time for his son's gymnastic practice. When he learned he only had one afternoon appointment at 1:00 PM, he told his receptionist that he wanted to make it the last one for the day.

At 1:45 PM John finished his last scheduled appointment and shrugged on his coat, but before he could leave, he learned that Hank Wilson had insisted he see John that afternoon. His receptionist didn't refuse Hank's request because he had a huge account with John. She also knew Hank was Andy's brother, and Andy Wilson was a deacon at their church and John's best friend.

John stood in the reception area and looked out the large, storefront window that stretched from one side of the Edward Jones reception area to the other. Swirling snow already covered walks and roads with four to six-inch drifts. Traveling to the high school would take a little longer. He pulled out his cell phone and called Hank. "Hi Hank, I'm scheduled to coach my son's gymnastics practice right now. Do you have a trade order for me, or can we schedule a meeting for tomorrow morning?"

As he waited for Hank to reply, he saw Hank walk in front of the office windows with his cell phone to his ear. "Hey John, I'm right here. I'll take just a minute of your time." Hank looked through their storefront window and waved at John.

John motioned with his hand for Hank to come into the reception area. As he took off his coat, he tried his best to hide his irritation. Hank could be long-winded and consume large chunks of his time. At one point in their relationship, he welcomed Hank's requests because his account generated a huge percentage of his income. Today, he tolerated him because of his friendship with Andy.

A flurry of snow blew in the doorway as Hank entered the reception area. Hank smiled broadly and thanked John for seeing him. As Hank settled in a chair in front of John's desk, he promised John he'd be done in twenty minutes. John reckoned that would never happen. Hank told John how much he appreciated the fabulous way Edward Jones managed his money. They had made him millions and gave him the ability to retire at age fifty. He appreciated the life of ease he had, but he just wanted to check on market conditions that affected his investments. He read on Facebook that Kennedy had gained significant support in his bid to run for President. If RFK Jr. became President, he would help bring unity and stability to the nation. That would help the stock market, wouldn't it?

John bit on his lower lip. Before John could say anything, Hank stood and reached across the desk with his phone to show John pictures of his new wet bar and indoor swimming pool. When John admitted he hadn't heard about Hank's recent Caribbean cruise, his appreciative client showed him more pictures. Hank's idle lifestyle bothered John. He hadn't become an investment advisor just so men like Hank could spend their days on social media and waste their money on luxuries. While Hank chatted, John prayed silently that he wouldn't be so late that David became angry with him.

An hour later as John navigated the snowy roads to the high school, he said another quick prayer that David would be proud of his dad. John arrived 15 minutes late for gymnastics practice. He apologized profusely, but he could tell David felt embarrassed and mad. A lot of good his praying did.

John threw his jacket on the back of a chair along the wall and put on his tennis shoes. Five fourteen-year-old boys took turns swinging from the rings, attempting to make something happen. Mostly they stood around chatting and pretending to be busy while older boys worked on the mat, high bar, parallel bars, or pommel horse. The freshmen needed someone to encourage them and show them how to perform the basic moves.

John walked over to the rings and called the five freshmen boys to gather around so he could learn what skills they had mastered. David and one other volunteered to perform basic ring dips and skin the cat moves. As the two demonstrated their moves, the others clapped and cheered. At first, John thought their hurrahs came as a form of mockery because the moves were so elementary. He challenged the other boys to show him what they could do.

The other three boys made excuses for not wanting to do basic exercises. Observing the boys further, he changed his mind about their reasons for not wanting to perform their routines. They appeared to lack motivation, and John figured they set their goals way too low. Though many of the moves on the rings required massive strength, John thought they could learn moves that relied more on flexibility or timing and coordination.

Though John hadn't worked out to keep in shape, he was thin and wiry, so he thought he might be able to do a basic kip move. He needed three attempts to perform a kip, and his form stunk. He assured them they didn't need to use muscle power. They just had to have the correct timing. He explained the exact moment in their swing when they should snap down with their arms.

When he asked them to try doing it, he noticed the tops of David's ears turn red. None of the boys budged. John felt like a jackass for forgetting to form a good relationship with them first and failing to assess the level of their ability. He told them they could perform whatever they wanted as long as it lasted between 30 to 60 seconds.

When nobody moved, he waved for them to stand up and form a line. A skinny boy got shoved to the front of the line. When he failed to even get his body to swing more than two feet, the rest of the boys called him a geek, a wimp, and several other names.

John criticized them for mocking their teammate and reminded them that they should act and talk like a team. That meant encouraging one another. The boys had a long way to go in learning to respect people's feelings. At the end of practice, as David headed into the locker room, John told his son he'd wait outside in the car to give him a ride home. David said that he wanted to walk home. John could tell he had his work cut out for him to repair his relationship with his son.

Later, at home, John checked his watch as he sat reading the newspaper on the sofa. They lived three miles from school. Walking slowly, David should have arrived home in an hour. However, by the time David appeared, two hours had passed, and Leah already had dinner on the table. John had no time to clear things up with his son. Throughout the meal, David remained sullen and gave one-word responses. After dinner John gave David an hour to think by himself in his room. That also gave John time to collect his thoughts and pray for him.

Two hours later, John walked out of David's bedroom having gained nothing from his talk with his son and feeling more alienated than ever. John's throat tightened. What made him think he could help coach gymnastics? Asking God to intervene hadn't helped. Proverbs said that in an abundance of counselors, there was safety. He thought about his friend Andy. He had raised four children successfully, and he never passed up an opportunity to chat over a cup of coffee. Maybe Andy could counsel him about David and pray for him, too.

And you shall know the truth, and the truth shall make you free.
John 8:32 NKJV

Chapter Four

At Caribou Coffee the next morning, John and Andy found comfortable, padded armchairs on the second floor in front of a fireplace. The only other customer sat on the opposite side of the second floor. While the artificial fire gave an illusion of warmth, real comfort settled over John from sips of hot coffee, aromas wafting the various brews created on the first floor, and a heartfelt connection with his friend.

Andy laughed when he heard what happened between David and John. "If that is the only wrinkle you have in your relationship with your son, you can consider yourself abundantly blessed by the Creator of the universe."

John smiled and stared at the artificial fire. Andy had a valid point, but that didn't mean he should ignore the problem. "Uh, I don't want the wrinkle to become a huge tear."

"That's true! The teenage years can be extremely difficult to navigate." Andy took two slow, deep, easy breaths and then muttered, "Prayer is the only thing that pulled me through those times."

"Man, I'm sunk then. My prayers feel like spitting before an approaching tornado. If I am aimed in the right direction, the spit vanishes in the wind. If I pray in the wrong direction, it's just plain nasty. And, if I'm standing next to the tornado, I'm scared spitless."

Andy chuckled. "I know the feeling. I believe the best way to improve your prayer life is to increase the amount of time you spend praying with others. You and Leah come every Saturday, but you should also find someone with whom you both can regularly agree on in prayer for your family."

"Right. . ." John took a slow sip of coffee. He hesitated to say more because he didn't want to insult him. As head of the prayer team, Andy took his job seriously. However, prayer in a group setting felt like wasted verbiage and effort. Few things tested his patience more than people praying with him for the same people or situation but for different outcomes than he did. He glanced over at Andy, whose eyes were focused on him.

Andy cleared his throat. "If you want to learn what the Bible teaches about prayer, you and Leah should join me every Tuesday morning on Aurora Bluff. It's just me up there, so we'd be free to discuss whatever we wanted to focus our prayers on for the day."

John leaned back and folded his hands behind his head. "I'll ask Leah, but she's not a morning person."

"Try to encourage her with the idea that she'd increase in her ability to pray. Let her know that before we start, we can decide which Scripture verses to apply to the situation."

"Yeah, if we have Bible verses on which to stand in faith, God will answer our prayers. On top of that, we have the power of agreement in prayer. Jesus said, '…if two of you agree on earth concerning anything that they ask, it will be done for them by My Father in heaven.'[2] When we agree on something the Bible says is right, it's a done deal." John glanced at Andy to see whether he detected the sarcasm in his voice.

"Ah, I don't think it's quite that simple." Andy shook his head. "I could find a Bible verse that says God wants to bless his people and then ask for a yacht. That's why the Bible exhorts us to agree with others on what to pray. We hold each other in check."

"Yeah, I suppose." John hoped something would light a fire in his soul for prayer.

Andy sipped on his coffee and stared at the fireplace. "Ya know, people in our church have faith in Christ for the forgiveness of their sins, but most of us fail to love the way God requires. We're all a bit selfish to some degree. That means—even when two of us agree — we could easily be deceived."

John stood to leave. "Why bother praying with others then?"

Andy extended and flapped both of his hands, signaling for him to sit back down. "I'm just saying we need to check our heart attitude before we apply promises in the Bible to our prayers. Simply

---

[2] Matthew 18:19

praying more with me or with others will not increase your faith or keep the goal of your intercession in line with God's will. Love, on the other hand, will. Galatians 5:6 says that the only thing that matters is faith which worketh by love. If we act and talk motivated by love, then love makes faith work effectively, and our prayers get answered, sometimes miraculously."

John questioned whether Andy and his right-wing conservative friends had compassion for the poor and suffering. "Okay, Yoda, what's stopping people from loving others so their faith brings results?"

"We often fail to receive answers to prayer because we aren't patient enough. In our culture we are used to having everything instantly. You'd think with all the timesaving devices that we'd have massive amounts of time to wait for God's answer. However, God gave everyone free will, but many in our church use their free will to distract themselves with shopping Online, social media, video games, entertainment, sports, you name it.

John bit his lower lip. Ouch! Andy's comment about sports hit close to home, but maybe sports provided a clue to the solution. John pointed his index finger upward. "Joy could be the key that makes our prayer effective. Everybody naturally does what brings them enjoyment, so they do it often and enthusiastically. Joy could be the catalyst that brings a powerful move of God to Bluffview."

"Sure," Andy said, "but I think our pleasure has to be focused on Christ so our joy springs from the love of God and not from our emotions."

John scratched his chin. The source of his pleasure came from several places—sports, food, family, and entertainment. Did those things distract him from loving God and others? He thought others needed to love more, but he had to examine his own heart. His critical attitude toward his right-wing friends required a course correction. Perhaps, weak love for God lay at the root of his lack of answers from God.

He didn't love God as he should because he didn't make knowing God a priority. How could he love Someone properly if he didn't take the time to know Him? He needed to have patience, and that challenged his natural tendency to rush through things. That needed to change if he wanted to receive answers to prayer.

"Okay, Andy, I'll try meeting with you on Tuesday mornings." John hesitated because he worried that they'd disagree with what God wanted them to pray.

Andy pumped his fist in the air with delight. "Yes! You are an answer to my prayers. I've been asking the Lord to send people to join me in praying for our town of Bluffview."

"Well, I'm not sure if I'm the kind of answer you'd be excited about." John considered Andy's enthusiasm for prayer. Andy's voice waxed passionate whenever he declared that real intercession should focus on lost souls. Maybe some of Andy's zeal for prayer, or intercession as he liked to call it, would rub off on him.

Andy leaned forward and stared intently at a point to John's right. "As I interceded for our town last Tuesday, God revealed strongholds of the enemy in different spheres of influence. The enemy's strategy involves extensive webs of subterfuge to undercut God's kingdom. The Lord wants to use our prayers to form a covering that blankets our town and dismantles Satan's schemes. Coming from above, armed with the knowledge of Christ, enables what I call prayers of suprafuge." Andy raised an eyebrow and gazed at John.

John held his gaze and exhaled sharply. "Ah, that sounds powerful. Maybe while we are at it, we can ask God to intervene in Ukraine. What time do you meet on Tuesday mornings?" John braced himself for his reply. Though Andy still worked as a mechanic, he was semi-retired, working out of his tool shed and setting his own hours. Andy could start his day late, but he likely didn't because he lived most of his adult life rising early.

"I start at 7:00 AM." Andy raised both brows and smiled.

John grunted. "Okay."

\#   \#   \#

John Greenberg climbed into Andy Wilson's pickup truck at 7:00 AM on top of Aurora Bluff. He nodded at his friend and tried to act happy that they were going to pray at this hour. Andy reached over and slapped John's upper arm with the back of his hand. He exhorted John to increase his faith. John explained that Leah had no desire to join them at that hour in the morning. Besides, she needed to make sure their children arose, ate breakfast, and made it onto the school bus on time. Consequently, praying for their family would have to come later. For now, John planned to concentrate on improving his ability to pray.

Andy described the focus of their intercession for the lost souls who lived in the East End of Bluffview. Then Andy quoted Bible verses they should wield as swords to slash into pieces the devil's schemes. Since Andy was head of the intercession team for the Evangelical Free Church, John didn't question his focus or the Scriptures he chose. After all, he came at this unreal hour so he could learn.

They prayed together inside the car for a while. Then they stepped out of the car and walked to an overlook as the morning sky lightened. They quietly prayed to themselves as they gazed at the city of Bluffview. Tall church steeple and apartment buildings caught the first rays of sunlight. Arrowhead Bluff towered over the other side of the East End, leaving the homes below in darkness except where occasional street lights broke through. A brisk breeze swept across their sightseeing location, and John shook his shoulders to generate body heat and jammed his hands into his coat pockets.

He contemplated praying and then singing praises to God or yelling at demons to release souls that were enslaved to sex, drugs, and despair. Instead, he just stared down below as the sun rose over the treetops and dispelled shadows on the East End's crime and drug-infested streets. At this hour without coffee, he struggled to pray through the early morning mental fog.

Andy said that he hadn't seen any results from all his efforts. Though he had been on the bluff every Tuesday for the last two months, he hadn't experienced any changes when he talked with people in the East End. John didn't respond to Andy's comment, though several reasons for not seeing results occurred to him. As Andy explained a few days ago, a lack of faith, love, and patience all undermined their prayers. They might also fail to understand what they needed to pray against to defeat the works of the evil one.

John turned to Andy. "Why do you keep praying for the people on the East End?"

"Because God's love moved me to pray for them."

"If God hasn't answered the prayer, maybe God wants you to pray something else."

Andy nudged John's shoulder. "Do you have something else you would like us to pray for?"

"How about praying for America's involvement in the war in Ukraine? I have a client who is freaking out over it."

"I thought you came up here so you could learn how to pray for your family."

John shrugged. "Yeah, but perhaps I need to practice on something not so close to home."

"Really?" Andy replied with obvious disbelief. "Besides needing a mountain of faith to change the direction of other nations, you'd also have to have a lot more wisdom. Maybe you should start with things that God's love is moving you to pray. Until you get things squared away with David, we ought to spend time praying for him."

"Well, God's love for my client moved me to pray for the end to the fighting in the Ukraine." John had prayed for David, but he hadn't seen any answers. He figured he could increase his ability to get results when he prayed over distant needs. Then he could pray with more faith for something where he had much more at stake personally. That sounded illogical, but that's the way he felt.

John walked to the side of the Aurora Bluff that overlooked the central downtown area and left Andy to intercede for the East End. John grimaced as he sat on a frigid park bench and rubbed his leg to generate heat. Andy prayed all the right words, but if Andy prayed in faith, wouldn't his prayers bring results? John wanted to avoid religious prayers that accomplished nothing.

John talked to the Lord about City Hall, downtown churches, and the public schools. Shortly, he felt alert, and he called out demons by name and commanded them to loosen their grip on the people in the central part of the city. He thought his words had power, the kind that could do damage to the devil's schemes. However, he prayed like that before. He believed God promised to answer prayers when asked in faith without doubting. Andy said that faith works by love. Maybe that was the key ingredient he lacked. He hoped getting up at 7:00 AM plus being part of the prayer team would teach him to let love motivate his prayer.

Whatever things you ask when you pray, believe that you receive them, and you will have them.
Mark 11:24 NKJV

Chapter Five

On Saturday evening, John and Leah left David in charge of his sister, while they joined the other five members of the prayer team —Doug and Mary, a young couple, John's friend Andy with his wife Eileen, and Janet, their neighbor. They prayed faithfully every week over the needs of the church and the community. Long before the meeting started, Andy opened the room that doubled as a Sunday school classroom and pushed the low, oblong table and several elementary-school-sized chairs into the corner so they could sit in a small circle on padded, adult-sized, folding chairs. Located in the basement of the church, the room had two small windows near the ceiling and a bright overhead fluorescent light. A whiteboard on one wall had Proverbs 3:5 written on it. "Trust in the Lord with all your heart, and lean not on your own understanding."[3]

John pondered Proverbs 3:5 and tried to apply the exhortation of the verse to his life and Bluffview Evangelical Free. He needed to trust God more when it came to prayer. Who didn't? Certainly, the former church members should not have leaned on their own understanding when a schism broke out over carpeting the classrooms. John considered the tile flooring they had. Carpet would have kept the sound level down, but the basement was too damp for anything but tile. Besides, grade school and nursery kids required floors with easy cleanup properties.

Andy started the meeting by asking whether anybody had special requests they wanted the team to intercede for. Everybody except John mentioned people or situations that needed prayer. While

---

[3] NKJV

others then prayed, John sat and mulled over the various reasons he failed to receive answers from God.

He stopped brooding for a few minutes when he heard Andy boldly asking God to intervene on the East End. Andy asked God to deal with the fornicators, drug dealers, and freeloaders living off the government dole. Then he asked the Lord to convict the Blacks and the poor of their laziness and failure to be responsible fathers. John twisted his rump from side to side and back and forth. Andy's prayers bothered him. Had love moved Andy to pray? Love certainly hadn't motivated John's critical attitude. However, Andy should have listened to the Holy Spirit before he prayed.

Did Andy realize the people in John's middle-class neighborhood needed prayer? They may have different sin issues, but they needed to be delivered from their bondage to materialism, greed, and selfishness as much as East Enders needed freedom from poverty, drugs, and illicit sex. Despite his best intentions to give Andy the benefit of the doubt, he couldn't accept that love had motivated Andy's intercession. He had to confront his judgmental attitude toward Andy. Otherwise, the political polarization would sour their friendship.

After the meeting, John talked with Andy as they walked to their cars. "Your prayers for the East End irritated me. Many evangelical Christians adopt the Republican Party narrative just because of the Pro-life issue. How can Christians ignore the tax cuts Republicans give the rich, their indifference toward healthcare, and their neglect of the environment? Then they support a Presidential candidate who spins out lies with every other sentence he utters."

"Whoa, John! Where did this come from?"

"I want to learn intercession from you, but I don't buy into Republican politics."

"You have to put love first. You can't put intercession first."

That made sense to John. God would show them the truth as they allowed Him to guide their intercession. "Republicans appear to lack love, but the Democrats fail in that department just as much. Both parties allow their desire for power to govern their actions. That causes increased divisiveness and ranting from people on both ends of the political spectrum."

"I just felt attacked by you. If love motivates your words and actions, you'll bring unity and not division."

John looked up at the sky. "Okay, Andy, I will work on being more loving."

On the drive home, John talked to Leah about his impatience with Andy.

"You are so impulsive at times," Leah said. "It's hard to be loving when you're in too big of a hurry. I've watched you run right by your next-door neighbor Willy completely ignoring his needs."

John swallowed hard. He had to be more patient with Andy and more considerate of Willy.

#   #   #

During breakfast five days later, Leah lamented the demise of their next-door neighbor's marriage. She had waited until the children left for school to get John's opinion on what to do.

John read news from an app on his phone and didn't respond except to mumble, "Yeah, that's terrible."

"Janet says she's going to file for a divorce," Leah said.

"That's too bad."

"Gumby! Is that all you can say? 'That's too bad?'"

Her use of the nickname from his college days caught his attention. He received the nickname for being kind-hearted and flexible. The disgusted look on Leah's face revealed he lacked a little kindness. "I'm sorry. What am I supposed to do about it?"

"I mentioned Willy to you on Saturday. Have you prayed for him in the last few days?"

John took a deep breath. He had turned a callous ear to the plight of his neighbor. A month ago, he'd talked with Willy about neglecting his wife. Willy just shrugged it off as though he wasn't the problem. Willy called himself a Christian, but he hardly ever attended church. John thought Willy would learn how to solve his marital woes if he attended church. At church he'd learn how to treat his wife and get life in order.

Meanwhile, God meant for John to love Willy enough to make Willy's marriage the focus of his prayers. Through prayer, Willy would be open to listening to him. God had set Willy right in front of him, but he had been too self-centered to love his neighbor. He couldn't excuse himself because he had doubts about prayer. He could have at least said a simple one-minute prayer.

After breakfast, John kneeled by the guest bed in their office to pray for Willy. Sun broke through the clouds and warmed the bed's white duvet where he rested his elbows. With his stomach full and his eyelids heavy, John's head sank onto the warm bed, and he fell asleep. The next thing John knew, he saw Willy watching Monday Night Football. Willy's wife called for him to stop their two boys from fighting before they ruined more furniture, but he made light of her request. At ages fifteen and seventeen, he claimed they didn't need a parent trying to protect them, and if they broke anything, they'd have to replace it with their own money.

John didn't have any idea how much time had passed when Leah called to him from the dining room. "Honey, lunch is ready!"

Now lying on the bed, John stretched his back. "Coming!" he yelled.

He only worked at the downtown office three or four days a week, but he didn't usually go back to sleep after breakfast on the days he worked from home. Maybe his early mornings on Aurora Bluff were taking their toll. He didn't mind getting up before dawn. In fact, he welcomed the change. Their lives had become pretty predictable. After breakfast, he would check the stock market, and she would talk to friends on the phone. In the evening after dinner, they would get occupied with their separate hobbies and then would watch the late news together.

The Holy Spirit had been nudging him to set aside more time to pray, especially to pray with Leah, but he kept finding new hobbies. Recently, he discovered the joy of baking cakes and cookies. Food had been a constant distraction for him. He wanted to put baking aside for a season. If that boosted his faith and his ability to pray, he would do it gladly. For now, he needed to get to lunch quickly. After all, God didn't want him to irritate his wife when she went to the effort of making a nutritious meal.

During lunch John told Leah about his dream. He thought the dream meant he should talk to Willy about being more attentive to his children. Before he talked to Willy, he wanted Leah to pray with him, that Willy would have an open heart. Leah had errands to run in the afternoon but promised to pray later in the evening.

While Leah ran errands, John knelt again by the bed in his office and asked God to show him how to encourage Willy to do the right thing. John bounced through a wide range of emotions. He considered himself a compassionate person, but these emotions were unusual for him. First, he wept for his friend Willy. Then joy bubbled up from within. He thought the Holy Spirit prayed through him, and that meant God desired to deliver Willy.

The sensations coursing through his mind and body defied description. Amazement, hope, and fierceness coalesced to motivate his prayers. He then sensed the enemy opposed his prayers, and he had to expand his intercession. He asked the Holy Spirit to show him better ways to pray for Willy.

Suddenly, John buckled over and groaned. He prayed as the Spirit moved him, and he wasn't sure he understood what came out of his mouth. After groaning and speaking unintelligible words for several minutes, John lay on the floor, stunned. Was that experience what the Apostle Paul meant by the Spirit himself interceding for us with groanings too deep for words?

"Holy Spirit, was that You that moved me to pray?"

John waited a few minutes for the Holy Spirit to indicate to him some kind of answer. He didn't know how he expected the Holy Spirit to communicate to him. John thought of Bible verses that described how Christians should live. "Holy Spirit, Paul said that You have not given us a spirit of fear but of power, love, and self-control.[4] A little while ago, that did not feel like self-control."

John reflected on that verse from Second Timothy. His version of the Bible translated the word as *sound mind* instead of *self-control*. He doubted, however, that his experience could be called sound thinking. The whole thing felt creepy. He would have to talk with Andy about it.

---

[4] II Timothy 1:7 ESV

For the love of Christ compels us, because we judge thus: that if One died for all, then all died; and He died for all, that those who live should live no longer for themselves, but for Him who died for them and rose again.
II Corinthians 5:14-15 NKJV

Chapter Six

At 7:00 AM on Aurora Bluff, John stepped out of his car and climbed into Andy's old pickup truck wide awake. He had missed the Saturday prayer meeting, so he still wanted Andy's opinion on what he experienced four days ago. Andy had his heater on high and the fan blowing full blast. The truck felt toasty warm, so John turned the fan down to help him hear what Andy said in reaction to his experiences last week at home.

When John finished describing how he groaned, he asked Andy if he thought the Holy Spirit had been praying through him as the Bible talked about.

"Wow! I don't know what to tell you. In the Bible Paul exhorts us not to be ignorant of the spiritual gifts." Andy opened his Bible and pushed on the switch for the cab light. After he had turned through several pages, he stopped and read. "In Second Corinthians, Paul says that he wishes that we all spoke in tongues. I think what you experienced could be tongues, and Paul affirms that. However, he calls tongues a lesser gift and urges us to seek greater gifts that build up the church. Before he wrote that comment about tongues, he wrote that famous chapter on love that we often hear quoted at weddings."

Andy paused and looked John in the eye. "Whether you are talking about spiritual gifts or interceding for others, the rock-bottom basis for what you do has to be love—love for God in gratitude for what He has done for you and love for your neighbor or for whomever you are praying."

John slowly nodded. He needed to grow in his love for God and others. Self-centeredness choked God's love from flowing through him. He too easily saw the faults in others and tore them apart in his mind.

Andy turned back through more pages in his Bible. "Jesus described a good way to determine whether God produced your experience. He said that you will know them by their fruits. Your prayer will be answered if it was God who caused you to pray as you did. Also, you should feel love, joy, and peace flowing from your heart."

"Okay, we'll see if my prayer for Willy gets answered. What should we focus on for prayer this morning?" John wanted to change the subject because his groanings troubled him. His heart seemed selfish and unloving, dark and joyless, and confused and anxious. He appeared to be an unlikely candidate for any spiritual gift. Unless God desired to use an unlikely person, he doubted God would use him through the gift of intercession for Willy in an unknown tongue.

Andy suggested they focus their prayers on public schools and the school board meetings. Normally, John would have perked up at that suggestion because he felt passionate about what the teachers taught his children. Today, his thoughts whirled around his inadequacies in prayer. Maybe his poverty of spirit was what Jesus referred to when He said that the poor in spirit were blessed. Certainly, shortcomings helped keep him humble. He could only hope that the Lord would look at his needy condition and have mercy on him.

John hardly heard the reasons Andy wanted to focus on the Bluffview schools or the Scripture verse he sought to apply to their prayers. Andy did most of the praying. Whenever Andy paused, John interceded for the teachers and school board in very general terms, asking the Lord to bless them and give them wisdom.

As soon as he could tactfully leave, John stepped out of Andy's truck to pray by himself at the overlook facing the East End. The school his children attended wasn't anywhere near the East End. He should be in with Andy passionately interceding for the school. His kids' education—their lives—hinged on the policies and materials shoved at them by their teachers. Yet, he hesitated to pray with Andy. Had he elevated the importance of prayer too high? His faith seemed to crash as he questioned whether begging God to move on his behalf made any difference at all.

The cloudy weather moderated the temperature, but the dreary skies dampened his attitude. A breeze on the bluff whipped around John, forcing him to pull the collar on his jacket around his neck and face away from the East End. "Lord, I am stymied over prayer. What piece of the puzzle am I missing?"

John walked over to the other side of the bluff where he hoped to find inspiration to pray and less wind. The wind felt even stronger there, so he rejoined Andy in his pickup. After praying with Andy for another 15 minutes, John told Andy he had to leave.

On the drive home, John imagined Leah cooking bacon and pancakes, and he hummed the tune "Blessed Assurance" until he landed in the driveway. He could practically smell the bacon from where he parked the car. When he entered the kitchen, he discovered Leah had cooked his usual fare of oatmeal and a boiled egg. He looked past the egg and at her with his mouth open, but he said nothing.

Leah looked up from the devotional on her lap. "Is something the matter?"

"No." John flashed her a smile. What could he say? God had to be dealing with some part of his selfish nature. He should be flattered that the Lord cared that much about teaching him how to pray.

Before they ate, John said a grace and added a quick prayer for the school board. Leah added a prayer for their children and Willy. John bit on his lower lip. Her prayer convicted him of his neglect of praying for them.

John gobbled breakfast and didn't bother to linger over a cup of coffee as he usually did. He went up to their home office and turned on the computer to check his emails and the digital version of the *Wall Street Journal*. After reading for ten minutes, he sensed he should pray instead.

John kneeled next to the guest bed and asked the Lord to forgive him for seeking to pray as an obligation he wanted to fulfill. He realized he should pray because love motivated him.

"Lord, my kids need Your help at school, and my neighbor Willy needs You to turn his life around even more. Willy has hardened his heart. He won't speak to me, and he appears to ignore his two sons and his wife. Have mercy on him. Forgive him, Lord. Give him the gift of repentance."

John's heart grieved for Willy's blindness. Compassion for Willy swept over John as he planted his face on the carpet. Soon, his gut ached so hard he couldn't breathe. Then everything went blank. John felt light as a feather. He floated toward the ceiling, and he looked down at his body, collapsed on the floor of his bedroom.

"Whoa!" John gawked at his motionless body. "I'm dead? That's not supposed to happen when you let the Holy Spirit intercede through you for a friend."

John then found himself floating fifty feet above his home with a view of the whole town as though hang gliding but frozen in time. "Father, I'm thrilled to be joining You with Jesus in heaven, but what will happen to Leah and the kids?"

"John, you are not dead. You have been temporarily transported out of your physical body so you can intercede from a position of knowledge."

"Oh!" John looked behind him where he heard the voice. A light shone so brightly from someone that he had difficulty determining their features. "Are you going to show me how to pray from here, Holy Spirit?"

"I am an angel, but the Holy Spirit will show you what He wants you to pray for." The light around the angel burst in a flash of intensity and then faded along with the image to nothing.

John looked down at Willy's home. "Lord, am I supposed to see something from here that will show me what to pray?"

Immediately, John entered Willy's bedroom and saw Willy pull up pornography on his computer. "Will, what are you doing? That stuff is poison to your marriage and your soul." Willy didn't a hear word John said.

John looked heavenward and stretched out his arms with his palms up. "Lord, why are you letting me see this? It's disgusting! He knows better than this. That hypocrite! I've heard him millions of times denounce Christians for being phony and call his coworkers perverts for viewing porn."

Now you know how to pray for him.

John woke up in his physical body, lying curled on the floor. His shoulder felt stiff from the odd way he lay, but he sprang up and waved his arms as he prayed against the spirit of pornography. He paced back and forth in his home office, binding the spirit of lust and passivity in the name of Jesus and commanding those spirits to loosen their hold on Willy. He continued to confess God's word over Willy for several minutes until he felt in his spirit that the bondage had been broken.

John landed on the stuffed armchair. Whoa, this went way beyond praying in another tongue. Where did it talk about this in the Bible?

\#   \#   \#

Willy's eyes were riveted to the screen of his laptop computer, his heart pounding from the screen's seductive appeal to the flesh. Two minutes later, a chill blasted his body followed by an electric charge that zapped his mind. He looked at his computer. Shocked by the image on the screen, he slapped the laptop lid down. "That's gross! I don't need that. . . Ever!" Willy opened his laptop again and deleted the website from his favorites. After that, he put parental controls on his computer to prevent him from having unwholesome visits.

As soon as he had finished setting the parameters, John called. "Will, we need to talk."

> *Judge not, and you shall not be judged. Condemn not,*
> *and you shall not be condemned. Forgive,*
> *and you will be forgiven.*
> Luke 7:37 NKJV

Chapter Seven

Willy heard the phone buzz and saw he had another text message from John. For over a week, John had been texting or calling and asking to talk with him. Each time John called, he sounded like he had an ominous message he wanted to lay on him. In the past, John hassled him for giving up on his marriage, and Willy didn't want to hear John preach at him anymore. Besides, after he had an epiphany about his porn addiction, his relationship with God and his wife changed dramatically. The freedom from that perversion felt amazing. No way would he ever go back to lusting after illicit sex.

Janet had mentioned how she had noticed a change in him. At work in 3M's marketing department, things were still tense. The secretary went from smiles to scowls whenever he walked past her desk. That would take some time for him to overcome. He had dished out inappropriate stares and innuendos for over two years. He just hoped and prayed that his work never uncovered the struggles he had with his pornography addiction.

When he realized the stupidity of watching lewd sexual sites on his company laptop, he downloaded the necessary office documents and scrubbed the computer as clean as he could. He didn't like lying to the IT department, but he told them he had forgotten his computer at the library over the weekend. By the time he remembered where he had left it, somebody had used it to open questionable websites that caused the computer to crash. They became upset when he told them of his neglect, and they almost fired him for failing to notify them sooner that his computer had been compromised. They seemed somewhat mollified because he had already bought a new one with his own money out of his remorse for being so negligent.

That was ancient history now. He had confessed his sin to the Lord. God had forgiven him and revived his heart. What business did anybody at work have in dredging up sins the Lord had removed as far as the East is from the West? He was a new creature in Christ now. Old things were passed away. All things had become new. He was not about to let people at the office dredge things back up. They would never know what had once consumed him. He made sure of that.

The receptionist informed him that John was waiting for him in the employee lunchroom. Willy sighed and checked the text message John sent him a minute ago. He couldn't avoid facing John any longer, but he had to make it quick. Over the past three months, his addiction had gotten much worse and work had suffered numerous delays because of his inattention. He needed to focus and get things turned around.

Willy walked into a lunchroom empty of people except for John, who sat in the far corner with a stern look on his face. Willy eyed John warily. His hopes for quickly dismissing John's concerns seemed unlikely. "What's so urgent, John, that you had to come to my office to talk with me in the middle of my workday?"

"Sit down, Will." John drilled Willy with his eyes. "You may want to deny what I'm going to talk to you about, but the best thing for you to do is just 'fess up."

Willy looked around the lunchroom and sat. "Okay, John, what's up?" Something was eating at John. He was glad nobody else was there, nor would anybody likely be there for another two hours.

John scowled. "Man, you are fooling yourself if you think everything is okay. Until you get things right with the Lord—"

"I have. God and me, we're good." Willy tilted his head to one side, disgusted that John would think otherwise.

"I'll get right to the point. I have been interceding for your marriage, and I wonder what's the point? Do you even want to save your marriage?"

Willy sighed. "John, I think God is beginning to turn our marriage around."

"I know different." John splayed his palms down flat on the table. "You can't fool me."

Willy snorted. "Boy! I thought super-Christians like you weren't supposed to be judgmental."

John leaned forward. "I don't need to judge you to know you should listen to what God has surely been talking to you about."

"You think that just because I'm having marital problems, I am rebelling against God!" Willy scrunched down and scanned the room to make sure nobody else was there to hear him.

John's nostrils flared. "Okay, I'm going to tell you what makes me think you're at risk for getting divorced."

Willy shook his head. They had been next-door neighbors for a long time and good friends for an even longer time, but he couldn't believe his arrogance. "Fine, John, lay it on me. Why is my marriage doomed?"

John hesitated and looked up. "Jesus said that out of the abundance of our hearts the mouth speaks, and you can know a tree by the fruit it produces."

"So," Willy said in a mocking tone, "you looked into my heart and thought my heart produced some rotten divorce fruit." John's assumptions unnerved him at first, but Christ had forgiven and cleansed his heart. John was wrong. Willy stood and leaned forward with his hands on the table. "You can leave now, O holier than thou, neighbor and former friend."

"Sit down, Will!"

Willy continued to stand.

John spread his palms out facing Will and spoke with a grave, hushed voice. "Have it your way, but I've gotta tell you I know you have latched on to some heavy porn that is going to destroy more than just your marriage."

Willy locked onto John's gaze. John stared back. Willy blinked and looked at the tabletop, groping for a response. "That's crazy! You know me better than that!" Willy let out a quick, high-pitched laugh.

"Are you denying it?" John's eyes widened.

"Yes, and I don't have to stand here while you judge and insult me."

"Will, I'm not judging you. I have spent hours interceding for you and your marriage. God took me in the spirit into your office in your home. I saw you in front of a screen, drooling over some hard porn."

"Really!" Willy attempted to snicker and mock his friend. He didn't know the Bible as well as John, but he was pretty sure God didn't send people to spy on other people. "Oh, did you enjoy what you saw? Maybe you wanted a link to the website."

John grabbed Willy's sleeve. "I'm not kidding here. I'm your friend. I want to help you, set you free."

Willy glanced at his friend's face for a second. He saw nothing but compassion in his eyes, which forced him to avert his gaze. Willy looked up at the ceiling. He couldn't let John see the guilt he still struggled with, even though he knew he'd been forgiven. "Great!" he said after a few seconds. "I have a former friend with a suspicious imagination."

"Will, I saw you as plain as day. You were wearing your Vikings sweatshirt and had latched on to a website that said, 'My body is Waiting.' Does that ring a bell? You fast-forwarded past the brunette, and you replayed the blond twice."

Willy could feel John's eyes scrutinizing his face to see if that had brought any reaction. He exhaled sharply, not daring to look John in the eyes for fear he would see any lingering guilt. "Is that a website you like and dream about? I imagine you must enjoy blonds."

John stood. "Hand me your laptop. I bet I can help you locate the site."

Willy smiled and looked John in the eye smugly. "You could step into my office and check out my laptop if you were still my friend."

John raised an eyebrow. "I had hoped to make you realize that if you confess your sins, God is faithful and just to forgive you and cleanse you of all your sins. If you don't confess your sin, you aren't going to be walking with Jesus."

"Ha! Really?" The pitch of Willy's voice raised an octave.

John glanced at him and walked to the door without saying another word.

"Thanks for the word of encouragement, . . .ex-friend!" Willy exhaled sharply. Could John read from his face the guilt he felt inside?

Therefore if the Son makes you free, you shall be free indeed.
John 8:36 NKJV

Chapter Eight

John sat in his car after he left Willy's workplace. He expected Willy to deny his addiction at first, but when he called out the details of what he saw, he thought maybe that would convince him he'd been caught in his sin. John understood the addicting power of pornography. Before John became a Christian, he lived in a college fraternity house and joined in a couple of stag parties where hard porn had come out along with the booze. Some of the explicit sex acts in those movies burned a permanent image in his brain and served as a reminder of the dangers of X-rated movies. John had needed to confess his sin to God and to his best friend at the time. Only then, with the help of his friend and the Holy Spirit. was he able to break free.

John squeezed the steering wheel. The Holy Spirit stirred in him a love for Willy, and he hated to see him bound by that perverted addiction. God showed him Willy's pornography addiction because John experienced firsthand the difficulty of breaking free from it. Unless Willy confessed his sin, Willy didn't stand a chance of getting victory over it, and from the looks of it, Willy didn't seem inclined to admit he had a problem.

John didn't think Willy would likely speak to him for a long while. As John drove home, he realized unless God did a miracle in Willy's heart, his vision of Willy's addiction didn't seem to have served any purpose. John entered his home office and closed the door so he could pray. Before he kneeled he looked out the window at a gray, overcast sky. The room felt chilly, so he turned up the thermostat a notch. Then he kneeled and waited for the Lord to guide his intercession. When he didn't receive any guidance, he cried out, "Lord, show me how to pray!"

A minute later, even though he didn't feel any direction on how to pray, he sang praises to the Lord, starting with the Doxology. Then he sang, What a Friend We Have in Jesus. God loved his friend more than he did. God had poured His love for Willy into John's heart until he thought his heart would burst. Willy's marriage had to be on the verge of imploding. A wonderful Christian wife like Janet and his two teenage sons deserved better. Instead of opening the door for the devil to destroy his family, Willy should be defending and protecting them.

After praising God with several refrains from All Things Are Possible, John quoted Bible verses over Willy, confessing Philippians 1:6 and John 10:27-29. Then he thought he'd spend time in prayer. Strangely, he still didn't feel any unction from the Holy Spirit about what to pray. John lay out prone on the floor and begged God to have mercy on Willy.

"Lord, show me how to pray for him. Pray through me. Your word says that we don't know what to pray for as we ought, but the Spirit intercedes for us with groanings too deep for words."

John waited, but nothing happened—no guidance, no words, no groaning. Just silence. For several minutes he begged God to help him pray for Willy. He received no assurance that God had taken care of the situation, so he asked the Lord for more guidance, a vision, or a Bible verse to stand on. In his heart he felt Willy still listened to lies, so John spent an hour binding the spirit of deception and lies. John waited a few days before paying Will a visit at home to determine if his prayers had made any difference.

# # #

Willy watched John leave the lunchroom in stunned disbelief. After standing a minute by himself, Willy made his way to his desk and slumped in front of his computer. Did God give John of vision of him while he looked at pornography? Why would God do that? He valued John's friendship. He needed help with his marriage, but not with porn. How could he ask John for help when John wanted to fix a problem he no longer had? If he spent any time with John, Janet would discover he had been into porn. That would devastate her. It would destroy his marriage for sure.

Willy hid his face in his hands and cried. "Lord, you delivered me from my addiction. You gotta save my marriage. If John talks to Janet, it'll be all over, my career, my marriage, my kids—"

"Willy, are you okay?" the receptionist stuck her head in his cubicle.

Willy turned to a file cabinet to his left to avoid looking at her. "Yeah, I'm fine. John is a good friend of mine, and we just had a huge misunderstanding. I am praying that God will work it all out soon."

Willy chewed on the corner of his lower lip. He hoped John would steer clear of him and his family if he came down hard enough on John. Maybe in six months he could patch things up between them after he had repaired the damage he had inflicted on his marriage and family.

# # #

John prayed for Willy for over a week after confronting him at his office. His lack of guidance from the Lord troubled him during that time. As he sat in his office, he applied Philippians 1:6 to his prayers so God, who began a good work in Willy, would keep on perfecting it. At that moment, John's heart burst with a sudden surge of hope. A minute later, his cell phone rang.

Janet apologized but wanted to know what happened between him and Willy. Leah had told her he had prayed for Willy and recently met with him. The change in Willy had been nothing short of miraculous. For the first time in over a year, she had genuine hope for their marriage. Willy asked to pray with her before he left for work, and his prayer showed a sincerity she hadn't seen in years. He prayed for God's protection over them and His blessings over her day. He had taken an active interest in the son's lives too.

"It was like somebody flicked on the God switch," Janet said. "But the strange thing is that when he came home from work a week ago, he complained about you being a jerk. I thought it would blow over, but it hasn't. What happened?"

John clenched his jaw. Had the accusations he had flung at Willy over a week ago just destroyed their friendship for no good reason? No, he felt sure God had given him the vision. Perhaps God's earlier guidance in prayer explained Willy's dramatic changes. Nevertheless, Willy needed his help if he indeed wanted to get free from pornography.

"John, are you still there?" Janet sounded offended.

"Yes, I was recollecting what likely set him off. Have him call me."

#   #   #

The following evening when John parked his car in the garage, Willy called to him from his side of the white picket fence that separated their properties. John walked over to him and immediately saw that Willy had fear written all over his face.

John took a deep breath. "Several years back, I wrestled with the same demons that you have, and I needed the help of friends to get complete victory."

"I'm glad you got the victory," Willy replied in a tone that sounded more angry than glad. "But don't come here projecting your history of battling sin onto me."

"Wiily, Satan will lie to you. He is the father of lies. If you think you can beat him, you are in for a big fall."

Willy jabbed his index finger at John's face and walked backward, keeping his finger pointed at him. "Stay away from me! . . .and from my family, too."

When Willy turned and stalked back toward his house, John blurted out, "You need help from your wife, from me, and from the Lord."

Willy stopped but didn't turn back around.

John continued. "If you keep it hidden, how can we help you? Satan is telling you that if the truth gets out in the open, your marriage will be ruined, and you'll get fired at work. Don't listen to the enemy. He knows if the truth gets out, you will be set free."

Willy's shoulders slumped, and he bowed his head.

"Jesus is the way, the truth, and the life. Satan thrives on hidden sins. Expose the lies, and he will be defeated."

Willy turned halfway around so John could only see the left half of Willy's face. "I no longer have the problem you had. I confessed it, and God forgave me. End of story." Willy spoke softly so John could barely hear him.

"If that's true, then let's talk about it." John waited a second for that to sink in. He figured if Willy had complete freedom he wouldn't sever their friendship.

Willy continued to look at him for a few seconds with the one eye that faced him. Then he looked at the ground and without saying anything further, he turned and walked into his house.

John's heart ached for Willy because of the shame, fear, and guilt he suffered. When John sat in the stuffed armchair in his office, he sensed the Holy Spirit wanted to pray through him. At first he thought the Lord would have him intercede for Willy and their friendship, but something else stirred him. The Spirit seemed to say that He had already taken care of Willy's addiction and his marriage. John laughed and praised God. "What an awesome God You are!"

Then he thought he had to be mistaken, that he misunderstood the Spirit. If Willy had truly been set free, wouldn't he have hugged him instead of going inside with his head bowed down?

John sensed the Holy Spirit still wanted him to pray for something else. The thought of receiving the Holy Spirit's guidance thrilled him, but he grieved over Willy's condition. Was Willy's thin veneer of good behavior covering a cancer that was eating away at the core of his marriage? What could he have done better to help John?

It is impossible to govern the world without God.
It is the duty of all nations to acknowledge the Providence
of Almighty God, to obey his will, to be grateful for his benefits
and humbly implore his protection and favor.
George Washington

Chapter Nine

After talking with his receptionist at Edward Jones, John learned his afternoon appointment had been canceled. He sat in their office at home and sensed God wanted him to use the time to pray. What a thrill to have the Holy Spirit guide him! John kneeled by his armchair and told the Holy Spirit to teach him. Shortly, John agonized from deep within his gut. He gasped and moaned, not from physical pain but from an intense discomfort in his soul. The agony continued, and he struggled to breathe. "Holy Spirit, what are we interceding for?" John grasped his stomach and chest, and he looked heavenward as much as his bent-over condition would allow. "How can I join You in earnest prayer if I don't know for whom we are praying? Show me and fill me with Your love for them."

Immediately, love poured into his heart for hundreds of thousands of people. He sensed people wheezing and gasping to catch their breath in hospitals and homes throughout the country. John prayed forty minutes for the healing of countless hurting people. When he stopped, he asked the Lord why he experienced such agony, and God transported him out of his body, just as the Spirit had when He showed him Willy's problem with pornography.

John looked at his physical body from the ceiling of their office. "Lord, this is pretty weird, again. What are You going to show me now? A dozen lifetimes would not be sufficient for You to take me to everyone for whom You had burdened me to pray."

In an instant, John hovered in the corner of a conference room where men in business suits sat around a long table arguing over methods to increase profits. They seemed to be brainstorming ways to manipulate medical insurance requirements and pharmaceutical demands to garner maximum income. The discussion heated up over concerns about getting caught, legal boundaries, and public perception.

John noted that none of them discussed the welfare of the patients. Above the men, a mist appeared that carried an odor of burned clothing or garbage. Then he heard voices that sounded like harsh whispers —

Yes, create fear in the minds of the public. Fear will make people cry for government intervention for vaccines.

Puuurrfect. State aid and medicine will replace God as a source of safety.
Fear, fear, fear! Oh, I love what fear does.

Yesss, superbugs and pandemics will intensify fear and create a clamor for federal solutions that will have them begging to relinquish their freedoms. Fear will make them demand that Congress spend billions to fund solutions without proper testing or any liability for drug companies.

Mmmmm, fear will force them to censor anyone who sheds light on the truth about the vaccines or confronts fallacies propagated by government agencies. Heh, heh, fear will stop their ears and blind their eyes.

John couldn't see who whispered, but he suspected demons influenced these executives that he saw below. Then he noticed Congresswoman Hartwood sitting at the table.

"So. . . ," Congresswoman Hartwood said, "if fear makes them reject even expert scientists and real scientific procedures, they will accept whatever the CDC, the President, and Congress say is true. The public won't balk at masking, closure of businesses, and vaccine mandates, no matter how much it defies common sense or past medical practices."

> *That's right, that's right! Expert epidemiologists like Peter McCullough and Computation expert Jessica Rose have challenged the lies you have spun, but mainstream news media has squashed them. They have convinced the entire world to label those challengers as crackpots and conspiracy theorists. Tens of thousands of doctors and scientists have signed the Great Barrington Declaration opposing vaccine mandates and other government narratives. But who even knows about the declaration? Nobody. And nobody ever will. Ha, you are thoroughly protected from having the truth discovered.*

"Even if a few expert scientists like Drs. Pierre Kory, Jessica Rose, and Robert Malone have some statistics that invalidate our conclusions," another man said, "we have plenty of people in Congress and the Administration who will support our efforts to suppress their evidence."

> *Ho. . . You have major medical journals, medical licensing boards, and medical complexes receiving finances from Big Pharma. They will condemn anyone who challenges your data as a source of misinformation. Those challengers will lose their license to practice and get fired from their jobs. Oh. . . , the fear you generate will keep you safe and prosperous.*

A thirty-something man at the head of the table stood with his hands planted on the table. "Our people will simply label anybody who tries to expose our program as conspiracy theorists and quacks, sources of misinformation."

Yesssss! On top of Big Pharma controlling the data, mainstream media will cover up anyone who dares to provide evidence to the contrary.

Congresswoman Hartman leaned forward. "That's right. Dr. Peter McCullough has testified before both houses of Congress multiple times and warned of the dangers of the vaccine and its ineffectiveness. The mainstream media always ignores his testimony. We have the media in our back pocket."

John shivered. He realized that several of the men had been verbalizing conclusions based on suggestions he had heard murmured from the ceiling. Those whispers came from demons who had been influencing the men sitting around the table. The demons knew which tactic to use for each person sitting there. On some they used the desire for protection, with others they used greed, indifference, or self-aggrandizement. John shook his head. Those men were devastating the nation's healthcare and destroying the lives of millions of people worldwide. He needed to do something. But what? Pray? How could his prayers affect their schemes?

Immediately, John returned to his body lying on the floor. Though his watch indicated only a few minutes had passed, the ache in his left hip made him feel as though he'd been lying on the floor for hours. John stood and stretched, flexing at the waist. Then he paced back and forth in their office as he interceded for the nation's healthcare by asking God to convict the men he saw of their greed and selfishness. After praying for five minutes, he felt overwhelmed. He asked the Lord for help, and shortly, Leah knocked on the door.

"Am I interrupting anything?" Leah poked her head in the doorway and smiled.

"No, in fact, you are an answer to the prayer I just prayed."

"Oooo, I like that."

"Well . . ." John hesitated. Lately, she had thought him weird whenever he went into deep intercession for someone, and she had even suggested that maybe dark spirits had influenced him or at the very least had let his flesh take him to dark places.

"Did God show you something sinister while you travailed in prayer?" Leah's tone of voice mocked him, though her eyes showed concern.

John looked at the ceiling. No way could he jump right in with a description of what he just witnessed. He went over and put his hands on her shoulders. "You know I have been praying for Willy?"

Leah put her palms on John's chest and stretched on her toes to kiss him. "I'm sorry. I don't mean to make fun of how you pray for people. It is just that lately. . ."

John put his arms around her back and hugged her. "Lately, God did a miracle in Willy's life. After I prayed for him, the Lord worked in his life supernaturally."

"Yeah?"

"Well, I hope so."

"I am sure God changed the situation because of your prayers, too, and the prayers of dozens of other people." Leah pulled her head away from his chest and looked up at him. "I just don't think God is into all the groaning I've been hearing here."

John grabbed her shoulders and looked into her eyes. "Why do you think God inspired Paul to write Romans 8:26? It says, 'Likewise the Spirit also helps in our weaknesses. For we do not know what we should pray for as we ought, but the Spirit Himself makes intercession for us with groanings which cannot be uttered.'"[5]

"That verse says the Spirit groans, not people."

John sighed. He saw no use in reminding her that the Spirit dwells in us. That was why Paul wrote the Scripture—so when people heard groanings they wouldn't be freaked out. "Do you want to hear how I think God broke the enemy's grip on Willy and Janet's marriage?"

Leah nodded and eyed him cautiously. "Is this something I should know?"

"Yes, because I won't share what broke loose but *how* God broke it loose." John motioned with his head for them to sit down. Leah sat on their stuffed armchair next to the desk while John sat on the desk chair. He slid his chair next to Leah's knees and held both of her hands.

John waited thirty seconds until he felt Leah calm her spirit. "God visually showed me a hidden sin in Willy's life so I could break the power of it over him. Now, he won't admit that he had a problem, but I think breaking the power of it healed his marriage."

---

[5] NKJV

"Okay, I know the transformation in Willy was dramatic. Janet told me as much, but why do you think it happened just because God revealed some secret sin of his?"

"Willy confirmed what I saw..., but not at first. When I gave him the specific details of what I saw, his face told me I had told him the truth. But that is not the supernatural part God wants me to share with you."

John looked for a good way to describe what God did. She would probably think he was crazy. God had prompted Leah to knock at the door as an immediate answer to his prayer for help. The Lord must want her to pray with him, so God would change her attitude toward how the Lord operated in intercession.

"Remember what Paul said in First Corinthians chapter twelve, where he described a vision of going into the third heaven?"

Leah frowned and cleared her throat.

John squeezed her hands gently to reassure her. "Paul wrote the Scripture for various reasons, and one reason was to let us know that such visions were possible."

Leah pulled her hands out of John's hands and sat back. "I suppose you are going to tell me that God took you into the third heaven."

John chuckled. "Leah, why are you looking at me like I've lost my marbles? Do you think all the miracles that happened to people in the Bible couldn't happen today because those were special people." John waved his arms above his head. "God is still the same. He hasn't changed, and He's all around us, in this very room. The only thing that prevents Him from doing the same thing today is our unbelief."

Leah's brow furrowed.

John slapped the arm of the armchair. "When I prayed, I believed God would answer me when I asked Him to show me how to pray for Willy, and He did. He gave me a vision so realistic that I felt like I was in heaven looking down on Willy while he sat at home."

Leah pulled farther away and bit her lower lip.

John bounced up. "I can't begin to describe how exciting that was. Can you believe it?"

Leah stood and walked backward toward the door gawking at him as she left. "No, I don't believe it. I am afraid you are either crazy or you have been deceived."

"Leah! I've never been more sane in my life." He reached out to hold her.

Leah shook her head. "No, we are done here. I am going to the family room to pray for you."

After she left their office, John flopped down in the armchair. "God, you have to talk to her. She won't listen to me."

In his mind John reviewed the conversation he just had with Leah. "Lord, I thought having her knock on the door—right after I prayed for help—was a sign that You had provided Leah as an answer to my request. Did I get that wrong?"

*It's easy to stand in the crowd, but
it takes courage to stand alone*
Mahatma Gandhi

Chapter Ten

John stood and opened the door to call Leah back, but he changed his mind. God had to change her heart, not him. John closed the door and stretched out prostrate on the floor before the Lord. "God, if my wife won't believe me, who can I get to help me?"

If what he saw and heard in his visions had any basis in reality, Drs. McCullough, Malone, and Kory likely received plenty of rejection and censorship. They ought to be eager to state their case to anybody willing to listen. John quickly prayed for the Holy Spirit to guide him and went to his computer to look up their contact information.

Epidemiologist Peter McCullough had a website that provided a telephone to contact someone on his team. After talking with an associate, John received data that implicated the media, the federal government, and Big Pharma in an unconscionable coverup of the truth that caused hundreds of thousands of people to suffer a horrible death. In addition to McCullough, Drs Paul Marik and Pierre Cory also reported effective results with Ivermectin or hydroxychloroquine when administered with doses of Vitamin C and D. These were not obscure scientists postulating theories based on results from laboratory mice. In randomized controlled trials that included over 2,100 patients, they demonstrated that ivermectin produces faster viral clearance, faster time to hospital discharge, faster time to clinical recovery, and a 75% reduction in mortality rates.

John thanked Dr. McCullough's associate for the information and went to his computer to investigate more. Big Pharma did not control the whole world, and John found some countries chose to do independent research. In August 2020, India's largest state, Uttar Pradesh, which has some 230 million residents, added ivermectin to its recommendations and distributed the drug for home care free of charge. The state of Bihar, which has 128 million residents, also started recommending ivermectin. By the end of 2020, Bihar and Uttar Pradesh had the lowest and second-lowest COVID-19 fatality rates in all of India.

Why had the US ignored those results? Both McCullough and Malone had testified before Congress of the effectiveness of Ivermectin and hydroxychloroquine. Though Congress then questioned Anthony Fauci on his refusal to accept those drugs, they didn't do anything to change government policies. In John's mind, that confirmed that those demons hadn't made empty boasts. Big Pharma and the mainstream media's ability to control the nation had help from evil forces.

Dr. Robert Malone was an internationally recognized scientist and physician. He was the original inventor of the mRNA vaccination as a technology, yet the media ignored him or wrote him off as a crackpot. Instead, the media held every word that Anthony Fauci said as the best medical advice available even though Fauci's formal education was only that of a medical doctor. John couldn't find any way to contact Malone on the Internet. The media had seriously censored Malone, and banks and social media had dealt him huge financial losses.

John looked up Dr. Pierre Kory online next. Like McCullough and Malone, he had been fired from his job and had his license pulled because he refused to accept the narrative of the NIH, CDC, FDA, and Anthony Fauci. Thousands of doctors and scientists joined them in signing the Great Barrington Declaration in October 2020. Many of the other signers also lost their jobs. John had to ask himself why. They would only put their livelihood on the line if they believed they were taking a stand for the truth that was worth the price they were paying. The courage and integrity of Kory, Malone, McCullough, Marik, et al, in 2020 should have made people listen. John staggered under the weight of the evil involved as he considered the hundreds of thousands of lives that were needlessly lost over the last three years.

John yearned to expose the corruption surrounding Big Pharma's lies and the mountain of evidence that the government and mainstream media ignored. Who would believe his story if he told them about traveling in his spirit body? Certainly, hundreds, if not thousands of people knew our country was being lied to. The members of our congress are the ones to be blamed for not correcting the lies. The collusion of Congress with Big Pharma infuriated him, so he kneeled in front of his armchair to pray. A pain gripped his insides, and he felt compelled to intercede for the members of Congress. "Lord, if You want me to intercede for the members of Congress, You have to show me what to pray."

    John's stomach cramped, and he buckled over on the floor, lying in a fetal position. After a few minutes, he struggled to his knees again and cried out to God. "No, Lord, I am too angry at those politicians to pray for them. How could they betray the public trust as they must have done? I want to pray judgment on them and for people to replace them."

    John continued to sense the Lord wanted him to pray for certain US Representatives, but he couldn't do it. He realized he should, but he'd be a hypocrite if he just went through the motions. Besides, there wouldn't be any power in those prayers. He had to wonder, though, if any of his prayers had accomplished much, despite the visions he received. However, he had to do something, so he decided to write letters to the editor to expose the greed and self-serving attitude of the men he overheard. Maybe he received those visions just so he could publicize the problem.

    The following afternoon, John sat in front of his computer stymied by what he wanted to say and what he couldn't say because he couldn't back up his assertions with hard facts. John deleted his document and went onto Facebook. He saw his cousin ranting about the President's "Badonomics" and figured he could join the crowd and do some of his own ranting. Maybe this is the means God provided to broadcast the problems. He had over 500 friends, so any comments on Facebook would likely influence more people than any letter to the editor. John grinned as he revealed on Facebook all the corruption he saw. Then he turned to Twitter or X and let the rants, rip, rock, and roll.

> Our Congressional Representatives are in cahoots with Big Pharma. They force everybody to take a leaky vaccine with unknown complications because they expect people to succumb to fear. They tell us people everyone has to have the vaccine even though it's established that COVID is a danger

only to senior citizens and the immunocompromised. Our elected officials are listening to Big Pharma with its hand on your wallet, employment, and freedom.

John smiled and posted his rant. He had only just begun, and he already felt invigorated. Drug companies, media sources, and politicians escaped criticism for using fear tactics because people had lost faith in God as a source of peace, a source that past generations relied on. That would be the source of his next rant —

Why do people let the media intimidate them into giving up their freedom of speech? They don't even bat an eyelash when social media removes any voice that contradicts the running narrative. Fear. That is the only explanation. People are terrified of getting sick, losing their jobs, or being labeled as antisocial or anti-vaxxers. They let fear rule their lives because they have lost faith in God. But faith wasn't lost. It was thrown out, at least the Christian faith was. It started with the public schools. They can teach Wicca or New Age religions, just not anything about a God who loves and cares for them.

John contemplated including a Bible verse but decided against it to prevent the post from becoming too lengthy. Without God, people were bound to lose a sense of purpose and peace. People were so lost nowadays that they would likely skip reading Bible verses anyway. He grinned and hit the Post button. He felt buoyed and ready to write more.

He needed to get specific now and name names. The drug companies he saw represented around that conference table needed to be exposed for what they were—greedy mercenaries who stole from honest taxpayers and stuffed their coffers. John didn't care if people got mad at him. He had a right to express his opinion and pass on information without revealing his sources —

I overheard conversations between Congresswoman Hartwood and William Bates from Bradlock Corp that revealed how they made millions of dollars for Bradlock by allowing drug companies to pay the deductible for patients because they knew that nobody would be able to pay the $19,000 per pill they charge for their latest chemotherapy concoction. Nobody, that is, except the American taxpayers. Hartwood, chairwoman of the House Investigation Committee, simply agreed to look the other way if anyone brought up the matter. Time to vote someone else into office.

John looked over what he wrote and clicked Post. He didn't want to pick on just Hartwood. Plenty of others deserved a little exposure for colluding with Big Pharma. He almost finished his next post when Leah appeared at their office door with her arms crossed in front of her chest.

"Gumby, you can't be passing along unsubstantiated rumors about our Congresswoman. You will make most of our neighbors who voted for her mad at you."

John turned in his chair to face her as she stood in the doorway. "I know firsthand that Hartwood colluded with Bradlock. Agreements like the ones she made have caused our medical costs to rise astronomically."

Leah tilted her head sideways and scrunched her nose. "Firsthand. Really? You're kidding, right?"

John stood and waggled his right index finger heavenward. "That's what I was trying to tell you yesterday. I saw and heard them talking in a small conference room."

Leah's eyes popped wide open with concern. "Gumby, I don't recall you leaving Minnesota in the last two years. When and where did this conversation take place?"

"You think I am crazy, don't you?" John put his hands together as in prayer. "Then you should pray for me. If I'm not crazy, then you should talk to God about our corrupt Representatives."

"That is not the point. Everybody knows politicians are open to undue influence from lobbyists, but you can't be posting total fabrications."

"I'm telling the truth!"

"John, think! What are you going to accomplish?" Leah leaned her shoulder against the doorjamb. "Perhaps, earn the well-deserved animosity of Hartwood and our neighbors who voted for her? Maybe even get removed from Facebook?"

"Whether you think lobbyists corrupt our politicians, or you think I'm crazy, you should be praying with me and for her."

Leah's eyes widened. She grabbed her phone out of her pocket.

"What are you doing?" John waved his hands with his "catching-a-pizza-dough" motion.

"I'm calling Janet so I can pray with her. I'm worried about you."

"What! You would pray with her before you prayed with me?"

Leah took two steps forward and touched his cheek with a concerned expression on her face.

"At least pray with me first."

Leah nodded. "Sure."

"Let's ask the Lord how we should pray, and let's pray for Hartwood too." John took her by her wrists and pulled her into the armchair next to the desk. When he sat in his desk chair, he scooted his chair over so his knees were touching hers, and he bowed his head in an attitude of prayer. He waited for her to pray, but he silently asked God to show her what he experienced with his spirit leaving his physical body.

Leah waited quietly. "Aren't you going to pray?"

John opened his eyes and looked at her. Did she even want to pray? John sighed. "I am waiting on the Holy Spirit to help me pray. He probably hasn't shown me anything because he wants you to pray first."

"He hasn't shown me anything either."

"Have you asked him?"

"No."

"Then ask Him, and afterward, wait for His answer." John closed his eyes and prayed earnestly for Leah to be open to the Holy Spirit moving supernaturally in her life.

Leah chewed on her lower lip, unsure how she should respond to John's request. He could be so impulsive at times. She supposed she should at least ask God to help her pray. She didn't know what to think about John's weird thoughts, so she decided to pray for their Congresswoman. "Lord, show me how to pray for Hartwood."

She heard John groan like he had been punched in the gut, but before she could open her eyes, she felt like the wind was knocked out of her. Seconds later, she passed out. The next thing she knew, she felt lighter than air, floating at the top of the ceiling.

She looked over at John, who floated next to her. He appeared transparent, and both of their solid physical bodies were slumped on the chairs. "What have you done to us, John?"

"Incredible!" John looked at his wife. "I didn't do this. How in heaven's name do you think I could do something like this?"

"Are we dead? Maybe we've been drugged or hypnotized. Or have we been demonized?"

"Sweetheart, only God could pull off something like this. If I'm not mistaken, what happens next will blow your mind even more."

*Have respect unto the covenant: for the dark places
of the earth are full of the habitations of cruelty.*
Psalm 72:20 KJV

Chapter Eleven

They found themselves floating in a room at ceiling level, observing various clusters of people who stood scattered about in what appeared to be a large private home. The air seemed clouded, though nobody smoked nor did the air feel humid.

Leah gasped. "What is this?"

"You haven't seen the best part yet," John replied.

"They can't see or hear us?"

"Nope, but if the Holy Spirit shows you what He showed me the last two times this happened, you will learn things that'll help you understand the devil's mode of operation throughout the world." John didn't doubt that demons whispered in the ears of the men below even now. God just hadn't opened his and Leah's ears to hear them yet. He wished the men below understood how demons swayed their judgment.

"This can't possibly be God's doing," Leah said. "I've heard about New Age gurus who boast about astral projection." Leah reached for John's arm, but her hand passed right through the image of his arm. "John, get us out of here," Leah pleaded with a worried expression in her eyes.

"The Holy Spirit is in control, Leah, not me. Don't worry! Holy Spirit won't force anything on you that you can't handle. The Apostle James tells us to consider it all joy, when we encounter various trials.[6]" As John said that, the clouds thickened in the room. A stench like decaying fish assailed their souls and harsh whispers reverberated

---

[6] James 1:2 paraphrased by the author

off the walls. Men and women socialized in various corners of several rooms.

Yes, increase CEO benefits, said a pale demon with eyes that glowed red. *The better the CEO, the more they will find ways to play the system, and everybody wins! The employees, Big Pharma, insurance companies, stockholders. You all get richer!*

Two portly men tapped wine glasses and toasted to their mutual prosperity.

Pay no mind to the extra costs, said a hooded demon with his face hidden. *Taxpayers will cover the costs. You can't lose what you fought for in establishing your RVUs.*

In another corner a middle-aged woman chatted with a gray-haired man. "Doctor, your staff has done an excellent job billing at the highest rates allowable."

The doctor snorted. "Thanks. The lack of oversight on our claims has kept us in the ballpark with the current RVUs."

"What are RVUs?" Leah whispered.

"I think that stands for Relative Value Units. It is a tool doctors use to bill for their services." John replied. "Evidently, some doctors and medical facilities use the tool to pad their bill."

The money you invest in medical schools and government agencies is like gold. That investment influences the education of doctors and ensures the oversight of drug approval by federal agencies will suit your every whim. They have to, or they will lose half their funding and face bankruptcy. Ha, ha, ha! The demon's deep cackle rose ominously, as though it came from a bottomless pit.

A pale, round, chubby-cheeked demon whispered in the ear of one of two men in a corner. *Yesss. . . The middle class won't be able to afford insurance with your proposals. Liberals will clamor for the federal government to be the third-party payer for everybody, and conservatives will insist on paying only for what they choose. In the endless battle to determine the fate of the healthcare system, Big Pharma, the medical supply industry, and enterprising doctors will cash in.*

In another corner of the room, a short man with a loose-fitting suit complained about the lack of caution used in promoting vaccines. A large man in a sport coat and fingers bedecked with large jeweled rings stared at the smaller man as he listened.

"Look, Mathew," the large man said, "we have to have everyone believing the danger of getting COVID-19 makes getting vaccinated worth the risk."

"But COVID-19 presents almost no risks to infants or young children," Matthew said. "Scientists like Jessica Rose have reported on adverse reactions in infants and children. The news about that is bound to get out."

"What do you mean?"

Two demons clamored for the attention of the large man, one demon by each ear. One demon encouraged him on his right. *You have worked hard to create an atmosphere of fear and a pervasive sense of danger from the pandemic. The public will demand that the media silence any scientists who dispute your assessment of how to manage COVID-19.*

The other demon reminded him: *You don't have to worry. The mainstream media have totally hidden the facts. They have labeled Dr. Robert Malone, the original inventor of mRNA vaccination, as a spreader of misinformation.*

"Hey, you big-shot executives and bureaucrats," Leah yelled, "what about the children who are suffering from vaccine side effects? While drug companies and the medical supply industry rake in the cash, do you care that millions are suffering or dying without health insurance?"

"They can't hear you," John said.

"Don't they realize demons are manipulating them?"

He hovered closer to Leah as they listened for several minutes while demons bragged about their corrupting influence on the various drug companies. "If those CEOs could hear you, their hearts would still keep them from receiving your message. All they want is the easiest way to capture the most profit."

"Where are we, and why are we here?"

"I have no idea where we are," John replied. "For all I know, we might be listening to conversations that took place years ago, but wherever, whenever, and whatever we're listening to, I think the Holy Spirit wants to show us how to pray."

"That's crazy!" Leah looked at him, shaking her head.

A second later, John opened his eyes in his physical body, which had slid off his chair and onto the floor. His right hip ached from the way he landed on the floor. He sat up and looked at his wife. Leah's eyes fluttered. "Did I just dream that, or did you see what I saw?"

John held Leah's hand while he grasped her upper arm and helped her sit up straight. "You mean the demons? The ones who whispered in the ears of men standing around in a room and told the men they deserved the money they connived together and worked the system to get?"

Leah put her head in her hands as she leaned her elbows on her knees. "How can we pray against demons if unscrupulous men won't listen to us?"

"Leah, you know what the Bible says about our authority in Christ. Luke 10:19 says God has given us authority to cast out demons.

Leah protested. "He gave that promise to the apostles."

"No, he gave it to over seventy disciples who did just that." John extended both hands straight out from his sides. "Furthermore, when Christ gave us the Great Commission to make disciples of all nations, He said that these signs would follow us as we did that—that we'd cast out devils in addition to laying hands on the sick and seeing them recover and receiving protection from serpents and poison."

Leah stared at her husband without saying a word.

John studied her face for some kind of reaction. Now that she had experienced the same thing he had, she surely must be excited, too. "God showed you this so we could intercede together in unity. Matthew 16:19 says whatever we bind on earth will be bound in heaven, and whatever we loose on earth will be loosed in heaven. Matthew 18:19 says that whenever two of us agree on anything we ask, it will be done by our Father in heaven."

Leah cleared her throat. "Casting out *a* demon from a demon-possessed person was one thing, but we heard a whole gang of demons influencing dozens of people. Are you trying to do something that even Jesus wouldn't attempt? All sorts of demonic networks existed when Jesus walked the earth. . . .But Jesus didn't attempt to cast them all out. He lived among the Romans who worshipped idols and practiced all kinds of demonic perversions. Are you planning—

"Absolutely! Jesus said we would do greater works than He did." John thought of doing the craziest things within sight.

She looked at John. "How do you—"

"That's what I tried to tell you earlier." John held out his hands for her to grab. "How we will do it is described by Paul in Romans chapter eight. When we don't know how to pray as we ought, the Spirit makes intercession for us with groanings which cannot be uttered."

Leah shoved his hands away. "That is way too weird for me. Praying with groaning might strike you as a good way to pray, but I don't want any part of it."

"Leah, I groaned earlier, but I heard you groaning too."

Leah grimaced and left the office.

\#   \#   \#

Two days later, when Willy walked into the kitchen, Janet asked him about a strange conversation she had with Leah. "I had to admit you have been a new person the past few weeks, but I couldn't tell her what changed you because you won't tell me."

Willy looked at the dog's empty water dish on the floor. To stall while he thought of a suitable answer, he filled up the dish. He couldn't tell her about his decision to foreswear perverted websites. That would only hurt her. God only knew what John told Leah, though he doubted John would gossip about his pornography addiction, even to his wife. "What made her think that something special must have happened . . .other than I felt the Lord wanted me to be more loving toward my wife?"

Janet shrugged. "She said John hinted that he thought God had done a deep, cleansing work in your heart. What would that have been about?"

"How would I know?" Willy growled. "I will ask him when I see him next."

Janet's eyebrows drew closer together. "Don't get mad at me. I am thrilled with the change that's come over you."

Willy put his arms around her and kissed her. "I'm sorry. I just don't like John putting ideas in his wife's mind that cause you to wonder about me."

"Well, the transformation in you has been a super blessing, especially after the complete separation I felt over the past year." Janet raised her eyebrows as though she hoped for further explanations.

Willy kissed her forehead. "God has been talking to me about being a better husband."

"Leah seemed to think that God had made a breakthrough in your life through an unusual type of intercession that God had done through John."

Willy chuckled. "John imagines all sorts of fantastic super-spirituality." Willy pressed his cheek to her forehead so she couldn't read his expression. He stuffed his anger because he had no explanation for being mad other than John's words scratched through the thin crust of his fragile shield of faith. John's prayers may have broken the power of pornography in his life, but he didn't care to have John explain why he needed help.

Janet pushed at his chest, and he knew she wanted to get a better look at his face. He checked his watch like he had something important to do so she couldn't decipher his real feelings. "Hey, I forgot something I need to find in the basement."

"Okay, I hope you are ready to come up in an hour. Leah said that she and John planned to drop by at six o'clock."

Willy ran down the stairs to their basement. He had to invent an excuse for leaving the kitchen abruptly. Now he needed a reason to leave the house entirely for a couple of hours. He'd deal with John's hyper-spirituality without Janet around. For now, he'd take Janet out with him. Otherwise, she would invite them in, and they would still be here when he returned.

Willy thought of a perfect solution. He called up from the basement, "Janet, did you wash the slacks I wore to work yesterday?"

"Yeah, they are in the wash."

Willy yelled up from the basement. "Phooey!"

"What's wrong?" Janet said.

"I had some coupons that I bought from Nick at the parts store. It was a fundraiser for his son's Boy Scout troop. If you didn't find them, I must have left them at work." Willy walked back up into the kitchen.

"You can get them when you go to work on Monday, huh?"

"Oh, I just remembered them, and I thought you would like to go to the new Tom Hanks movie they are showing tonight."

"Wow, it has been forever since we went to the movies. When does the show start?"

But thou, O Lord, art a God full of compassion, and gracious, long suffering, and plenteous in mercy and truth.
                                        Psalm 86:15 KJV

Chapter Twelve

They left a note for their sons to help themselves to leftovers in the frig. They would be back late tonight. When they arrived at the theater, they were almost an hour early. Willy pointed out his "mistake" and apologized for not checking the movie times more carefully. As they stood in front of the concessions, choosing their snacks, the aroma of pizza and popcorn reminded Willy of dating before they were married. He squeezed Janet around the waist. "Why don't we get some pizza and call it our dinner? We can get dessert at the Perkins Restaurant afterward."

"We could have eaten dinner at Randy's cafeteria and still made it to the show."

"Yeah, sorry about that. I wouldn't have taken you to McDonald's or Burger King, but Randy's would have been quick and still not cheesy." Willy wanted to get out of the house fast before John arrived. If he had told her they had an hour before the show started, Janet would have insisted they either eat at Randy's or finish up leftovers at home. Since John loved Randy's salad bar, that also would have risked them bumping into John and Leah. "Eating pizza at the theater reminds me of the times when I had to get you home before your dad's curfew." He enjoyed the memory now, but he still thought it absurd that her dad put a curfew on her at age 29. He thanked God at the time because her dad's curfew likely kept other bona fide suitors away from her.

"Yeah?" Janet smiled and leaned her head against his arm.

"Yep, I wanted to give you the royal treatment due a princess —both dinner and a show—even though I didn't have time for both because of your dad's curfew."

Willy picked a pepperoni pizza and Janet chose cheese. They sat on a bench outside the theater room number seven where their movie was showing to eat their pizza. That way they wouldn't see the ending before the beginning. Willy liked the pizza. He could almost pretend the dimmed lighting of the theater hallway gave the atmosphere a romantic feeling. A cheesy poster for an upcoming horror movie that featured a chainsaw maniac spoiled the ambiance somewhat.

When they finished their pizza and beverages, Willy stood and threw their trash in the bin next to them. Then he glanced down the hall and saw John and Leah walking toward them.

Willy jerked back around, hoping they hadn't seen him. He stood in front of Janet with his back to them to prevent them from seeing her. "Hey Janet, let me show you this picture that one of my co-workers showed me." He pulled out his phone, hunching over it in front of her to keep John and Leah from noticing them.

"Hi Janet, hi Will," Leah said.

"Imagine seeing you here." John slapped Willy on his back. "We just stopped at your house to talk with you. Your sons said you had gone on a date, so we decided to come here. We haven't been to the movies in years."

"Wow, we haven't been to the movies for ages either, and then we bump into you two. What are the chances of that happening?" Willy tried to keep his frustration from showing. He smiled, but he doubted he looked happy to see them.

"Hey, you guys come for Tom Hanks's latest flick, too?" John asked.

Janet stood. "Yeah, we can sit together."

"Hey!" Willy replied in the most enthusiastic tone he could muster. "We haven't double-dated at the movie theater since we first met. That would be wonderful."

"Super, we can talk about why we stopped by your home while we wait for the movie to start," John said as people poured out of theater room number seven.

Leah sat next to Janet so she could talk with her. "Thanks for taking this time to chat with me. I'll move once the show starts." Leah could tell Willy was nervous, and she wanted to do everything possible to avoid squelching Willy's desire to be attentive to his wife.

Willy looked at people filing into the seats and frowned. "Sure, Leah, but if it's something personal, maybe you and Janet can find a better spot to discuss it."

"Of course, I just wanted to learn what God has been doing with you two."

"That is exactly what I would prefer you discuss later."

"Sure, maybe we can stop for coffee and pie after the movie."

Leah turned to Janet. "I'm happy to see how things have turned around for you and Willy. I'm looking forward to hearing the details after the movie."

Leah engaged in small talk with Janet, but her mind wandered elsewhere. She hoped that Janet would talk candidly about the turnabout that happened in their marriage. She hated the thought that John's scary out-of-body intercession was responsible for it. If it was, he'd expect her to join him in intercession, and she'd have difficulty refusing him. Traveling out of her body took her way beyond her comfort zone. With God, all things were possible. She just never thought the "possible" would be that insane.

After the movie they stopped at the local Perkins and sat at a booth in the back corner. The restaurant didn't have many customers at 9:30 PM, so they had plenty of privacy to talk openly.

After the waitress took their orders and left, John leaned forward and looked each one of them in the eye. "Is there an elephant in the room that we need to talk about?" John extended the palm of his hand toward Leah as though she knew what to say next.

"John's ideas are nothing but speculation or the result of a runaway imagination," Willy huffed.

"That's exactly the way I feel." Leah elbowed John. She had no idea why John thought he should discuss this with them now.

John threw his hands up in the air like a referee signaling for a touchdown. "Let's start by defining our elephant."

"Let's not!" Willy bit out his words.

"Why not?" both Janet and John exclaimed simultaneously.

Willy glared at John. "To preserve our friendship and my marriage."

Leah placed her hand on John's forearm. "Maybe this isn't the time or place to discuss this." Leah sighed. Sometimes John could be so insensitive. If nothing else, Willy's reaction proved the error of John's new way of interceding.

The waitress returned with three coffees and a tea. She left after she assured them she would be right back with their order.

"I don't think there will ever be a good time," Willy added.

"Willy, John expects me to join in doing what he does."

"Well, tell him, 'No'"

"What do you think about his out-of-body experiences?"

Willy sat back and looked back and forth between John and Leah. "What?"

Leah realized that John might be right about the elephant because Willy either ignored the elephant or didn't know it existed. "Has John told you what he does?"

"Not exactly." Willy's voice sounded as cold as the stare he gave John.

Leah didn't know how to describe it. She and John had entered a realm in which no sane person would want to be, and he longed for her to join in his madness. "Well, John wanted me to let you know that he wouldn't describe specific things that might aggravate matters between the two of you. I have no idea what those things were. I wanted to ask your opinion about another matter. John and I saw and heard strange things after we prayed for Congresswoman Hartwood. When I say *strange*, I mean something totally out of this natural world."

The waitress returned with two apple pies and two lemon meringue pies. Leah waited until she left to speak again.

While briefly describing her experiences with John, neither Willy nor Janet commented, but their faces appeared to register the same disbelief that she felt at first. How could they feel otherwise? When she finished she asked, "What would you do if that happened to you?"

Willy put his elbow on the table and bent his forearm up to rub the top of his head with his hand. "I . . . don't know."

"How about you, Janet?" Leah asked.

Janet looked back and forth between her and John. After a moment of silence, she took a deep breath. "I have always respected you, John, as a wise, mature Christian, but even the wise can be deceived."

John planted the palm of his hand firmly on the table. "I hadn't planned on describing in detail how I knew how to pray for Willy."

The waitress stopped at their table on her way back from checking on another customer. "Need anything else?"

Everybody shook their head, and Leah replied. "We're good, thank you." Their server was efficient and sweet. Normally, she would have made pleasant conversation with her, but she didn't want to delay hearing Willy's reaction.

John thanked God for their desserts and then asked their thoughts about the visions Leah had described.

Willy took a big bite of his pie, and he just grunted a noncommittal opinion.

Janet forked a piece of lemon meringue and knitted her eyebrows. "If God were in these visions of yours, wouldn't you be seeing God's angels as well as Satan's angels? I mean, I have been told that God has twice as many angels as Satan has."

"Maybe God's angels don't go where they aren't invited." John's frustration was evident from the tone of his voice. "Besides, the businessmen we saw had no doubt courted the demonic influence."

Willy swallowed hard. "Ah, if God's angels weren't invited there, what were you doing there?"

John wedged off a piece of apple pie and stabbed it with his fork. "Learning how to pray!"

"Do you need out-of-body experiences to pray?" Janet asked.

"Yes, sometimes we don't even know who needs prayer or how to pray for them. That's why the Bible says the Holy Spirit should help us pray."

Janet shoved a piece of her lemon meringue pie around on her plate. "Really, don't you have enough people close by to pray for, and isn't that why you ask and take prayer requests from people?"

John glanced at Willy and Janet. "Janet, God leads each of us differently in how we pray or serve Him. Some people fold their hands and close their eyes with their heads bowed when they pray. Others stretch their hands out and open their eyes, looking towards heaven." John raised his hands heavenward.

Leah pulled on his arms to get him to lower them. "Maybe we can talk about this some other time."

"The whole reason we wanted to talk with Willy and Janet was to settle in your mind whether these visions came from God to show us how to pray."

Leah glared at him, and she hoped he took that as a hint to drop the subject. "What did you think of Tom Hanks' performance?"

"Tom Hanks does what he does best," Willy replied without hesitation. "Whether he's a developmentally challenged soldier or a lonely, bitter, old man ready to commit suicide, he pulls it off masterfully."

John sighed. "Yeah, Hanks was great. Maybe we can talk later."

The secret of freedom lies in educating people whereas the secret of tyranny is in keeping them ignorant.
Maximilien Robespierre, French Statesman 1758-1794

Chapter Thirteen

On the drive home, John wanted to discuss their vision of spirit-body traveling. He tried to avoid discussing how their conversations with Willy and Janet had gone, but that's what Leah wanted to talk about. She asked why he hadn't outright asked Willy if his vision had inspired Willy's transformation. He had tried to avoid that because Willy insisted the vision had no basis in reality. Besides, the substance of what he saw wasn't something he could share.

When they stepped inside their home, John asked Leah one more time to pray with him against the demonic influence over Big Pharma which they discovered in their spirit-body visions.

Leah stopped at the entrance to the living room and shook her head. "Didn't Janet's remarks bother you?" Leah sounded worried.

"What? Do you think the devil would reveal what he is doing so we would know how to pray against his schemes?" John tapped his temple with his right forefinger. "He's smarter than that. Furthermore, God's angels weren't there because we have to pray for them to be there."

"Well, you don't want to talk with Willy about your vision, and I am not about to go back to listen to demons."

John shook his head. She didn't understand. They should put Willy's problem behind them for now because they had bigger issues to deal with. He walked into the living room and waved his hand at the sofa. "We don't have to watch demons anymore. We just need to pray for God's angels to deal with the situation. Psalm one hundred and three says that God's angels perform God's word, obeying the voice of His word. Our job is to be the voice of His will in this place on earth."

Leah remained where she stood and stared at him. "He doesn't need us to put angels into action. Besides, our children are probably sleeping. We'll wake them."

"The kids will be fine. God longs for us to intercede for others."

"Why?"

John walked back and grasped her hand. "Because God desires for His love to motivate our prayers. Having His love in us will empower our prayers to change other people and us."

Leah's shoulders slumped.

John drew her to their sofa. "Hey, what do you have to lose? If nothing happens when we pray for God and his angels to expose the things we saw in, then we will know God wasn't in the vision we experienced."

"Vision!" Leah shuddered. "That out-of-body experience of hearing demons spooked the daylights out of me. I'll never get used to that kind of thing."

John continued to hold her hand as they sat on the couch. "I am not asking you to do anything spooky. Just pray with me about what we saw and see if what we pray comes to pass."

"So, what will that prove?"

"If nothing happens, I will admit this kind of intercession was wrong, and I will never bring this up to you again." John believed if Leah agreed to pray with him, God would do His part.

"Okay, I'll pray with you." Leah exhaled sharply and bowed her head.

John bowed his head and closed his eyes. He remembered overhearing a demon boast about how he had arranged for Bradlock to buy out generic drug production and then jack up their prices so they could continue to make exorbitant profits on brand name products even after their patents had expired. That bothered John, but he sensed God didn't want him praying over that. Instead, the Lord led him to intercede for another issue. "Lord, send angels to expose schemes that allow Big Pharma to sponsor the copay for patients on outrageously priced drugs. Don't let them hide how that lets them keep the drug at sky-high prices. Reveal which politicians are aware of those schemes that leave taxpayers or insurance companies with inflated prices. Stop

Big Pharma from shielding drugs from market forces that drive prices down."

"Humph," Leah snorted.

John looked up at her. She didn't seem ready to put much faith into interceding.

Leah took a deep breath. "Yeah, God, I suppose if you are in this, then send angels to embarrass the politicians who refuse to bring the Big Pharma to task for buying out companies that manufacture cheap generic drugs. Don't let them raise the price of generic drugs so they can jack up the price of a brand name product."

An exciting chill spread across John's shoulder blades. The Lord stopped him from praying about generic drugs because He knew what Leah's heart desired to pray. When she ditched her indifferent attitude, God's desires could flow through her and make her prayers effective. Hadn't Leah realized that the Holy Spirit inspired her to pray?

Leah opened her eyes and held his gaze while she smirked.

John bowed his head and prayed silently. "Lord, how could she fail to realize the Holy Spirit inspired her prayer? With the amount of faith and effort she put into that prayer, will You still honor her prayer? What do You want me to do, Lord?"

He paused for a few minutes, waiting for God to reply, and not hearing an answer, he continued to talk to the Lord silently. "I can't force her to pray. Without faith motivating her, we are wasting our time."

John waited a few more minutes before he tapped Leah's knee. "Thanks for praying with me. You can go now, and I will continue to pray by myself."

# # #

Two weeks later, Leah received a dream as she lay asleep next to John. The images in her dream possessed vibrant colors that could only exist in heaven. In her dream John came up to her as she sat on a chair and asked her if she had seen the key. She shook her head, and John seemed to be bewildered and left. After he left, she stood and lifted the bottom of her chair seat which covered a tray. Inside the tray lay a box from which Leah removed a key. In the dream, Leah realized that she held the key John wanted, but up until that moment she hadn't actually seen the key. She just knew she sat on it.

Leah woke up alert. The clock displayed the time as 2:00 AM, way too early to get up for the day. She turned on her side and pounded her pillow. What did God mean by that dream? She hadn't lied to John. Was the dream meant to warn her of a future temptation to lie to John by neglecting to say something she knew the truth about? She decided the dream likely had no significance at all. She pounded her pillow again. No, she wronged John by only giving lip service to their intercession together.

Leah looked over at John, thankful he was still asleep. She didn't want to talk to him now. Two weeks ago, she sensed the Spirit had inspired her intercession, but now she felt terrible for failing to tell John that she sensed God inspired even her half-hearted prayer. That wasn't truly a lie of omission because she still doubted her prayer came from God. Besides, that was ancient history, and she didn't want to burden him with her doubts. Leah glanced at John and shuddered. She dreaded traveling out of the body too much to tell John anything.

Leah slipped out of bed and went to the kitchen to make some comfort food. She made macaroni and cheese and tried to ignore the extra calories she'd end up consuming. To heck with the diet! Leah banged the needed pan as she removed it from the cupboard. Why did John hound her in his search for effective intercession? Even when she read the Bible, she felt him needling her about faith and prayer. Jesus said repeatedly that according to her faith, it would be done for her. But what if she didn't want anything done for her? Despite being afraid, she had asked God to help her use any knowledge they might have gained from their visions.

John walked into the kitchen, appearing still sleepy. "Trouble sleeping?"

"How can I have faith if the out-of-body experience terrifies me?" Leah snapped. "Would God expect me to journey if I hear demons cackling and my hands tremble so badly I can't touch my mouth with my thumb?"

"Oops, I appear to have walked into a bad dream. Too early for that. I'll talk to you later." John turned around and left.

Leah pursed her lips. It was bad enough he caused her distress in her dreams. Now his physical presence threatened to spoil her binge on comfort food.

She couldn't confess what happened when John had prayed about politicians looking the other way. The jolt she felt in her gut could have been caused by anything, though it seemed to confirm he had prayed what the Holy Spirit wanted. But she had to proceed with caution because feelings could deceive us. She had sensed that she should pray against the thievery caused by buyouts of generic drugs. However, if God inspired either of their prayers, we would see an answer soon.

Leah took a bite of hot macaroni and cheese. Maybe John would drop his idea of having her join him in his idea of intercession if nothing came out of their prayers. Then John wouldn't expect her to leave her body so they could spy on corrupt politicians and business tycoons.

When Leah finished her comfort food, she went into the living room to pray on the sofa but promptly fell asleep. Three hours later, Leah woke, looked at the living room wall clock, and realized she needed to set out breakfast for the children. John would pray with Andy on the bluff that morning, so she cooked bacon for him as a peace offering.

John entered the kitchen as the bacon finished cooking and declared that the aroma drove him wild, so he better have a couple of slices before he headed to Aurora Bluff. He left with a smile on his face. The children ate breakfast and rushed out the door.

Leah set out a cup and plate for John's breakfast and sat at the kitchen table to read her Bible. After reading chapter two in Philippians, she prayed that the issues between her and John would be resolved quickly. Then she prayed for unity in Willy and Janet's marriage.

After asking God to heal relationships with other friends, Leah closed her Bible and sauntered into the living room. John hadn't picked up the daily newspaper from the front porch yet, so she put on her shoes and fetched the paper, shaking off a dusting of snow that had blown over it.

The headlines broadcasted the details of a robbery in a strip mall and a fire in a warehouse on the north side of the Twin Cities. Nothing new there. She turned to the section on national news and froze when she read a small article at the bottom of the page. An independent reporter described the Big Pharma schemes to escape market pressures that normally reduced the price of exorbitantly priced pills by paying the copay for desperate patients. The article described examples of costly cancer medications that meant impossibly high copays. The Bradlock Corporation paid the copay, which allowed them to pass the outrageous price on to insurance companies and, in the cases of Medicare, on to taxpayers. Bradlock merely added the cost of the deductible onto the already inflated price, and they looked like heroes though taxpayers via Medicare and insurance companies staggered under the weight of inflated healthcare costs.

This article was what John had prayed would happen two weeks ago. Leah's prayer hadn't been answered yet. Would John release her from her promise because only his prayer had been answered? She hoped he wouldn't read or learn about the article. To make sure he wouldn't, she cut out the article. If he asked her about the missing bottom part of the page, she'd tell him she clipped it off for an ad on some shoes. He'd never ask, anyway. John never paid much attention to the national news.

For unto us a child is born, unto us a son is given: and the government shall be upon his shoulder: and his name shall be called Wonderful, Counsellor, The mighty God, The everlasting Father, The Prince of Peace.
Isaiah 9:6 KJV

Chapter Fourteen

On the following Monday, Leah sat and watched John poke at his ground beef enchiladas, one of his favorite meals. The only words John spoke were to David when he said, "Good work on the rings today." Long periods of silence weren't typical of her husband. With Christmas a week away, he usually burst with enthusiasm over finding gifts for everyone and baking Christmas cookies.

Leah waited until the children asked to be excused and left the dinner table. She put her fork down firmly on her plate, creating a clunk to grab his attention. "What are you getting Rachael for Christmas?" Leah asked softly, using exaggerated lip movement so Rachael couldn't hear.

John held up both hands as though catching raindrops and shrugged.

"What's wrong? By this time, you have usually hidden dozens of creative gifts and found a new way to celebrate the Holidays."

"Maybe the trouble I am having with coaching David's gymnastics team has kept me from catching the Christmas spirit."

"Yeah? Maybe we should bake some of our favorite Holiday treats to break loose the Christmas spirit." Leah hated to see her cheerful hubby so down at the mouth. His sadness, however, likely prevented him from learning the news about Bradlock and how God answered his prayer.

Every day that passed without him learning about the article brought her a modicum of relief, but each day also increased her guilt. She believed he teetered on the brink of abandoning his new method of intercession because he had seen no positive results.

She asked God to keep the news from John. If God honored her request, didn't that mean He also wanted her to hide the news from John? Certainly, God would never make her do something beyond her level of faith. She struggled to watch John mope around, but if traveling in his spirit body had demonic origins, then she did the right thing.

John asked Leah to save the uneaten portion of his enchiladas, so she picked up the dinner plates. When she brought out a carrot cake, she called the children to join them for dessert. Rachael and David scarfed down their cake and left. When John dallied over his favorite treat, she decided to encourage him with a compromise. "I've been thinking that we should resume intercession together after we celebrate the new year. I am asking the Lord not to send me out of my body, and I'm pretty sure He won't. I am fine with you traveling somewhere in your spirit body. I am not sure your voyages originate from God, but if they don't, He can stop them from happening."

"You'll join me in intercessory prayer?" John's eyes widened.

Leah sighed. "Yeah," she replied in a barely audible voice.

"Don't sound so enthusiastic."

"If anyone except our closest friends overheard you describe your journeys, they'd send you to either the funny farm or an exorcist." Leah looked heavenward. "I not planning to float around like a ghost."

John pulled out his cell phone and paged through his Bible app. "You still doubt whether God would send us traveling. Let's review the Scripture basis for it."

Leah nodded, thankful that in his excitement he hadn't asked why she changed her mind. "There's nothing in the Bible about turning people into spying ghosts," Leah said, hoping to emphasize why she wouldn't be traveling with him in her spirit body.

"Paul describes the out-of-body experience in Second Corinthians 12:2." He turned to the page in his Bible and read it. "I know a man in Christ who fourteen years ago—whether in the body I do not know, or whether out of the body I do not know, God knows—such a one was caught up to the third heaven."[7]

---

[7] II Corinthians 12:2 NKJV

"That doesn't say anything about spying on people and seeing demons," Leah said. She believed the Scriptures did not encourage flying around in their spirit bodies to listen to evil spirits. She was right to question his desire to travel in his spirit body. Fear couldn't help but come when doing something you shouldn't do.

"I've wrestled with the same thought," John said. "Two verses later, Paul says in verse four: "'and he heard things that cannot be told, which man may not utter.'"

"Well, I guess that means you shouldn't be expecting me to do it or to be doing it yourself."

"I wondered whether I had erred in talking with you about it. But I think this verse means I should consider what I see or hear as something that should be held in strict confidence. This passage in Second Corinthians does suggest traveling out of the body is possible. Paul did it."

Leah avoided making eye contact with him. "I don't recall any place in the Bible recommending we listen to what demons are saying to people or to each other."

John covered her hand on top of the table with his. "Jesus listened to demons in Matthew 8:31 where the demons begged Jesus, saying, 'If You cast us out, permit us to go away into the herd of swine.'[8] If Jesus did, then it's okay for us too."

"But spying on people. . .? Nothing in the Bible about that!" As long as she had the Bible on her side, Leah justified keeping a safe distance from spirit traveling.

A day later, Leah noticed John seemed to perk up and resume his usual cheerful outlook on life. He discussed their Christmas plans and went over his Christmas shopping list for the following day. Though she still dreaded the risks of being connected to John's visions, she could live with her agreement to pray with him again.

#   #   #

John drove to the shopping malls the Friday evening before Christmas and joined a mass of men making their last-minute Holiday purchases. Buying gifts a few days before Christmas wasn't entirely new to him. He enjoyed the madness of trying to find the latest

---

[8] NKJV

electronic gadget, video game, or fashion statement. Though he could have ordered everything online, he rejected the concept because that seemed too sterilized from the Christmas spirit. Somehow, joining the mass of humanity inundating the malls seemed to embrace the joy of the season.

Amid shopping, he heard Christmas carols. He paused as he examined slippers for Leah. The carols reminded him of the reason for this season. Jesus came as a child to Earth, and as Isaiah prophesied, the government of the world was to be upon his shoulders. He was and is the Prince of Peace. Therefore, John could sing hallelujahs because Jesus was in control, and Jesus would bring His peace to squash the corruption messing up the world.

# # #

Two days later, John and his family attended the Christmas Eve service at church and afterward gathered in their living room to open their presents. They sang their two traditional carols around their brightly lit tree, and Rachael distributed the presents to everyone. John sat on the sofa and watched David and Rachael open their presents. Leah served them hot apple cider, and the aroma of cinnamon and apples enveloped John with contentment. Though this year's celebrations seemed subdued, he welcomed the ensuing peace. He could enjoy their reactions to their gifts because he left the problems of Willy, Big Pharma, and vaccines in God's hands.

Leah seemed delighted with the pink, wool-lined, furry slippers he gave her, and she gushed over the bread maker. She glanced at the recipes they included inside the box and smiled slyly at him. "This will fit well with one of my gifts for you."

"Oh? I can hardly wait." John ripped open the larger of his two boxes. He smiled at the wool-lined furry slippers. "Our feet are going to stay warm and comfortable together this winter."

John looked at Leah to sense her reaction. "What could be in this small box that will fit well with the bread machine?"

"Oh, there are three gifts in that small box. Only one of them fits the bread maker." Leah scooted next to him on the sofa and put her hand on his arm. "I know you don't like the materialism that surrounds much of Christmas, so this isn't a physical thing. I gave you the gift of my time."

"Wow! I like that!" John kissed her and opened the box. Inside the box he found three envelopes. He waved the first envelope in the air to be melodramatic.

Inside that envelope, Leah's card said: "I promise to make my husband sourdough bread at least once a month for a full year or until he tells me to stop."

"Yes! I love sourdough bread!" John forced a smile. He loved sourdough, but he bought the bread maker because their children loved homemade bread. They didn't love sourdough. More importantly, sourdough cultures would consume a lot of Leah's time, which he had hoped the bread maker would free up so she would pray with him more often.

When he picked up the next envelope, he held it to his forehead. "Ooo. . ., I wonder what it says." John imagined she changed her mind and agreed to travel in her spirit body with him at least once a month. Though he needed to spend more time with Rachael and David, God wanted him to have someone to join him in his spirit-body journeys.

He ripped open the envelope with a flair. The message read: "I will go on early morning walks with my husband up to three times a week during the summer."

"Wow! Really? Thank you!" John gave her a sideways hug. "We can talk and pray over our plans, enjoy the sunrise, inhale the fresh air." He smiled at her, hoping summer walks would include discussions of their experiences traveling in their spirit bodies.

John picked up the last envelope and placed it over his heart. Closing his eyes, John willed the last card to say that she promised to journey in the spirit once a week with him.

With shaky hands he ripped open the envelope and unfolded the card: "I promise to set aside one night a week for a full year to play board games with my husband."

"Oh," John said as he read the card a second time. "Thank you. I know you are not fond of board games, but I am. This is quite a sacrifice on your part."

"You don't seem very excited about it."

"Oh, I love games, but I mostly just relish spending time with you. I'll light a fire in the fireplace for us to enjoy together."

Rachael spent the rest of Christmas Eve learning to use her new calligraphy pen set, and David retired to his room with a new video game. Leah put on her new slippers and sat with John as they soaked up the warmth of the fireplace and discussed the aunts, uncles, and cousins who would arrive in the morning.

One aunt and uncle, with their adult children, decided to skip celebrating Christmas with them this year. The last family gathering for the Memorial Day celebration had erupted into vitriolic rhetoric over critical race theory and Donald Trump, which resulted in hurt feelings. John and Leah prayed for reconciliation for the hundredth time and prayed God would prevent anything like that from happening tomorrow.

Lots of good food and board games went a long way in making Christmas Day fun. Rachael and David wanted to spend a couple of days at their cousins' home during their winter break. John looked forward to enjoying some time alone with Leah.

Great men are ordinary men with extraordinary determination.
Abraham Lincoln

Chapter Fifteen

A week after they celebrated New Year's Day, John ate a leisurely breakfast in the kitchen with Leah. From where he sat by the window, he could see wind and snow blowing outside. Inside, the aroma and taste of coffee stimulated confidence in what God had planned for the new year. He reminded Leah of her promise to pray with him. He figured in the last-minute bustle of Christmas that she had forgotten about it.

In the recent flush of his success with coaching David's gymnastics team, John almost overlooked her promise, too. His extra work during winter break to supervise David's strength training had paid off. David excelled on the rings and their relationship flourished as well. Though John burst with pride over David, something inside of him relished even more the thought of him and Leah developing a new way of interceding for people and situations. He let Leah know how much he longed to pray with her.

Leah's brows narrowed. "Why do you feel compelled to pray differently than other Christians?"

John put her hand into his. "The Spirit didn't take us on journeys just to give us a thrill. I want to know why we haven't seen a manifestation of the answer."

"Can't you be satisfied with leaving the results in God's hands?"

"I want to see evidence of God's answers to our prayers." John hesitated before saying anything more. "Jesus said we should be wise as serpents. He promised in John 16:13 that when the Spirit of truth comes, He will guide us into all the truth. Whatever He hears, He will speak. The Spirit, who sees into the hearts of all men, sees what's going on. He'll show us what we need to know to be wise as serpents so we can pray accurately."

Leah frowned. "That is *not* saying He is going to turn us into spies."

John turned off his cell phone so they wouldn't be interrupted. "Are you going to pray with me?"

"I will pray with you again, one more time. If God takes your spirit someplace and shows you things that require our intercession, I'll pray with you. But, unless an angel from heaven visits me, it will be the last time."

John leaned forward. He felt like she was reneging on her decision to pray with him already. He put his elbows on the table and head in his hands. "I will pray, and you can join in with me when you are ready." John doubted they had achieved any kind of agreement. What sort of answer could they expect sitting at the breakfast table without having any kind of agreement on how they would intercede?

Leah put her hand on his shoulder. "Don't sound so discouraged."

John wanted to scold her for being the source of his discouragement, but he realized he had to own up to his lack of faith. "You're right! If I believe God would have us intercede like I say, then I should pray with confident expectation."

Leah smiled, and her eyes reflected a love that gave him hope that God was in this.

After ten minutes of praising God and thanking Him for His presence and purposes in their lives, they both stopped talking to God and just listened for the Spirit to reveal what they should pray. After five minutes of silence, John wondered if he should talk to God about the lack of guidance he felt, but he sensed he had to be quiet and listen.

After twenty minutes of silence, a gentle warming of John's heart made him believe God had strengthened his spirit. The warming sensation spread to his arms, and joy bubbled up from within his inner being. Tears of joy ran down his face as joy overflowed from within for another five minutes.

He glanced at Leah, and tears ran down her face as she looked heavenward. John wasn't sure how long they continued like that, but suddenly he sobered as an intense pressure squeezed his gut. He heard Leah gasp for breath and noticed that she grasped her stomach. John's

Journeys into Suprafuge by D. Henry Roome

pressure became so sharp that he doubled over and groaned. He saw and heard Leah do the same.

Shortly, John looked down from the ceiling at their bodies on the floor. Janet hovered next to him.

"Where do you think is God taking us now?" Leah sounded resigned to follow this through.

"After the joy and the urgency we just experienced, you can't possibly doubt that God is in this." John looked over at Leah, but he could no longer see her spirit or their bodies below. Instead, he seemed to be viewing a room in a huge yacht that rocked gently from side to side as though anchored offshore. Two men sat sipping beverages at a bar.

Within a few seconds of perusing his surroundings, Leah appeared.

"Don't ever leave me like that again." Leah sounded more exasperated than frightened.

"Don't blame me. Talk to the Holy Spirit about it. He's the one in charge." John turned and directed his gaze back to the men below. One of them reminded him of photos he'd seen of media magnate Jack Wilson and the other looked like multibillionaire Mack Smith.

Smith sipped his drink and pointed with his chin at a chart laid out on the table. "What are the alternatives?"
Wilson nodded pensively.

A pale, hooded demon whispered into Wilson's ear. *That's right. Don't let people accept as credible treatments any off-label medications. Keep the people fearful of a plague that could decimate entire populations. Make them so afraid of a dreadful death that they will demand that the entire population get vaccinated, children and adults alike. More profit for Bradlock, bigger cut for you.*

An obese demon suggested to Smith. *People will be so terrorized that they will beg the government to restrict their freedoms. They will ignore their privacy rights and their freedom to choose their medical care.*

They will believe those rights will be worthless if everybody perishes in a pandemic.

A tall, lanky demon hissed. *Less freedom means more vaccinations and more profits.*

Another demon with slime dripping from his mouth scoffed. *Keep the fear level elevated sky-high. People will ignore your efforts to crush dissent. They will despise anti-vaxxers for fear of the unvaccinated spreading a plague no matter how remote the possibility of asymptomatic people infecting others.*

The lanky demon assured Smith. *No worries. Your companies are protected by law from liability. Keep research to a minimum, neglect thorough scientific methods, and hide any potentially troublesome data. It will all add up to mega-profits.*

Wilson smiled and shook hands with Smith. "I will make sure readers stay terrorized by headlining daily death tolls and omitting comparisons of death tolls to normal seasonal flu. On top of that, I will smother opinions that challenge our data and label them as ignorant conspiracy theorists."

John waved at Leah to get her attention. "Fear is Satan's favorite tool. That is something we already knew."

Leah wrinkled her nose. "Ask the Holy Spirit to get us out of here."

Instantly they found themselves in a room with the heads of nations and the CDC, WHO, and NIH.

Demons clamored so loudly into the ears of the people that they seemed to be shouting.

Continue to push for WHO to have the authority to make the rules in every nation as soon as a pandemic is declared.

Ostracize any country that doesn't sign an agreement. Pass sanctions against countries that don't comply!

Remember the goal: one world government—a power you will control. Fear will drive citizens to believe the only way to save the Earth from environmental disaster is by turning over all the power to you. If people are scared, they will ignore the economic upheaval your green initiatives create and will beg for equity among the masses of all the nations. When riots break out, they will demand a return to law and order that only a powerful world government can enforce. Add to that increased international tensions with more wars and imminent threats of a nuclear holocaust. People will gladly surrender their nation's right to exist.

Leah shouted to John, "We have more than enough to pray about."

"I agree, John said, "we should begin interceding right away."

Immediately, their spirits rejoined their bodies slumped over the breakfast table. John's ribcage hurt where it pressed against the tabletop. He straightened up his back and studied Leah's face. "Was it any easier this time?"

"No, I wanted to return to my body as soon as possible."

"Why? Did you think the Holy Spirit wouldn't let you return?"

Leah shook her head and grimaced. "The demons disgusted me. I realized how precarious the condition of our country is. This is more than we can handle. We need other Christians to help us pray against this."

John stood and extended his arms from his sides with his palms up. "That's why Jesus sent us the Holy Spirit."

Leah stood and patted his chest. "We need more than that." She walked into the living room, sat on the sofa, and signaled him to sit next to her. "The Spirit showed us what to pray, *and* He will show us how to pray. But we need more people to join with us in prayer. The Bible says one will a thousand to flight and two will put ten thousand to flight."

John remained standing in front of her with both hands extended facing her. "Whoa! If you and I can put ten thousand to flight, why do we need more help?"

Leah grabbed his hand and pulled him onto the sofa. She waited for a few minutes before saying anything. "This is much bigger than either of us can handle."

John placed his other hand over the two clasped together. "We can do this, Sweetheart. If we discuss this with others, they'll argue about how to pray over information received from spirit-body traveling, or worse yet, they'll call our visions evil and want us delivered from demonic possession."

"Is that fear talking to you, or is pride making you think that you know better than everyone else?" Leah said. "You are always saying if you want to find joy in the life Jesus has for you, you have to stop trying to please other people."

John took a deep breath. Certainly, having many people praying would make sure all the points that needed prayer got covered. What's more, if others joined them, they could protect each other and guard their blindsides.

"Okay, Sweetheart, as long as we limit our intercession team to members of our church prayer team. Nobody else should be included." John rubbed the back of his neck. Having others join them seemed wise, but his heart told him big trouble lay ahead.

Though none go with me, still I will follow;
No turning back, no turning back.
from lyrics of *I have decided to follow Jesus*
written by Simon Kama Marak

Chapter Sixteen

On Saturday night, John and Leah met with the usual five other church members who gathered for prayer, but tonight, a new person greeted them. Andy introduced a friend of his, Carl, who had just moved to Minnesota and joined Bluffview Evangelical Free. Carl said that he looked forward to joining their prayer team and shared briefly about his involvement with an Assemblies of God church in another state.

After Carl fielded a few friendly questions, Andy asked if anybody had special prayer requests. As usual, several people requested prayer for health and relationship issues. Andy suggested concerns in the church, the community, and the nation about which they should ask the Lord to intervene.

After a brief time of thanking God for His goodness, everyone prayed over the personal requests for the next half hour. Each person focused on the individual needs of particular people. Then Andy moved the intercession to issues concerning their church, and they prayed for Bluffview Evangelical Free. Ten minutes later, the focus of the intercession moved to Congress and the President. The war in Ukraine and the border crisis weighed heavily on everyone's mind, and they interceded for those disasters for twenty minutes.

When nobody prayed anything for about five minutes, John looked at Leah, and she raised her eyebrows and mouthed the words, "Now is a good time."

He planned to tell everybody about their experiences, but with a new person on the team, he hesitated. However, since Carl came from a charismatic church, John was okay with Carl being there. Normally, Andy would start praying for the community, usually the East End, or somebody else would introduce an entirely different topic. Since they hadn't changed their focus yet, now would be the perfect time to tell the team about their experiences.

John cleared his throat. "I've got a prayer request of sorts. We need wisdom and guidance on something that Leah and I have experienced. John paused to be sure he had everyone's undivided attention. He asked people to turn to Romans 8:26, and he explained how God had pressed on his soul in a way that made him groan.

Andy looked at his watch. "Try to make your request as specific as possible."

"This will take another twenty minutes. Do you want me to wait and share this next week?" John asked.

Andy waggled the back of his hand at John for him to continue.

John read II Corinthians 12:2, and then he explained what happened to him and Leah. During his explanations, he sat on the edge of his seat. When he got to the part where they hovered in the air over their bodies, he stood and spread his arms like they were wings. He looked around at the prayer team. They all seemed engrossed in his story, so he sat and continued to describe the visions Leah and he saw the first night and then again a month later.

"You can imagine," Leah said when John finished, "we thought we had hallucinated."

John could tell Andy and Carl thought their out-of-body experience had not come from God. John stood and asked, "Does anybody have questions about our experience and our interpretation of the visions?"

John heard a snicker to his left and turned to Carl and Andy. "Comments, guys?" John tried to sound nonjudgmental and open-minded.

"Really!" Andy declared with an incredulous burst. "Do you expect us to believe that God gave you a special revelation like Paul's?"

Carl cleared his throat. "Did you receive an answer to your intercession in light of what you saw in your spirit bodies?"

Andy had a gleam in his eye and smirked. "Did an angel tell you to gather a thousand faithful followers for a trip to a deserted South Pacific island? Maybe we need to wait there for a new revelation from God."

"Thanks, Andy," John grinned. "No, no angels this time, but I've got some Kool-Aid for you to drink."

Janet raised her hand and waved. "John shared a vision he had over a month ago with Willy and me. He used the knowledge gained from his spirit-body journey to guide his prayers. He didn't tell us what he saw, but I can tell you the results that I saw in Willy and the change in our marriage can be described as nothing short of a miraculous work of the Holy Spirit."

John glanced at the other seven sitting there. He appreciated Janet defending his intercession. He just wished he could say his prayers had set Willy free. They all seemed a bit troubled, and Andy and Carl's comments didn't help matters. "What bothers you about what Leah and I experienced?" John addressed his comment to Andy and Carl, though he scanned the expressions of the others.

Doug, a young chiropractor, commented softly, "I can't think of anything in Scripture that would condemn John and Leah's experiences. The Apostle Paul talks about being out of the body and going into the third heaven. Acts describes Phillip being supernaturally transported to where God wanted him to go. Why couldn't both things happen to a Christian at once?"

"Leah, weren't you scared?" Andy's wife, Eileen, asked.

"Yes!" Leah replied. "The demons terrified me! I almost didn't agree to pray with John a second time for fear that God would send me out of my body again to listen to voices of evil."

"John and Leah aren't people who draw attention to themselves to start religions," Doug said.

"Oh, come on!" Mary huffed.

Andy looked back and forth between John and Doug. "Are you expecting us to join you in this or just pat you on your back and say, 'Well done, wonderful?'"

"We should take our questions and concerns to the Lord in prayer," Doug suggested.

Andy and Carl nodded, and everybody bowed their heads to pray.

For what seemed like several minutes to John, nobody said anything. John prayed silently: "God, I know You are the One who took us in our spirits to see the things we saw. Speak to these guys about it so they're not spooked out. Don't let them think we are crazy either. Calm their fears and give them your peace."

Doug broke the silence. "Lord, we know all things are possible with You, so if these out-of-body happenings are from You, will You just confirm that in some unmistakable way?"

"Give us wisdom, Lord, we ask in Jesus' name!" Eileen said.

A second later, Andy added: "We bind any spirit of fear, confusion, or deception, in Jesus' name."

John heard Andy emphasize the word *deception*, likely because Andy still doubted the authenticity of the visions. John took a deep breath. "Lord, keep us from pursuing something that would cause another church split. We don't want to be deceived here, but we'd hate to miss Your will for these times we live in because of fear. Give us Your peace."

"Lord, our hearts are so easily deceived," Carl lamented, his tone so melodramatic that John figured Carl believed with Andy that his journeys came not from God.

"Yes, Lord, our hearts are so easily frightened," Eileen quickly added. "Yet, You said that Your sheep hear Your voice and the voice of a stranger they wouldn't follow."

After a moment of awkward silence, John raised his voice with as much of an authoritative tone as he could muster. "Lord, You railed against two things, time and time again—the religious spirit that kept people from walking in love toward their neighbor and the failure of people to let love and faith operate in their lives."

"Jesus, we need to hear from You," Leah prayed.

After another minute of silence, someone said, "Amen."

Two others followed confidently with: "Amen!"

John raised his head and checked everyone's expression. Carl and Andy appeared to still have serious doubts. "How should we proceed?"

Andy looked at Doug and Carl. "Tomorrow, we should talk with Pastor Ron about John and Leah's vision."

"Is that necessary?" John doubted Pastor Ron would be impartial. Pastor didn't agree with him on numerous theological issues.

"That is why we have a pastor," Andy said. "He is supposed to guide us."

John rubbed his cheek. "Ah. . . I don't think he likes to referee our little skirmishes."

Andy zipped up the cover on his Bible as though the topic was settled and he wanted to go home. "We are supposed to go to him when we have questions about God or issues that need to be resolved."

"What more needs to be dealt with?"

Andy stood and put his jacket on. He turned to John and paused, making eye contact with him. "We have a pastor in our church as a covering over us so we don't go astray, right?"

"Yes," John replied, "but I think a lot of people in our congregation would be freaked out by our experiences."

"So?"

John stood and reached for his jacket and then looked at the others. "What do you think, Doug?"

Doug stood looking at John and Andy. "Andy is right. Actually, you both are, but regardless of what the repercussions might be, Andy should check with Pastor Ron."

John shrugged on his jacket and attempted to sound open-minded. "The last thing we need is another firestorm of controversy."

Andy glared at John. "Let Pastor Ron worry about that."

John tried to act nonchalantly and extended both palms up toward Andy. "Okay, have it your way. If what I shared this evening goes viral in our congregation, they'll be asking you about it. You lead the prayer team. I hope, however, you don't let the church lead the prayer team."

Andy frowned. "What are you trying to say, John?"

"Maybe everybody here should promise not to share what Leah and I experienced, and we should inform Pastor Ron of our commitment not to tell others and ask him to do the same."

Andy replied, "John, he's our pastor. He should call the shots."

Doug, already heading for the door, turned and faced them. "Andy, you're our leader. Do you think we should all agree to keep a lid on this until Pastor Ron says otherwise?"

Andy stood and stared at Doug for several seconds without saying anything.

John stiffened his head back. "You have someone besides Pastor Ron that you are itching to tell this to?"

"It doesn't hurt to get an objective opinion from somebody not involved here."

John kept his clenched fists at his side as he stepped toward Andy and looked straight into his eyes. "That's how gossip gets started."

Doug stepped between them. "Nobody from our team is going to go around and spread rumors." Doug turned and stared at Andy. "And nobody is sharing their version of the Greenbergs' experience with someone outside our group. Right, Andy?"

"I am not a gossip, Doug. You don't have to worry about me."

Many people, especially ignorant people, want to punish you for speaking the truth, for being correct, for being you. Never apologize for being correct, or for being years ahead of your time. If you're right and you know it, speak your mind. Speak your mind. Even if you are a minority of one, the truth is still the truth.
                                                            Mahatma Gandhi

Chapter Seventeen

John doubted their new kind of intercession could be kept secret. Besides dealing with the controversy it would generate, he feared that forces of darkness would stir up and hinder future spirit-body journeys. On top of that, his previously tenuous relationship with Pastor Ron would likely be driven past any semblance of tolerance on Pastor Ron's part. If the church hadn't desperately needed every financially contributing member to keep it afloat, Pastor Ron might have suggested Leah and he look for another church to attend several months ago.

God had filled John's heart with love for the people of Bluffview Evangelical Free, and he believed God desired to mobilize the church to advance the kingdom of God in Bluffview and in the nation. That would not happen if some of the "old guard" in the church got wind of what transpired.

John had seen too many church splits. To prevent one from happening again, he needed to convince Pastor to keep their experiences quiet. Nobody outside the prayer team should know about them. Pastor would only agree to that if John downplayed the out-of-body experiences. Leah and John prayed earnestly that Pastor Ron would not only commit to keeping their novel intercession to himself but would insist that everyone on the prayer team not share it with anybody.

# # #

On Monday morning, John entered the pastor's office at church. The office carpet, almost as ancient as the hundred-year-old church, created a noticeable amount of static electricity because of the dry air produced by antique radiators cranked up to heat the room past the comfort zone. When John reached to shake Pastor Ron's hand, a spark jumped between them. Pastor Ron jerked and grimaced. After shaking hands, he motioned for John to sit in a padded armchair facing the desk where Pastor Ron sat. Instead of making friendly chit-chat, Pastor Ron stared silently straight ahead with his hands folded on his desk.

After thanking the pastor for taking a few minutes of his time, John searched for a tactful way to start. "Has Andy mentioned what transpired at Saturday's prayer meeting?

"Uh-oh," Pastor Ron said, "is this something I should be hearing about from you, or should I be talking to Andy instead?"

"No, no, I thought maybe Andy had already spoken to you about it. I wanted to make myself available to explain the situation since what happened Saturday came because of things Leah and I experienced. I am sure Andy will be talking to you about it too."

Pastor Ron looked at John over the top of his glasses. "It isn't because you wanted to get here so I would hear your side of the story first?"

John couldn't help but detect an accusatory tone in Pastor Ron's voice. "No, I hope you don't feel that I am here to make you choose sides."

Ron scowled. "Andy has a different interpretation of what happened?"

John scooted forward to the edge of the chair to make his point. "Well, I don't know. He might. That's not why I—"

"Sounds to me like you want me to choose sides."

John took a deep breath to calm himself before he spoke. "The situation in question occurred just to Leah and me. We shared with the prayer team how God supernaturally showed us how we should pray. It only makes sense that you hear directly from the source."

Pastor held his palm up facing John. "Did what was shared affect the prayer meeting in a bad way? Is that why you're here now?"

John sighed. Pastor Ron had tried, judged, and convicted without even hearing him out. "I am not here to talk about Saturday's prayer meeting. That's Andy's place. He is the leader of the prayer team."

Pastor cocked his head to one side and raised one eyebrow at John.

John paused and leaned back in his chair. "A few weeks ago, I received a vision that showed me a friend's secret sin. When I learned the nature of his battle, I interceded accordingly. Pastor, I had been praying for him for over a year without any success. Within a week of receiving that vision, my friend did a complete turnaround, and he took steps to heal his marriage."

John looked for a reaction from Pastor Ron, a pastor who doubted God still gave visions to Christians. He considered elaborating on Willy's sin, but he didn't know how much credit he should take for Willy's deliverance. Janet credited him with causing a miracle. That would have to be enough assurance for him for now. They still waited for results from their intercession for justice with Big Pharma and Congresswoman Hartwood.

John cleared his throat. "I shared my visions with my wife. At first she didn't want anything to do with the sort of visions I had, but when she saw the miraculous change in my friend, she agreed to join me in asking God for visions. As soon as she agreed to pray like I did, she had a vision, too. The Holy Spirit uncovered sin in a public official. We both received the same vision. After that, we prayed according to the vision we saw. We haven't personally received an answer to those prayers because our visions dealt with politicians in Washington and national business leaders."

Ron pulled a notebook from a drawer and opened it. "Yeah, I suppose she worried that a little political bias might have crept in. Politics has ripped our congregation apart these past couple of years. Some issues have caused such division in our church that they can only be explained as an unadulterated work of the devil."

"The Lord probably wanted to show us why those church splits happened." John leaned forward in his chair. "Maybe that was why the Lord gave us these visions now of how Satan is using subterfuge against us, so we can pray against it and—"

"Do you think it's necessary to know details?" Pastor Ron said.

"Not essential but extremely helpful."

"The Bible says we're to be wise as serpents but innocent as doves." Pastor Ron picked up a pencil and started doodling in his notebook. "Perhaps knowing details will offend our souls, pollute our spirits. Certainly, getting too much information could vex us to where we fight our battles in the flesh instead of the Spirit."

John scooted to the edge of his chair again and tensed his hands in front of him like he held a basketball between them. He wished he could squeeze Pastor Ron's shoulders in his hands—or better yet, his head—and shake hard. John shook his arms in cadence with each word he spoke. "Ignorance is not bliss. We can't expect to get better results if we apply the same methods we failed with."

Ron took his pencil and slapped it on his desktop. "What did you and Leah see then?"

"We saw world leaders, and we heard demons whispering in their ears. Our experience seemed like more than just a vision. Almost like our spirit bodies had traveled there and witnessed the meeting."

"Whoa! That doesn't sound God-inspired."

"Do think that God couldn't do something like that?"

"John, I don't know where you are going with this. John 10:27, a Bible verse you memorized as a youth, gives us Christ's guidance in this. Jesus says: 'My sheep hear my voice, and I know them, and they follow me.'"

John sat back, deflated by Pastor Ron's condescending tone of voice. "Yes, Pastor, but Jesus also said that the voice of a stranger we would not follow. That implies we have a choice and could hear demonic voices, right?"

"Of course, but—"

"So we could hear the voice of the devil."

"I think Jesus meant the voices we have to reject are voices from our flesh and the world or our culture."

John felt Pastor Ron offered talking points that he didn't really believe but just spoke to counter whatever he said. John slid forward and squeezed his knees with both hands to keep himself from jumping up. "Are you saying Christians can't be tempted by the devil?" John fought against sounding incredulous at Pastor Ron's retort.

"No, no, of course, it is possible—it is just unlikely that Christians would hear demons. That's all."

"Then Leah and I *could* have heard demons. Jesus heard demons before He cast them out of the demoniac."

"Okay, you may have heard demons whispering into various world leaders. What did you hear them say and how did that help you pray?"

"We heard the demons encourage them to use the pandemics and worldwide problems as a springboard for launching a one-world government. Moreover, when troubles popped up, the demons urged them to exaggerate the danger so the leaders could implement their scheme to control our freedoms. Christianity, freedom of religion, and freedom of speech topped the list of things they sought to squash." John paused because he could tell Pastor Ron considered what he said.

Pastor Ron picked up his pencil and tapped the eraser end against his desktop. "Well, how did you pray then?"

"We bound the spirit of deception and lust for power over the leaders, standing on Luke 10:19 and we loosed a spirit of truth over them according to Matthew 16:19."

"Casting out demons and binding evil spirits. Humpf! You and I don't exactly see eye to eye on that. I will pray about this and get back to you."

"Of course, Pastor, I expected you would. Only, until you feel you have received guidance from God on this, please don't talk to others about it. I promise you I—"

"John!" Pastor said, interrupting him. "Andy needs to meet with the three of us together—you, me, and him—so we can untangle this."

John agreed, though he dreaded clashing with both Pastor and Andy at the same time. When they met, they would likely draw up sides, and that would cause people to talk too much. If gossip spread about his and Leah's out-of-body experiences, Pastor would kick them out of the church for sure.

Pastor Ron told John that Andy had an appointment with him in six hours, and John should be there. John agreed to come. He used the six hours to organize his thoughts and pray for God's Spirit to change Pastor's attitude.

For His anger is but for a moment, His favor is for life;
Weeping may endure for a night, but joy comes in the morning.
Psalm 30:5

Chapter Eighteen

Six hours after meeting Pastor in the morning, John settled in next to Andy as they sat together in padded armchairs. Pastor Ron sat facing them in an identical chair. The sun had just set, so minimal light came through the window. The light in the room mainly came from a lamp in the corner behind Pastor Ron, casting shadows on Pastor Ron's face.

Despite the dim lighting, John saw in Pastor Ron's countenance an assurance that hadn't been there six hours ago. That bode well for John unless he mistook the source of Pastor Ron's confidence. Instead of finding peace after praying, Pastor Ron may have found assurance by obtaining an ally in Andy, supporting a natural bias against what Pastor considered John's overemphasis on the supernatural.

After opening their meeting with a prayer, Pastor Ron paused and took a deep breath. "Thank you, John, for coming back to meet with us. After talking with Andy on the phone, I can imagine you understand. I am a bit concerned over what transpired last Saturday, or at least over what you shared with the *group*."

John swallowed hard. The emphasis Pastor Ron put on the word *group* made John realize he shouldn't have been timid about giving Pastor Ron more details. "Well, what did he tell you?"

Pastor Ron slapped the padded arm of his chair. "Really, John, if the tables were turned, wouldn't you, as a pastor, want to know the entire story? Anything less than the whole truth is simply a lie."

John squeezed the padded arms of his chair, turning his knuckles white. "Are you suggesting that I am a liar?" His voice dropped an octave as he pronounced each word distinctly.

"Settle down, John," Pastor Ron leaned back and glanced at Andy. "I'm sure you have a logical explanation for any discrepancies I heard."

John felt his face get warm. "How am I supposed to explain any discrepancies if I don't know what he said?." John pointed at Andy with his chin. "I am the one who experienced the vision. I hope you would give more weight to my description. My version hasn't been filtered through Andy who may have misheard and possibly filtered his report through his prejudices."

"Okay, John, let's get to the crux of the matter." Pastor Ron nodded at Andy. "According to Andy, you and Leah saw your souls float above your bodies and then float above a conference room where you witnessed world leaders conferring while demons whispered in their ears."

"That's right!" John affirmed without hesitation.

"You and Leah had an out-of-body experience with your souls!" Pastor Ron shook his head slowly. "John, what am I supposed to do with that? First, you come in here and tell me you just had a vision, albeit one that seemed real, that made you feel like your spirit bodies had traveled there. Then I hear the truth of it from Andy, that you had some kind of New Age astral projection."

John stared vacantly at the floor. Then he looked back up at Pastor Ron.

Pastor looked over the top of his glasses which had slid down on his nose. "Don't get mad at Andy. He's been a good friend of yours for years, and he's worried you might be deceived. You wouldn't listen to him, so he came to me. Andy wanted to give me the whole truth.

I believe you need to look squarely at your experience and see it for what it truly was, an apparition sent by the enemy to inflate your ego. This is not something to be ashamed of."

"Why do you assume the evil one caused it?"

"Did you lie, John?"

"I told you it was a vision. It seemed real. I don't know if we actually traveled in our spirit bodies or not. That's the truth!"

"Really? The whole truth?"

"Even Jesus, when He talked with the disciples as recorded in the Gospel of John said, 'I still have many things to say to you, but you cannot bear them now.' Jesus wasn't lying when he omitted something, nor did I when I didn't give you the details of my vision. In the same way that Jesus didn't think the disciples could bear the whole truth, I didn't think you could handle it if I suggested that my vision might have involved my spirit body traveling somewhere. In truth, I don't know how God revealed those things to us."

"Hmmm. . ." Pastor Ron looked back and forth between Andy and John. "What do you think happened? Did you just have a vision or do you feel your spirits traveled to someplace or other?"

"Either is possible. What did Paul say in Second Corinthians chapter twelve? He said that he didn't know whether he was in the body or out of the body when he was carried into paradise. What does that mean but that he had a vision? Like Paul, I had a vision. If it was more than that, I can't say for sure. It sure felt real."

"Are you comparing yourself to Paul now?"

"Are you saying the supernatural can only happen to the apostles?"

Pastor Ron leaned back in his chair. "Okay, suppose God wanted to use this type of supernatural phenomena. Why would He do this now and not in a previous century? And why just you and Leah?"

"I don't know." John stared at the floor between them. He asked himself those same questions. He looked up at Pastor Ron and offered the reasons he believed made sense. "Maybe because we live in an age where scientific advances bombard people with medical options, which creates numerous moral dilemmas. Another reason might be the morass of information dumps that hide seductive webs of unprecedented evil."

John's voice raised as he spoke passionately about the obstacles facing Americans. "The entertainment industry has anesthetized our senses and technology has freed hours of leisure time available to Americans, leaving us open to attacks from the devil."

John paused as he held Pastor Ron's gaze. "Dozens if not hundreds of people have had out-of-body experiences. Some of them have written books about what they saw. Last year you quoted one example from the book *Heaven is for Real* in a Sunday morning sermon."

Ron snorted. "Desperate times call for desperate measures, huh?"

"I'm sorry," Andy said. "Please forgive me for my part in causing this argument. I knew you disagreed with John about miracles, so I played up the supernatural aspect because I didn't trust John's vision. And I didn't trust his motive, but it was my motive that stunk. I feared losing control over the prayer team."

John nudged Andy's arm with the back of his hand. "I forgive you."

"Why weren't you both more upfront with me?" Pastor Ron frowned as he shifted his gaze back and forth between them.

Andy exhaled sharply and looked at John. "I feared the enthusiasm that always bubbles out of John. He spurs people on to participate in whatever his latest inspiration is. I worried we'd get caught up in emotionalism."

John slapped the palm of his hand on the armrest. "We wanted to avoid having the congregation take sides over the vision. That's why both of us acted like we had taken the last cookie out of the cookie jar."

"We'd hate to see another church split," added Andy.

"Men, I'm concerned about people reacting out of emotionalism, but I'm not opposed to God performing the miraculous. We can't let your adventure spread abroad. How do you propose to proceed from here?"

Andy and John exchanged glances. Andy took a deep breath. "I think we should commit to not talking about the vision to anybody outside the prayer team and you. That includes the church secretary and any spouses not on the prayer team."

Ron bit on his lower lip. "Okay, Andy, for now, while I pray further on this, I will trust you to deal with this in the most discrete manner possible. You are in charge of the prayer team, and I know you will impress upon them the importance of not blabbing this around."

"Of course."

"John, you will follow Andy's lead in this, right?"

John assured him he would; however, he mostly worried about Pastor Ron and his wife. He reportedly had a history of telling her everything, and he had no idea what she would do with the information.

> *Then he touched their eyes, saying, "According to your faith be it done to you."*
>
> Mt. 9:29 NKJV

Chapter Nineteen

At home John told Leah how Pastor Ron desired to pray further about their spirit-body journeys. He asked Leah to pray that Pastor Ron's attitude toward the possibility of miracles happening in the twenty-first century would change radically. John trusted that Pastor's desire to prevent gossip would keep Pastor Ron from sharing their vision with his wife.

Leah assured him that Pastor Ron's wife, Francine, rarely discussed behind-the-scenes controversies. Just in case that wasn't true, John urged Leah to invite Francine over to their place in a week for a chat. Leah was part of the controversial issue, so Francine might feel free to divulge whether Pastor Ron had revealed their intercessory experience to her. She might also say whether she had enlisted anyone to support her husband's point of view, and she might also reveal what that person's opinion was.

John had promised not to share his vision with anyone outside the prayer team, but that didn't mean he couldn't keep his ear to the ground to determine if the herd had reacted by stampeding toward the exit of the church. In the meantime, he focused his intercession on Pastor Ron and prayed that God would give Pastor wisdom on their out-of-body journeys.

After praying two days for Pastor during his free time, John changed his focus to interceding for the six other members of the prayer team individually. He longed for them to learn intercession by having their spirit bodies transported by the Holy Spirit. If they experienced what he and Leah did, they'd be less tempted to talk about it with others. At least, they wouldn't put a negative spin on it if they did.

On Thursday, John came home from work filled with hope for their new type of intercession. Leah met him at the front door and popped his bubble of enthusiasm. "You have to talk to Rachael about her new friend. I tried talking to her, but our daughter seems to think her mother is too old-fashioned."

John ran his hand through his hair. He doubted he would have more success than Leah, but he agreed to do his best.

# # #

Rachael sat at her desk, working on homework, when John entered her bedroom. John chuckled softly. Most parents would be thrilled to find their child doing homework when they randomly entered their child's room. "Hey. Partner, what's up between you and Mom?" John sat on her bed on the opposite side of the room.

"She has an issue with my friend Montana." Rachael turned around to face him. "She's judged her without even seeing her. How fair is that? David doesn't like her, so he bad-mouths Montana—"

John extended both hands with a stop sign motion. "Okay, why don't you tell me about her."

Rachael's eyes widened. "You'd like her Dad. She speaks very respectfully to her mom, and we talk a lot about God. Her mom believes in angels and the spiritual power of prayer."

"Oh, I'd like to hear more about that. Be sure to invite her over so we can meet her." John would have to find out what Leah and David had against Montana.

At dinner, John learned little from David, other than what he had already told his mother. Everything that Leah believed about Montana came filtered through David's biased opinion. John could only resort to holding Rachael up in prayer until he met Montana.

That evening, after praying for wisdom for Rachael, John turned his attention to interceding for Pastor Ron. He prayed Pastor Ron could put their vision for intercessory prayer in its proper place, but John struggled to stay focused during prayer. On Saturday John felt led to pray in the morning for unity between Pastor and the prayer team. Later in the afternoon on Saturday, Leah interrupted him while he surfed the Internet. "Have you talked with Willy since we went to the Tom Hanks movie?"

John frowned. He'd focused too much on seeking Pastor Ron's approval. If Willy was still hooked on pornography, he could easily slip back into sinful patterns. John needed to check up on Willy and keep abreast of his spiritual life. John pulled out his cell phone and called his neighbor. No answer. Maybe Willy still worried about getting confronted with his addiction.

John looked heavenward and prayed, "Lord, I don't know how to deal with Will anymore. You showed me what to pray about. I prayed, but he hasn't confessed or repented. He just denies he's got a problem. Lord, use me to intercede for him and open the communication between Will and me."

John sensed God wanted him to pray for something, but he didn't know for whom or for what he should pray. "Lord, do you want me to pray for Janet, too? Or is it Ron, or Andy, or Rachael?" He didn't hear the Holy Spirit telling him what to pray. John gritted his teeth. His conscience needled him over his lack of patience to sit quietly because he often sensed the Holy Spirit wanted to tell him something, but instead of waiting, he would rattle off a list of concerns he had. Ten minutes later, he'd realize his complaints had kept him from hearing the Spirit. At other times, he found himself distracted with things around the home or on the Internet. By the time they had to leave for the Saturday evening prayer meeting, John had received no leading from the Lord on how to pray, so he left the issue of Pastor Ron and the new method of intercession in God's hands.

When Leah and he arrived at the church for the prayer meeting, John believed that at some point in the evening, Andy and at least one other person on their team would learn a new way of interceding. Before the meeting started, John wrote Bible verses on two whiteboards.

Doug and Mary called and said that they'd be ten minutes late because Grandma, their babysitter, arrived late. While they waited, John told the team that he thought someone would experience a vision during the meeting. Though Andy doubted that, he said he wouldn't try to stop it from happening.

When Doug and Mary arrived and settled in their seats, Andy thanked everyone for coming and opened the meeting with a brief prayer. Then he held up his Bible and said that the word of God and the

Holy Spirit controlled the direction of their meeting. After Andy said that, he informed them John wanted to say a few words before they took prayer requests.

The prayer room's wall-mounted whiteboard faced half of the chairs in the circle set up for the prayer team. For the other half of the group, John positioned the portable whiteboard so they could see it. On both boards he had written:

> But if we hope for what we do not see, we eagerly wait for it with perseverance. Likewise the Spirit also helps in our weaknesses. For we do not know what we should pray for as we ought, but the Spirit Himself makes intercession for us with groanings which cannot be uttered.
> Romans 8:25-26 NKJV

> I know a man in Christ who ...was caught up to the third heaven—whether in the body or out of the body I do not know, God knows ...and he heard things that cannot be told, which man may not utter.
> II Corinthians 12:2a, 3, 4 NKJV

John stood and pointed to both whiteboards. "I wrote these verses so everybody could see and meditate on them as we prayed, regardless of where they sat. Note the first sentence on top. It says if we hope for something we can't see, we should persevere in our prayers and we should do so eagerly. The Bible teaches that without faith, we cannot expect to receive anything from God.

"Last week Leah and I shared the vision we had when we interceded, a vision so real it felt like what happened to Paul—we couldn't tell if we were in the body and just dreaming, receiving a vision, or if our souls had left our bodies. Some have expressed doubts as to the source of the visions. This evening I felt the Holy Spirit wanted other members of our team to experience a supernatural intercession. They could verify the validity of praying this way. I checked with Andy before the meeting." John extended his hands out as though checking for raindrops. "Much to my delight and surprise, he agreed."

John glanced at Doug. He could tell Doug wanted to believe in this. Mary and Janet appeared stoic.

John gazed at Andy who was grinning. He believed Andy looked back at him with eyes that glowed with an expectancy that God would show them how to intercede in a way that truly demolished principalities and powers of evil. John swallowed hard. The dramatic change in Andy caused John to stumble getting back to his chair. John glanced around to see if others experienced the same thing. God had already begun answering his prayers.

Andy rubbed his hands vigorously. "Okay, If God is going to do something tonight, let's get started."

*Make sure you are doing what God wants you to do—
then do it with all your strength.*
George Washington

Chapter Twenty

Doug leaned forward in his chair, resting his forearms on his knees. "My brother, Rick, had a stroke a few weeks after receiving a COVID-19 vaccine booster. Now he is wheelchair bound and his medical insurance has maxed out. He has serious ulcers on his bottom, and he needs nursing care but lacks the money to pay for it. He had a strong Christian faith, but his faith was crushed under a mountain of anger and despair. Currently, he bounces between hating his employer for mandating the vaccine, ranting against Pfizer for not acknowledging their vaccine caused his stroke, and attacking the government for granting Big Pharma immunity from liability for pushing an unproven drug that crippled him."

Andy opened his Bible and read II Timothy 1:7 (NKJV). "For God has not given us a spirit of fear, but of power and of love and of a sound mind." Andy paused as he considered how to expound on the verse. "Some translations substitute *self-control* or *discipline* for the word *sound mind*. Whichever version you use, we can apply this verse in praying for Rick. If the Spirit so leads, we might pray for the gift of repentance for Rick for any sins he needs to confess. I feel we should pray through this thoroughly before addressing other prayer needs. I hope the rest of you don't mind waiting with your requests."

Andy looked at each person sitting in the circle, waiting until each person either shrugged or nodded. "Okay, then," Andy announced enthusiastically, "let's see if we can get at the root of Rick's problem."

John asked, "Can I make a suggestion?"

"Fire away!" Andy replied.

"Before anybody prays aloud, let's wait in silence for at least ten minutes to hear how the Holy Spirit wants us to pray."

After five minutes of silence, John heard Andy and Doug take deep gulps of air as though they had trouble breathing. He sensed that the Holy Spirit had moved on Doug's and Andy's hearts in such a way that they couldn't speak. Then he looked up and saw Andy fall to his knees, groaning—followed by Doug, who did the same thing. Listening to them groan, John could tell the extent of Rick's need went deep. Like an invasive weed that propagated through the spread of its root system, Rick's suffering had sent out tentacles that would take extensive intercession.

John rose and went over to lay his hands on Andy to pray with him. He caught Leah looking up at him, and he pointed with his forehead at Doug for her to do the same thing with Doug.

As John prayed with his right hand on Andy's back, he felt as though a vacuum sucked his hand into Andy's back. Andy buckled over and moaned deeply. Then a jolt, like a collision in a carnival bumper-car ride, separated John from Andy, and Andy fell sideways on the floor motionless.

Shortly, Doug groaned intensely, buckled over, and crumpled over on the opposite side of the circle of chairs.

After they lay there for a few minutes, Mary asked, "Are they all right?"

"I don't see either one of them breathing." Carl bounded over to where Andy lay.

"You don't need to worry about him. He's fine." John put his hand out to stop him.

Carl shoved John's hand aside and kneeled next to Andy. After giving Andy's limp arm a shake, Carl put the back of his hand under Andy's nose. "He doesn't look so okay to me. I'm not feeling any breath!"

Carl put his fingers on Andy's neck where a carotid pulse should be detected. After waiting thirty seconds, Carl shook his head. "I'm not feeling any pulse either!" he yelled.

Carl sprang up and shoved John. "What have you done to my friend?"

John's heart raced as he stared at Andy. "He's my friend, too! I'm sure he's fine!"

"Fine! How can you say that?" Carl whipped out his phone. "We need to call 911."

"Look!" John pointed at Andy. "Does he appear to be dead? His skin is pink." John kneeled and put his hand on Andy's face. "And he feels warm. Case reviews have shown in the excitement of seeing someone collapse, even trained medical professionals fail to detect a pulse."

Carl hesitated a second and then shook his head. "What do *you* know? By the time his skin turned pale and cool, we would have lost precious time that could have been used to save his life by calling for an emergency responder."

Mary rushed over to Doug and checked his pulse.

Carl dialed 911 and put the phone on the speaker while he positioned Andy to do CPR. He looked at Mary. "Do you know how to do chest compression?"

While Carl talked to the 911 operator, John shot up a silent prayer. "Lord, getting an ambulance here would upset the whole church and create a firestorm of controversy. Please bring back Andy and Doug right away."

"Where are the two unconscious people now?" the operator asked.

"On the floor of a classroom in our church basement." Carl breathed heavily, his eyes wide open.

"The address of your church?" the operator asked.

Carl turned to Eileen. "What's the address here?"

John heard Andy huffing on the floor. "Look, he's moving and getting up!"

"Just the name of your church will be fine," the operator said.

Carl gawked at Andy sitting up and Doug moving on the floor. "Oh, I'm sorry, lady. I've made a terrible mistake. Both men are up and alive." Carl quickly disconnected.

Carl knelt next to Andy and put his hand on Andy's shoulder. "What happened to you? You had me scared out of my wits."

Andy sat with one leg bent upward with his elbow draped over it. "It was like what John described to us. I saw my body lying next to John while I floated over the room. Doug joined me in the air, and the next thing I knew, we hovered in an office where three men conspired over the COVID-19 vaccines. Two appeared to be media moguls of some sort and a third represented a drug company.

"The moguls discussed their effectiveness at smothering reports about the vaccine causing thousands of deaths worldwide. A conference in Romania had threatened to break the news to the rest of the world, but media moguls made sure the conspiracy theory label remained stuck over the hearts of terrified citizens, preventing people from learning the truth. One mogul questioned the morality of giving vaccines to children for whom no risk of harm from COVID-19 had been found, while side effects from the vaccine had serious repercussions for children.

"They argued about the harm to children at considerable length. The Big Pharma guy acknowledged that vaccines lacked efficacy even with adults, and he admitted they altered DNA molecules in the body which caused cells to produce particles that the immune system could attack several months or years later and weaken the entire body. I think the man who waffled on the morality of what they were doing had a grandson who had received vaccines and boosters at age five.

"Then they argued about how to convince our country to join the WHO so the elites could control the pandemic mandates. The men schemed with WHO to change the terms of their pledge after countries agreed to the WHO proposal. Later, they would instruct countries to surrender their sovereignty, denying they ever said anything different. They snickered at the public's short memory. In the middle of a pandemic, the fear they instilled in people would shorten their memory even further. They believed people would beg to surrender their freedom in exchange for safety from the horrors of COVID displayed every evening on TV."

Carl turned to Doug, who was sitting on a chair. "What did *you* see?"

"The exact same thing. We talked with each other as we watched, and they couldn't hear us. It was the strangest vision. It had to be from God. Otherwise, we wouldn't have seen and heard the same thing." Doug's eyebrows drew closer. "I think our spirit bodies may have actually been—"

"Oh, you might want to rethink that," John suggested. Although John felt validated that other people experienced what he had, a mere vision would be more palatable to Pastor Ron than out-of-body travels.

Mary pointed to Carl. "While your bodies lay on the floor, Carl here freaked out because he thought you were dead. Your bodies lay here while you had your vision, but I don't think your spirit bodies had time to hover elsewhere."

"Really?" Doug looked incredulously at Carl.

"Yeah, I thought John's insane vision had killed Andy, so I called 911."

"No way!" Andy put his hands on the top of his head.

"Don't worry, you came back to life before I gave them our address, so I told them I had made a mistake and hung up."

"All this begs a bigger question." John sat next to Andy and glanced at Mary whose eyes seemed to bulge out. "If our out-of-body experience is just a vision, then we need to be more careful in how we interpret it."

"I think we have an entirely different problem," Andy said.

John sensed everyone turning their attention toward Andy because of the serious tone of voice Andy used.

"I just remembered something I saw at the beginning of my 'vision.' I saw Carl jump up and check my nose with the back of his hand. Did that happen?"

Carl and John nodded slowly.

"I think it had to be more than just a vision," Eileen said.

"Uh, visions could depict present as well as future events," suggested Mary.

"It sure didn't feel like a vision," Andy said.

Truth will ultimately prevail where there is pains taken to bring it to light.

George Washington

Chapter Twenty-One

Andy landed on his chair in the circle of eight where he sat before his spirit went traveling. Despite the exhaustion he felt, they needed to pray about the things they saw and heard. He would worry about what to tell Pastor Ron later.

"Are you okay, Andy?" Eileen looked at her husband with worried eyes.

Andy smiled at Eileen and gave her a thumbs up.

"Do we need to pray for you?" John asked Doug.

Doug shook his head and patted the chair next to him, encouraging Mary to sit down.

As soon as everyone sat down, Andy said, "Doug and I should lead out in prayer because the Spirit showed us what needed to be addressed, but the evil I witnessed makes me shudder and boil in anger at the same time. We need people, whose souls haven't had their flesh riled, to pray in the Spirit."

"You and Doug pick the issue to focus on," John said. "The rest of us will take it from there, as the Spirit leads."

"Let me describe what happened," Andy said. He took a deep breath to settle his nerves and put a lid on his anger. When Doug floated next to me, I couldn't doubt God did this. The whole thing shook me to the core, but once I acknowledged God's hand was in this, we immediately saw the office with the three conspirators.

"Doug and I hovered on the ceiling, listening. The demon whispering in their ears repulsed me. Demons urged one of the media moguls to maximize profits on their investments and seize as much control as possible from the plebs. Other demons scoffed at the mogul who balked at the harm done to children and reminded him to consider the greater "good" they would accomplish by convincing nations to surrender their sovereignty to the WHO. If they controlled pandemics, people would gladly surrender their freedom. When they eliminated wars, they wouldn't need money gained from the military-industrial complex. They could accumulate wealth by distributing limited resources among the masses and keeping their due share for themselves."

After he talked for a few minutes, Andy couldn't contain his anger at the greed and selfish lust for power he saw. He shouted, "In Jesus' name, I bind the demonic spirits of deceit, greed, selfishness, oppression, arrogance, and murder! I command them to loose those moguls and to cease corrupting them and anyone they employ. Lord, I pray for any of their employees, that You would convict the employees of the harm their lies of omission have caused and give them courage to speak the truth."

Andy pled the blood of Jesus over all the media and thanked God in advance for the victory he was confident that God's word had been accomplished. He praised the name of Jesus, and he confessed Jesus was the name above all names, the name at which every knee shall bow and tongue confess that He is Lord. Andy stopped to catch his breath and realized that someone else should pray, someone whose flesh wasn't riled and who could pray in the Spirit.

John started praying, and Andy sensed that the Holy Spirit inspired his prayers. After he prayed for a while, Eileen prayed what Andy believed were also Spirit-anointed prayers. When she finished praying, John prayed again for a few minutes. Then prayer alternated between John and Eileen, with the others contributing a prayer occasionally. That went on for an hour.

Then Doug jumped and praised the name of Jesus as he bounced up and down, waving his hands in the air. "Lord, thank You that You are the truth. I pray the truth about the thousands who died from the vaccination will be revealed. That people will stop reading and listening to the false narrative of the media. Bring those to justice who are responsible for the needless loss of life."

When Doug finished praying, Andy realized that besides praying against the evil trying to control the world, they needed to pray for men of integrity to take action. "Lord, raise up honest men and women who care more for their fellow citizens than for their personal well-being. God, give them courage and wisdom. Open doors of opportunity for them to lead our nation back to a country where Your name is honored and freedom reigns."

For the next two hours, Andy heard Doug and the rest join him in interceding vigorously. When he felt calm in his soul, he believed that they had finished praying for what the Lord wanted for that night. He figured they had interceded for an hour, but his watch said 11:30 PM. He could hardly believe four hours had passed.

The meeting broke up after they petitioned the Lord concerning urgent local needs that couldn't wait until next week. As the team left, John sensed Andy bubbled with excitement in his spirit, though his body looked exhausted. Since the rest of the team had left, Leah said she would wait in the car for him. John wanted to help Andy put chairs away, and he desired to ask questions. Once they were alone, John asked, "What do you think is going to happen now?"

"Well, we prayed, It's God's move now. He is in this, so He will make what we prayed happen."

"Is it really that simple?" John wondered aloud, half to himself and half for Andy's sake.

"The Bible gives the reasons prayers aren't answered." Andy stacked four chairs in the corner and turned to John. "Either it is because we ask amiss and selfishly, or we ask without really believing God heard us. Since God showed us what He wanted us to pray, we know we didn't pray selfishly or amiss. As a result, we prayed in faith without doubting."

John dragged the last of the chairs into the corner. "What about the decisions of other people? God gives each person a free will to choose right or wrong. He won't violate their freedom. That is why when leaders try to force their will on everybody, we know their schemes are from Satan. The evil one seeks to put everybody in bondage. Jesus is the One who sets us free.

"This evening, we bound several demons and their activity. I'm sure many more demons come into play on the world scene, so our work is hardly done in that regard." John paused, contemplating the world's needs. "I think God wants hundreds of other Christians to join us in intercession. The spirit-body traveling may have shown us the problem, but that's not the same as knowing how to pray against it. He still has to teach us how to pray once we see what we are fighting.

There are other prayer teams in America that a better trained to intercede."

"Our prayers are just what God wants them to be," Andy said.

"As far as our prayers go, I'm sure they are fine, but God longs for us to grow stronger in faith."

"Do you think God has led other Christians to have experiences similar to ours?" Andy's jaw dropped as he turned to John. "What do we tell Pastor?"

*Whoever walks in integrity walks securely, but he
who makes his ways crooked will be found out.*
                              Proverbs 10:9 NKJV

Chapter Twenty-Two

Pastor Ron sat in the church lounge that doubled as the library and reception area next to his office. The ladies there peppered him with questions about the lesson he had just shared with the women's weekly afternoon fellowship. He taught them about the importance of mothers and grandmothers spending time on their knees beseeching the Lord for the salvation of their family members.

Right away, when they asked him practical questions, he realized his mistake in waxing eloquent in his message. Many of them were grandmothers who couldn't kneel unless they had someone nearby to pull them up afterward. After asking him about other postures for intercession, they asked about praying silently versus out loud, group prayer versus alone, and saying written prayers versus extemporaneous prayers.

Pastor Ron had avoided women's groups for too long. Francine begged him for months, maybe years, to speak at one of their meetings. He had no idea of the paltry amount of knowledge they possessed concerning prayer. In truth, Pastor Ron resisted talking to women's groups almost as much as he resisted joining prayer meetings. Their last church split originated from a women's intercessory prayer group that met on Mondays. They were a bunch of gossips. It should have come as no surprise when they sparked a division that left a third of the church heading across town to worship with the Lutheran and the Assemblies of God churches. Then there was the time when the women who did most of the serious praying in the church left over the troubles with their youth pastor. However that division occurred, Pastor Ron had to admit those women seemed to know how to pray. Maybe their efficacy motivated the devil to undermine them with a spirit of strife.

Pastor Ron pointed to one of the younger members of the women's fellowship. He hoped she would ask a quick question that would allow him to exit shortly.

"Can you recommend some books on prayer we could study as a group?"

"Yes, *With Christ in the School of Prayer* by Andrew Murray is a classic. Another good one is *Prayer* by Tim Keller. Both of those books can tell you much more than I ever could. Perhaps Francine can help you decide which book would be most appropriate for you." Pastor Ron scooted to the edge of his chair. "Thank you so much for inviting me to speak with you and for your keen interest in interceding for our church."

Pastor Ron stood and smiled at Francine. "I'll be excited to hear how it goes with whichever book you ladies choose."

Two minutes later, Pastor Ron slumped in his desk chair. Of all the topics they could have chosen, why prayer? Was God trying to tell him he needed to be more serious about prayer? Certainly, with John's visions threatening to create the next cataclysmic war in his church, he needed to study the books he recommended. He hadn't read books about how to pray since he graduated from seminary. A bigger problem lay in his lack of faith in prayer. Consequently, he didn't preach or teach much about prayer. That didn't mean he was a hypocrite. He talked to God, but he never received any answers that anyone would classify as miraculous.

None of the books he remembered from seminary said anything about the kind of visions that John claimed to have seen. Pastor Ron turned his desktop computer on to search for books about prayer. If only Andy could have taken care of the whole matter. He trusted Andy. John, on the other hand, worried him. Evangelical Free churches were supposed to be open-minded to a wide range of Christian beliefs. John would turn us into an Assemblies of God congregation if he had his way.

Pastor Ron pushed away from his desk and knelt for the first time in a long time. Before he went any further, he needed to ask the Lord for help. Serving as a pastor meant he helped people find God. He hadn't entered the ministry on an idle whim. In high school God radically turned his life around and rescued him from the path of addiction and prison. After seminary he hoped God would use him to save youth in the same way others had done for him. Several churches later, God or circumstances led him to this church, and he presided over the exit of most of the young families. His youth minister departed in ignominy, which left them attempting to enlist volunteers to take over youth ministries. Pastor Ron was too old to be an effective youth minister or supervise younger volunteers. Pastor Ron longed for the current congregation to grow and have a healthy faith in Christ. Without younger families, Bluffview Evangelical Free faced an existential crisis.

God needed to do a miracle. The church no longer had enough financially contributing families to hire a new youth pastor. They had too many senior citizens on Social Security. The retirees who had extra income were snowbirds and spent four months out of the year in Florida where they tithed to the churches there.

Given the church's financial situation, Pastor Ron reckoned his best alternative consisted of cutting back the hours they gave Suzi, the church secretary. If she only worked two mornings a week, she would likely then look elsewhere for employment. That couldn't be helped. He hoped a volunteer would pick up some of Suzi's duties. Even if Suzi left, her salary was too small to free up enough money to hire another experienced youth pastor. Consequently, Pastor Ron prayed they would be able to hire someone right out of seminary and desperate enough to get experience that they'd take the tiny salary their congregation could offer. Without a strong youth program, their church would die a slow death.

Pastor Ron clasped his hands together in prayer. "Lord, we need someone who can ignite faith in the teenagers of our community, a person recently graduated from seminary with zeal to save troubled kids, someone without much financial need themselves. I suppose a single person would be best. A young married couple without any children would work if their spouse pulled in a good income. Unlike our previous one, Lord, they have to have a pure heart and follow our guidelines.

"God, whoever You find for us faces a huge challenge. Most Christian youth in Bluffview attend youth activities at the Assemblies of God church, which is fine. A new youth leader will have to connect with other youth who aren't involved in church activities. Youth bend so readily to peer pressure that pulling them away from the herd is next to impossible. Yes, I know nothing is too difficult for You. We need a gifted individual who can connect with an unreached clique or bring deliverance to a kid whom others will follow into Your kingdom and our church.

"In the meantime, bring revival to the rest of our church and keep us from divisive controversies. And Lord, give Andy wisdom about those wild visions of John's. Give Andy the courage to confront John with the likely source of his out-of-body visions. Another church-wide controversy would destroy us, and the devil knows that, Lord.

"And God, tell me whether this new way of interceding comes from You or Satan. I think the enemy is behind his vision, but I need You to confirm that. If John is wrong, show me Scriptures that put John in his place without chasing him out of the church."

Pastor Ron waited in silence for God to impress particular Scriptures that he could use. After five minutes of waiting quietly on his knees, Pastor Ron heard nothing and failed to receive any direction. Growing impatient and uncomfortable, he rose and sat on his chair. Pastor Ron looked at his computer and hoped that God would speak to him later.

# # #

At 6:00 PM on Wednesday, Pastor Ron sat on a padded armchair in his office, facing Andy and John in identical armchairs. Andy appeared nervous, and John seemed so animated that he looked like he might launch from his chair at any minute. That didn't bode well for Andy reporting he'd contained the rumors or had convinced John to abandon his visions.

Pastor Ron gripped his armrests. "Andy, tell me how Saturday's prayer meeting went. I haven't heard any horror stories about heresies being spawned there, so you're keeping John's adventure from causing wildfires."

Pastor Ron saw Andy glance at John like he wanted clues on how to proceed. Andy balked, so Pastor Ron spoke first. "I am confident that God revealed to you what came from Him and what came from the devil."

Andy glanced again at John and exclaimed, "Absolutely, Pastor Ron, the best possible way for me to determine whether John's vision came by inspiration of the Holy Spirit occurred—God took me through the same experience as John and Leah."

"What?" Pastor Ron said, stunned by Andy's news. He couldn't imagine a worse scenario. John had won Andy over with his craziness. "How do you know what you experienced came from God?"

"The Lord did something so spectacular with such profound revelation that it had to come from God."

"Do you realize that being caught up with something spectacular increases the likelihood that the devil deceived you?"

Andy leaned forward and shook his head. "God confirmed that the visions were from Him."

"How so?"

"When I floated above my body, I thought I experienced a vision at first. Then the Holy Spirit transported me to an office where He revealed schemes of the devil."

"Wait," Pastor Ron interrupted, "you saw a vision, but then you thought God actually transported you."

"But God did!"

"You are talking about astral projection. You are mature enough as a Christian to know that New Age witchcraft is not from God.

John scooted to the edge of his chair and extended his hands as though he were shaking a basketball. "Would the devil reveal his schemes to Christians who would pray against them?"

"To have them pray amiss," Pastor Ron replied. "For sure, he'd love to inflate you with pride and cause a church split."

"Pastor Ron, do you think Satan has the power to teleport a Christian somewhere in violation of God's will for them?" John waved his right hand like an airplane taking off.

"No, but he could deceive you into thinking the vision he gave you was real. And, boy, would he love to use you to divide our congregation." Pastor Ron took a deep breath. His heart pounded in his chest, and he sensed his blood pressure had skyrocketed.

Andy looked at John and then faced Pastor Ron. "We have proof my experience happened."

Pastor Ron put his forehead in his left hand and shook his head. "Really?" he muttered. "Could this get any worse?"

"While God showed me media moguls who schemed to deceive the public, Carl thought the body I left behind had died. After he checked for a pulse, he called 911 for an ambulance."

Pastor Ron jerked his head straight up. "What! An ambulance came here?"

John extended his hands with his palms facing Pastor Ron as though he wanted to calm Pastor Ron's concerns. "Don't worry. Before Carl could give him our address, Andy and Doug's spirits returned to their bodies."

Pastor Ron collapsed against the back of his chair and shook his head. "Doug experienced the same thing?"

"Yes!" Andy exclaimed.

"Which is more confirmation that God was the One who transported us," John added.

Pastor Ron stood and walked behind his desk to sit on his swivel-rocker. He needed to take control of this ticking time bomb. "So, if God made all this happen, how did the Spirit's revelation help you pray?"

"We prayed that the lies media told about the efficacy and safety of vaccines would be exposed, and the truth—"

Pastor Ron slammed his desktop with his hand. "Absolutely not! There's no way God would want you to pray for that!"

"That's how the Spirit led us!"

"Are you certain it was the Holy Spirit you heard? Did you wait and listen long enough to know it was God you heard from?" Pastor Ron eyed both of them.

John pursed his lips and looked at Andy.

Andy cleared his throat. "Nobody can be one-hundred-percent sure, but we all felt that—"

"You were all moved by signs of the spectacular sent by the devil."

John slapped his armrests with both hands firmly. "Why would Satan transport both Andy and Doug to reveal his schemes?"

"The evil one is clever. His enemy is the church. We barely survived the rift between the maskers and the non-maskers, and we just smoothed out the rancor between vaxxers and the anti-vaxxers. God wouldn't show you lies from the media that would split our church again."

"God could treat us like Gideon's army and whittle our numbers down to prevent us from taking credit for what He does." John stood and chopped the air with his hand like an axe. "But I don't think He wants to do that. His heart longs for us to pray in the changes that He wants to make."

"Sit down, John," Pastor Ron said, irritated at John's constant use of animated hand gestures. "Maybe you misunderstood their conversation, and they spoke in jest."

Andy stood next to John. "We heard and saw demons urge those media moguls to follow their evil plans."

Pastor Ron rocked back in his chair. "You saw demons," he muttered. "Did it occur to you that those demons might be the source of your madness?" he said in crescendo volume, ending in almost a shout.

John planted both hands on Pastor's desk and leaned forward. "God is in this. Demons couldn't transport Christians against their will."

Pastor Ron stood and leaned toward John. "Demons couldn't, but Satan could trick a person into letting him do it!"

"Could he trick four Christians? And one of those persons didn't believe in it?" Andy asked. "Pastor Ron, the whole prayer team believes the Holy Spirit orchestrated the entire evening."

"Ah, you are *all* deceived!" Pastor Ron shouted.

Andy said, "But we all prayed and felt—"

"I don't care what you prayed. You just better pray now that word doesn't get out about this to anyone else. Period." Pastor Ron sat and pointed to the door. "Go home and call everyone on the prayer team. Tell them that they are not to speak of this to anyone. I'll come on Saturday to explain my feelings on the matter."

I have yet many things to say unto you, but
ye cannot bear them now.
The words of Jesus in John 16:12 KJV

Chapter Twenty-Three

Leah put the last ingredient into a pot of stew when John walked into the kitchen. "How did your meeting with Pastor Ron go?" Leah waited for John to say something, but he looked somber and remained silent. Not a good sign. She studied the look in his eyes. "That bad, huh?"

"Worse than bad. Pastor Ron accused us of being deceived by the devil."

"Everybody?" She could hardly believe Pastor would be so hasty in pronouncing judgment."

John shook his head and said that he was going upstairs to the office to pray. When he returned for dinner, he said grace and ate without saying much to Leah or the children. Leah wanted to get details about what transpired with Pastor, but she knew she would need to find another subject to discuss first. "How's the stew?"

"Hmm. . ." John grunted.

"It's your mom's recipe."

"I'm sorry, Honey, I don't mean to ignore you. The stew is delicious. I just can't believe Pastor Ron's reaction." John looked at Rachael and David as they busied themselves eating beef stew. "We can talk about it after dinner?"

John asked David how gymnastics was going and then asked both kids about school assignments. When David finished his supper, he asked to be excused from the dinner table. Rachael followed him five minutes later.

As soon as Rachael left, John placed his fork on his plate and shook his head. "How can Pastor Ron be our spiritual leader if he relies totally on his feelings and doesn't trust the Lord to protect his flock?"

"He is our Pastor, so we should respect his reasons." Leah winced after she said that. John hated it when she defended Pastor Ron, but she realized how difficult being a pastor could be, especially when John, one of the pillars of the church, contradicted his decisions.

"You saw for yourself at the prayer meeting on Saturday. Both Doug and Andy said they experienced the same thing we did. Everybody on the team felt God caused the whole thing, including you."

"You have to remember who you are talking to, a very traditional minister who shies away from anything remotely charismatic. Most of our congregation is like that. That's why they hired him."

Leah watched him shove cold stew around in his bowl. Though she empathized with him, she searched for words to convince him to adjust to Pastor Ron's theology or at least acquiesce to Pastor Ron's comfort level.

John washed down a mouthful of stew with milk and firmly placed the glass on the table with a thud. "What if God wants to teach Pastor Ron a valuable tool that will bless the church as well as our nation?"

"Leave the care of our church in Pastor's hands."

"But we can't abandon what God wants to use to turn our nation around."

"Will you let Pastor call the shots for Bluffview Evangelical Free?" Leah studied John's reaction. By the time they finished cleaning up the dinner mess, she believed he would leave the care of the church in Pastor's hands, but he didn't seem likely to let up on out-of-body excursions. His desire to learn how to intercede for the country appeared unabated.

Naturally, she wanted to pray for her country and support her husband. However, it would be wrong for her oppose their pastor. On top of that, she dreaded the backlash she'd experience from all her friends if she backed John's beliefs instead of Pastor's. Somehow, she would find a way to keep both men happy.

# # #

On Saturday before the prayer meeting, John sought to change Leah's mind, but she insisted God wanted her to stay home and intercede for the confrontation that was due to happen between him and Pastor Ron. Now he had one less ally in defending God's strategy for overcoming corruption in America.

At times, he thought the wickedness propagated in America went beyond God's ability to redeem. Like Sodom and Gomorrah, the Lord would have to destroy the nation. The words of chapter eighteen of Revelations seemed to describe America exactly and God's judgment that was due her. Nevertheless, John believed with God all things were possible, and His mercy and love were unfathomable. That meant the Holy Spirit's new strategy for intercession might save America from destruction. The Lord could well use out-of-body experiences to rescue the entire world from Satan's schemes.

Andy had asked John to put out the chairs for the prayer team, so John hoped to arrive at church early and pray while he set up the folding chairs. After he failed to convince Leah to come, he barely had time to take of the chairs and write Bible verses on the two whiteboards. When he finished writing on the whiteboards, he prayed, pacing back and forth in front of the whiteboards. He believed the Lord would have to convince Pastor Ron to stay through the entire time of intercession. During that time, God would have to transport someone's spirit where they learned things for which we would intercede, and finally, Pastor Ron would need to witness an answer to our intercession in some spectacular way.

Andy arrived two minutes before the start of the meeting, and a minute later, Pastor Ron walked through the doors.

"How long have you two been here?" Pastor Ron asked, sounding suspicious.

"Just arrived a minute ago," Andy replied. "Doug and Mary said they'd be a few minutes late because grandma was late arriving to watch their kids."

Pastor Ron nodded upward once.

"I'd been here by myself for ten minutes before Andy came." John waited to take a seat until Pastor Ron found his seat so he sat next to Pastor Ron. Pastor seemed suspicious of his influence on Andy, so he wanted to keep several chairs between Pastor and Andy. He also wanted to sit close enough that he didn't miss any nuances in Pastor's communication.

Carl entered and greeted them two minutes later, and Doug and Mary arrived five minutes after that.

Once everyone sat, Pastor Ron smiled at each person individually. "Before you begin, Andy, I wanted to give a brief explanation of my stance on what occurred last Saturday."

"I am truly sorry for calling 911." Carl dipped his head like a dog who deserved to be beaten.

"Carl, God seemed to have rescued us from that fiasco," Pastor replied.

Eileen's face lit up. "Pastor, you should have seen it! God did much more than save us from embarrassment. We thought Doug and Andy had died. Then they came back to life, and what the Lord showed them transformed the way we prayed."

"Hmmm, Eileen, that's what I wanted to explain. I'm not sure God did what you think He did. I have to—"

Mary leaned in and turned to Pastor Ron. "If you had been here, Pastor, you would have seen that the Holy Spirit guided our prayers because of what Andy and Doug experienced."

"Let our pastor finish," John said. "He came tonight so he could decide for himself. We need to hear him and accept his judgment on the matter. That's why we hired him to be our pastor."

John thanked God silently for answering his prayers for the Holy Spirit's intervention in working out the details of the evening. Not only did John not have to defend what God did last week, but God allowed him to defend Pastor Ron.

"Thank you, John. I do plan to observe what happens tonight, and I am certain the Lord will show me if things are amiss here."

Andy pointed to the whiteboards. "John wrote the same verses for us last week. John, would you review the significance of these Scriptures?"

"Don't review the verses on my account."

John smiled at Pastor Ron. "I'm sure you are familiar with both of them, Pastor. I just wanted to remind the others of four things Romans 8:25-26 teach us." John walked over to the whiteboard.

> But if we hope for what we do not see, we eagerly wait for it with perseverance. Likewise the Spirit also helps in our

weaknesses. For we do not know what we should pray for as we ought, but the Spirit Himself makes intercession for us with groanings which cannot be uttered.

Romans 8:25-26 NKJV

John pointed to the second half of the first sentence. "First of all, notice that Paul assumes we will wait with perseverance. Second, we should wait or pray eagerly. In other words, God probably won't use us if we aren't eager for it to happen." John then underlined the words —*helps our weakness*—with his hand. "Third, these words inform us that what God does in prayer is not about how spiritual we are. It's all about God doing it. And fourth, we learn we don't know how to pray as we should, but the Holy Spirit will intervene for us and teach us how He does it."

Pastor Ron walked next to John and jabbed his finger at the last part of verse 26. "This verse says the Spirit 'intercedes for us with *groanings.*' It doesn't say anything about astral projections." Pastor Ron stammered in John's face. "Does. It."

John stepped back to put a little space between him and Pastor Ron. "Well, how do we interpret 'groanings too deep for words' in this scenario?"

"Good grief! Certainly not with—"

"Pastor," Doug interjected, "last Saturday, the whole out-of-body thing happened right after Andy and I began groaning in the Spirit."

"You what?" Pastor Ron turned and glared at Doug.

John motioned with his hands for Pastor to return to his seat. "Pastor, keep an open mind and at least pray with an expectation that the Holy Spirit might be working in the fashion that we described. Remember, He isn't making you do this, but He may want you to witness Him operating in this manner with others."

"Hogwash," Pastor Ron huffed. Grabbing his coat, he stomped toward the door. At the door, he stopped and turned. "I will be praying for this thing you are doing, and I will get back to you on what I feel the Lord is saying to me. In the meantime, don't be sharing your spirit voyages with anybody outside of this room." He turned and slammed the door.

John returned to his chair and sat with his elbows on his knees and his head in his hands. The meeting had started with such promise.

He could only hope that God touched Pastor Ron's heart through a different means.

After a long moment of silence, Andy suggested they start the prayer meeting and trust the Holy Spirit would touch Pastor's heart. They prayed for Pastor Ron and then took prayer requests. When Eileen shared about a ten-year-old granddaughter who wanted to become a boy, Carl, Mary, and Andy argued about whether transgender problems came from the devil or just the fallen condition of the world.

"Whoa!" John said. "Maybe the Holy Spirit wants us to intercede for the entire nation about this problem."

"Excellent suggestion," Andy said. "Let's wait silently for the Holy Spirit to show us how to pray or do the same thing He did last Saturday."

*Nations do not die from invasion;
they die from internal rottenness.*
                                    Abraham Lincoln

Chapter Twenty-Four

As they waited for the Holy Spirit to guide them, John thought things would happen much quicker this time. The transgender issue affected lots of children, and he knew God wanted the church to deal compassionately but scripturally with the problem. The controversy caused huge rifts among young Christian parents as well as with parents in the general population. Christians should lead the charge in bringing healing there.

After waiting ten minutes, silence seemed to cocoon the entire room. He could faintly hear the battery-operated clock tick on the wall above the whiteboard. An occasional gust of wind outside the window reinforced the warmth he felt in the room. Shortly, a peace enveloped John that made sound and other senses withdraw to a different place. Soon he heard someone groaning. Then another person exhaled sharply, like he had been punched in the gut.

John glanced up to see Carl groaning and Eileen gasping to catch her breath. After five minutes of groaning and gasping, Carl and Eileen lay motionless on the floor. Mary rose and checked on Eileen.

"She's all right," Andy said. "We need to focus on praying for them while their spirits are gone so they learn what we are supposed to pray about."

After ten minutes, John asked the Lord what was happening. Andy and Doug had stayed away less than five minutes. John figured that in the Spirit, time flowed at a different rate, so he wondered what caused the delay this time. Maybe their prayers moved the Spirit to show them an abundance of things. God didn't have to worry about dealing with one of them calling 911 this time. The long lapse of time, however, stretched his faith. He knew how long a body could go without breathing, and their chests didn't appear to be moving.

Thirty minutes later, Eileen and Carl's bodies moved. John exhaled sharply. He hadn't been aware of holding his breath, but the last few minutes must have made him tense as he struggled to trust God to bring Eileen and Carl back.

"Man!" Carl took a deep breath. "It felt like we were gone for days."

"Yeah, you had us worried, too," Andy said. "You were gone for 41 minutes."

"What did you see?" John stood and helped Eileen up.

Eileen staggered to her feet. "Wow! Where do I begin? We went all over the place, and I think we traveled back into history and then returned to current events."

"That would explain why you took so long to return to us," Andy said as he guided Eileen to a chair. "With God, all things are possible, and He lives outside our restraints of time. There's no reason why God couldn't take you into the past, or He could give you visions of something from history. Likewise, He could also have that all happen in what seemed like several hours to you but only 41 minutes to us."

"We spied first on a conversation that took place in an office in 2005." Eileen turned her head in Carl's direction, leaning in to see around Andy who blocked her view. "Did you notice the date on the desk calendar, Carl?"

"No, I didn't look. Traveling away from my body freaked me out so much I struggled to think clearly at the first place we visited."

"Not me! I immediately sensed God wanted us to gather as much information as possible so we could battle effectively against the schemes of the evil one."

Carl leaned forward with his elbow on his knee. "I just remember hearing a head of the Psychiatric Department in a hospital getting fired for opposing gender transitions in adolescents."

"The men we listened to complained that the hospital had no legitimate reason for dismissing the man." Eileen's eyes widened as she appeared to be envisioning the scene. "One of the two psychiatrists who chatted appeared terrified that he would lose his job as the other man had if he didn't toe the line with the transgender movement directives. The one who was fired cautioned the other man about getting upset. Evidently, the hospital had legitimate concerns because some patients with gender dysphoria had deep hurts and feelings that began long before anyone could have influenced them with their ideas of what gender meant. The suicide rate went right off the charts for those individuals."

Carl scoffed. "The psychiatrist who wasn't fired discounted the statistics trans activists used, but he planned to retire soon and wouldn't make things difficult for others. He struggled with altering people's bodies when for decades, he and most psychiatrists helped patients adapt their thinking to reality. Now they mutilated their bodies to align it to their messed-up way of thinking."

"Uh, that last part, Carl, wasn't exactly the way he said it."

"Whatever! The main thing I learned about the methods transgender activists used at the first place we visited could be summarized in one word: *fear* and *intimidation*."

"That's two words. We didn't learn the exact number of psychiatrists and psychologists who felt intimidated. The next place we visited did provide some hard data. Before 2001, only 0.001% of the population had been diagnosed with persistent feelings of gender dysphoria at an early age, and of those 99% were male. Then we saw sociologists gathering current data that showed gender transition at upwards of 24% in some school districts. Those sociologists wrestled with the dramatic uptick of adolescent females complaining of gender dysphoria, but when they attributed it to social contagion, they were shot down by their bosses.

"The last several places we visited disturbed me the most. We saw distraught parents trying to reason with their daughters. Typical of teenagers, they ignored their parents' feelings and advice. Two of the girls received encouragement from school authorities, and the parents had no say in their daughters' lives. The anguish of those parents so tore at my heart that I could hardly stop myself from crying. Then we saw people selecting only favorable statistics that supported their opinion to make it appear that the effects of hormone blockers could be reversed. They also edited data to show improved feelings of self-worth and decreased suicide rates."

"Christians need to kick out all the politicians who support the trans agenda," Carl declared.

"Carl, remember, there were a few, usually boys, who have legitimate feelings of gender dysphoria. As Christians, we should lead the way in showing compassion to those who are tormented about who they are."

"Good point, Eileen." John had heard enough, and he didn't want to get sidetracked with arguing over the transgender issue. "We need to hear from the Spirit on how to pray for this issue. What else do the two of you have for us before we go into intercession on the transgender controversy?"

Eileen frowned and took a deep breath. "We witnessed those liars suppress a ton of data. Accurate statistics revealed between 80 and 95 percent of children who expressed a discordant gender identity came to identify with their bodily sex when natural development was allowed to proceed. On top of that, transitioning treatment has not reduced suicide rates among people who identify as transgender. People who have transition surgery are 19 times more likely to die from suicide than the average person. Many kids who feel distress over their bodily sex know they aren't really the opposite sex. I couldn't hear the exact number. Carl, did you catch how many—"

"That's okay," John said, "we don't need to hear all the statistics."

Carl shook his head. "I didn't hear the number either. My temper rose when I saw all the anguish the parents suffered. The tears they cried, the self-incrimination, frustration, confusion, and despair they experienced upset me so much that I had to fight to keep my anger under control. Likewise, I struggled over those parents' sense of helplessness when school staff threatened to sever their relationship with their son or daughter. Listening to case after case of children being ripped from the protection of their mothers and fathers tore me up."

With his elbows on his knees and his hands over his face, Carl's voice broke as he described what he saw. "One mother wept and moaned, overwhelmed by her daughter's transition. Previously, her daughter liked to climb trees, practice martial arts, and play hockey, but she also relished being a queen, wearing makeup, dancing, cooking, and sewing. Her daughter had always expressed pride in being a girl. Then, as a teenager she connected with girls who thought transitioning would spite their parents, and that would give the parents what they deserved. Her daughter had never been rebellious before. Now she wanted to do anything to fit in.

"To watch that mother agonize saddened my spirit beyond words. She cried to God that her daughter didn't know what she was doing, or what she was losing. 'Have mercy, Lord' she pleaded. My spirit shuddered when she learned her daughter was taking hormone blockers. I begged for the Lord to take us back to our bodies after the mother learned the effects of the hormone blockers were to a great degree not reversible. I heard her crying so hard she could hardly catch her breath."

John fell to his knees. The pain zealous transgender activists caused parents and their children hit him like somebody knocked the wind out of him. "We need to take a break here and ask the Holy Spirit to show us how to pray for children and adults who suffer from gender confusion. Better yet, let's ask the Holy Spirit to pray through us. We have to pray for His love and truth to reign in this situation."

John returned to his chair and waited until Andy, who had been standing with his hand on Eileen's shoulder, returned to his seat. "What do you think, Andy? Are we ready to pray God's truth and love into this?" John extended his hand toward Andy to encourage him to lead the group on how to proceed in their intercession.

Andy nodded. "I think the Lord would have us wait again in silence for five or six minutes so we don't pray out of our emotions. God has pinpointed an open wound in our country that He wants to heal, and we can't let anger, grief, or a spirit of offense motivate our prayers."

John sensed God's assurance. Though he felt the gravity of the problem, the presence of the Lord caused the joy of the Lord to bubble up from within him. Andy said exactly what he had hoped he would say. John could tell Carl wanted to rain down fire and brimstone on anyone promoting the trans agenda. That could lead to problems.

For God is not the author of confusion but of peace,
as in all the churches of the saints.
I Corinthians 14:33 NKJV

Chapter Twenty-Five

After two minutes of silence, Mary prayed with a loud voice. "Heavenly Father, thank You for revealing the grievous injustice done to our children. We pray Your justice be served to those who rob our children of their very identities. Don't let them get away with all the harm they are causing."

John stood and extended his arms wide. "Yes, Lord, the deceptive evil perpetrated in the name of compassion crushes our hearts to where we struggle to respond." After he prayed that he sat and silently prayed. "Lord, help us wait on You so Your Spirit can pray through us." He hoped Andy would say something if people started praying out of their emotions instead of hearing for the Holy Spirit.

John recognized Carl had been upset by what he had seen, so he looked up at him. Carl sat with his eyes closed and his mouth shut. John figured that he was reluctant to give full vent to his emotions because he had only joined the church a month ago. John thanked the Lord for that.

John believed much more to the transgender issue existed than just some overzealous activists. The Holy Spirit revealed corruption He wanted them to pray against, but God had Carl and Eileen view hurts that required healing and restoration that only the Lord could provide. John longed for the Holy Spirit to guide their prayers. He knew the enemy would love for them to pray according to their ideas, or worse yet, according to their emotions. That would be a total waste of Carl and Eileen's visions, but worse, it would open them to attacks from Satan.

Mary prayed for two minutes and doubled over on the floor. Then she cried out in a loud voice. "Oh God, bring justice to these ungodly people who have corrupted our youth. Heal those who are trapped in lies of the devil."

Carl kneeled and pounded the floor with his fist. "Lord, stop those teachers in schools who are separating children from their parents. Give parents boldness to stand up against them."

After a minute of silence, Doug cleared his throat. "Lord, this is beyond my comprehension. I don't know how to pray. Ugh!" Doug went to his knees and then curled on the floor, holding his stomach.

A few seconds later, Doug muttered words to himself that were not of any language that John recognized. John thought he understood their meaning, however, so he spoke them out. "Bring compassionate people to help those children who are confused, give courage to those who are intimidated, expose the deceptions of the liars, and anoint Your church to offer compassion, hope, and deliverance to those who feel trapped."

To the right of John, Carl prayed, and John sensed Carl's prayers sprang from the intense pain he felt from what he had witnessed. While Carl prayed, he heard Janet calling on the Holy Spirit to intervene. Carl pounded on the tile floor and shouted against the plots of the devil. His words reverberated off the walls and floor. That didn't sound very inspired by the Holy Spirit to John's way of thinking. The prayer time seemed to spill forth with more confusion than with anything spiritual.

After an hour of bedlam, Carl and Mary quieted, and he heard only Andy praying. "Lord, we declare You reign in our nation, and we confess Your Lordship over our church and our time of intercession. Holy Spirit, continue to guide us and anoint us as we seek to offer compassion to the hurting, present truth to the confused and deceived, and bring justice to those who lie and corrupt our youth for selfish reasons. In Jesus' name we pray."

When Andy finished his prayer, he looked at John and gave him a weak smile. John rubbed his lower lip with his top teeth. John believed their intercession had been a mixed bag. God could work with some of their prayers, but the most passionate ones sprang from anger or hatred toward the perpetrators. For sure, God hated the evil that they propagated in the name of love, but many of those activists acted out of their hurt. They needed to find God's compassion for their lives just as much as anybody else.

John lingered behind to talk with Andy after the rest had left the prayer meeting. "What did you think about our prayer time?" John asked as they left the building.

Andy stopped as they approached John's car. "The information Carl and Eileen provided us from their out-of-body trip didn't get used properly."

"Some of us may have let our emotions guide us instead of our spirits."

"Humph!" Andy snorted. "None of us asked God how we should pray, at least, not as far as I could tell. If they did, they must not have listened or waited long enough to hear God answer.

John crisscrossed his arms over the top of his head and looked up at the cloudy night sky. "I have this foreboding that we may have stirred up a spiritual hornets' nest. I wished we had been more effective tonight in destroying strongholds of wickedness."

For whatsoever is born of God overcometh the world: and this is the victory that overcometh the world, even our faith.
I John 5:4 KJV

Chapter Twenty-Six

Leah hung up the phone after a half hour of trying to avoid probing questions from the pastor's wife. Francine wanted to know why Ron came home complaining about the mess John's ideas made for the prayer team. He refused to give her details and just griped unceasingly about the problems John would cause and the bad influence he had on Andy. Francine insisted Leah knew exactly what Ron complained about, and Leah repeatedly tried to act ignorant of the whole matter.

Leah thanked God repeatedly for keeping her home last night and for helping her avoid Francine after the church service the following morning. Since she hadn't been at the prayer meeting, she could rightly say she didn't exactly know what made Pastor Ron so mad. At the end of their conversation, she had to get a little huffy with Francine. She knew that Pastor Ron didn't want her to tell Francine, so she had no business telling it to Francine.

Francine sounded upset and would likely give her the cold shoulder for a few weeks. Their friends would likely talk, and that would leave her on the outside of their circle looking in. Leah wished she hadn't participated in any of John's visions, and she hoped she could stay far away from them. However, she didn't think she could leave the prayer team without creating even greater problems.

Leah knelt by the sofa in the living room and begged God to intervene and protect Bluffview Evangelical Free. She sensed evil forces of wickedness coming against the church, so she went to the spare bedroom where she could shut the door and pray uninhibited by concerns of being overheard by David and Rachael. After closing the door, she interceded with a fervency she rarely felt. Leah pled the blood of Jesus over their congregation. Then she prayed, binding several evil spirits in Jesus' name. Soon, she lay on the floor and prayed against several evil principalities and powers that came against their church.

After twenty minutes of interceding, pain on both sides of her head hit Leah with such intensity that she could scarcely breathe so her cry for help came out as a mere squeak. When her pain abated, she gulped for air. She never had headaches. Was she having a stroke? She wanted to intercede more, but she feared any movement would send the pain level through the roof again.

John came home from watching football at Andy's an hour later, and she still couldn't move without sharp pain shooting through her head. She wanted to call out to him but feared the ensuing pain would be unbearable. John discovered her in the office a few minutes after he returned home, and when he learned the reason she lay on the floor, he commanded the enemy in Jesus' name to take his hands off his wife. Leah felt the pain leave immediately. She twisted her head around and bent it side to side. "Wow, I guess we know what caused the pain."

"How long had you been lying there?"

"It was terrible Honey, I prayed against evil spirits attacking our church. Then an intense pain hit my temples, and I could hardly breathe." Tears flowed from Leah, and she felt powerless to stop them. This all happened because of John's desire to do spiritual warfare, and she hated that she had agreed to join him in his craziness. Why couldn't they be like normal people?

John wrapped his arms around her. "You are safe now. God didn't abandon you, and He never will."

Leah shoved his chest with the palm of her hand. "It's all your fault. If you hadn't gotten Pastor all riled up, Francine wouldn't have needled me for half an hour to tell her why Pastor Ron acted angry."

"You didn't tell her, did you?"

"No, but you probably caused me to lose all my close friends."

"Well, they wouldn't be real friends if they would leave you for refusing to share a secret."

Leah batted his chest with her hand. "Your crazy visions are the cause, and friends shouldn't keep secrets from friends. You have to stop those out-of-body travels."

"But Honey, God is using—"

"Don't 'but Honey' me. You are going to cause a church split. Does that sound like something God would want?"

John helped her up and seated her in the armchair. "God wouldn't, but the devil would."

"Are you joining in what the devil is trying to do?"

John sat and looked at her. "I am joining God in praying for what he desires for the church and our nation. If some members of our church are not happy with that, then they will have to ask God about that. That's not my problem."

"Well, it is *my* problem. How would you feel if all your friends left you? You have to stop seeking for God to take you traveling in your spirit." Leah studied his expression. She usually appreciated the enthusiasm that always bubbled out of him and spurred people on to join his latest insight. How could she convince him of the havoc his latest inspiration caused?

John put his hand on her shoulder. "You can't blame me if your friends want to leave you. God desires to use spirit-body journeys to show us how to pray. If God is for this, how can you ask me to stop?"

Leah glared at him. He could be so impossible at times. "Just stop!" She wanted to add the 'If you loved me, you would,' but her conscience kept her from trying to manipulate him. His often-repeated mantra haunted her: "If you want to find joy in the life Jesus desires for you, you have to stop trying to please other people."

John took her hand. "The Holy Spirit makes this happen. My response has to be the same as Peter's when Jewish rulers commanded him not to preach anymore about Jesus. 'I cannot help but speak what He has commanded me.'"

Leah gritted her teeth. She could tell arguing with John would accomplish nothing. Equally obvious, she would have an impossible task when she next met with Francine and the rest of her friends.

The thief does not come except to steal, and to kill, and to destroy.
John 10:10a NKJV

Chapter Twenty-Seven

Shortly after midnight two nights later, John's cell phone rang. He went to grab it quickly, hoping to catch it before it rang again and woke Leah. Not remembering where he left the phone, he patted the lamp table next to his bed to search for it. The phone chimed again. It was in his pant pocket.

Leah twisted to face John. "Gumby, that's your phone. Get it!"

John sprang over to his chair where he had draped his pants. By the time he fished his phone out of his pants, the call went to voice mail. John berated himself for failing to silence the phone before falling into bed. He had a feeling, however, that maybe the Lord wanted him to check the message because whoever called had a serious problem.

John took the phone into the living room so he wouldn't disturb Leah. The voice message was from Doug:

"Hey John, sorry to bother you in the middle of the night. Mary just had a nightmare. Actually, she called it a demonic visitation. She insisted that I call you now because she knew the Lord allowed the attack to warn us that we had entered into the enemy's camp. Give me a call as soon as you hear this. Mary and I will be interceding for our prayer team in the meantime."

John set his phone down to pray before he returned the call. Doug sounded worried and goaded by Mary to call him. Undoubtedly, the dream terrorized Mary, and she likely wanted us to either stop traveling in our spirit bodies or cease the chaotic praying the team members did afterward. The latter would suit him fine. He'd fight any suggestion that they quit the out-of-body reconnoitering. The Holy Spirit wanted to use it. If God was for it, who had any right to stand against it?

John prayed for the Holy Spirit to give Doug and Mary peace, and he asked God to guide their conversation. John picked up his phone. Another thought came to him. Maybe Mary would quit as a member of the prayer team. That would solve several problems. Mary did a wonderful job marshaling prayer support from the rest of the congregation, but he hardly considered her a team player. Too often she insisted on steering the Saturday evening prayer in a different direction than Andy had laid out.

John looked at the ceiling of the living room. "Lord, forgive me for my critical attitude of Mary. You are in charge here." John pressed the icon to call Doug's phone. "Wow, Doug, sounds like you guys had quite a night," John said as soon as Doug answered.

"The horror that Mary suffered went way beyond what a mature Christian should experience." Doug's voice quaked with anger. "Jesus would never allow that to happen unless we had stepped someplace where we didn't belong."

"Ah, let's pray about that," John said. He figured fear triggered a fight or flight response that produced the anger that he heard in Doug's voice. John wanted to turn that anger into motivation to fight the devil, not flee from him.

"We *have* prayed! That is why we called you now. We prayed, and the Lord said to stop the spirit traveling."

"I see. I would like to ask Mary some questions." John prayed silently for Mary to answer honestly while Doug asked her to talk with him.

"Yes," Mary huffed.

"I don't want you to recount the nightmare to me, Mary." John tried to sound as calm and reassuring as possible. "I just want you to tell me the exact words Jesus said when He told you to stop the spirit traveling."

"Well, for Pete's sake, John. I didn't hear an audible voice from heaven. But the Lord impressed upon me very strongly that He didn't want us involved in out-of-body voyaging."

"Mary, you sound upset, and I would be too. Let's talk about this in the morning."

"There's nothing to talk about. You heard me, stop the spirit-body traveling."

"Mary, why are you telling this to me? I am not in charge of the prayer team."

"Fine, I'll call Andy."

John heard Mary or Doug fumbling with the phone.

Doug's voice came on. "John, Mary's upset, as you can imagine. We'll set up a time to meet with Andy. Can we meet together with you and him this evening?"

# # #

John tried to call Andy several times, but he never answered. Eileen didn't respond to his messages either. He received a text message from Doug that told him to meet with them and Andy at the church at 6:00 PM. That didn't bode well because it sounded like Mary had connected with Andy, but Andy hadn't contacted him. If they met at the church, Pastor Ron would join the fray. That thought provided some relief. Pastor Ron wouldn't let Mary bluster her way into insisting they listen to her because she had "heard from God" on the matter.

Since he had received Doug's text message at 11:00 AM, he had plenty of time to pray in between the two appointments he had scheduled at the downtown office. He left early for the church, hoping to talk to Andy before the meeting started.

When he arrived at 5:30 PM, Suzi, the church secretary was still there. She greeted him absent-mindedly as she fussed around the office.

"Have you seen Andy yet?" John asked her.

"Yes, no, . . .I don't know."

John had known Suzi for years and had never seen her so flustered. Something filled the atmosphere with fear and confusion. "Suzi, what happened here?"

Suzi dropped the programs in her arms onto her desk. "Oh, John, you would not believe what happened right after I came in this afternoon. A rock crashed through Pastor Ron's window with a note on it. 'Transphobic people and churches will bear the consequences of their hate!' Why would anybody do that?

"It is insane. Why would they target *our* church? We haven't attacked the transgender agenda. Pastor Ron has always sought to strike a balanced approach to controversial issues. He knows we have church members at both ends of the political spectrum."

Suzi took a deep breath and released a verbal flood bursting from an overstressed damn. "We love people of all persuasions here. They should know that, John. Why would they think otherwise? Have they even talked to Pastor Ron? I cleaned up the shattered glass. Pastor taped a piece of wood to keep the elements out. What do you think they will do? Am I in any danger?"

"I'm sorry, Suzi. A message like that is horrifying, but God has angels around you." John put his hand on her shoulder to reassure her, but he balked at the suddenness of the attack by the evil one. "Can I talk with Pastor Ron?"

"I'm not sure you want to him. He is madder than a wet hen."

"Thanks for the warning." If Pastor Ron reacted like he did when stressed, he would be in a rage and difficult to reason with. However, the rock message might turn out to be a blessing. If Pastor Ron reacted with fight instead of flight, he would be less than receptive to Mary's warning.

When John knocked on Pastor Ron's office, a disgusted grunt from within seemed to indicate John could enter. Pastor Ron sat behind his desk and glared, daring John to say something.

"Suzi told me about the broken window and the warning."

"I wanted to know who talked to whom about your intercessory prayer meeting last Saturday. Then this afternoon, this happens." Pastor Ron pointed to the patched window. "Coincidentally, less than an hour after Mary calls, insisting on having a meeting with me, you, and Andy."

"We are fighting powerful demons that seek to destroy our children." John curled his fist in front of his chin to suggest they should fight and not cave into pressure. "We can't let Mary's demonic dreams intimidate us. Jesus put us in a spiritual battle that we dare not abandon because demons attack us."

Ron faced his palm out toward John to stop him. "Fine, but a person wrote that note and threw the rock. That person could cause our church all sorts of problems. I thought everyone on the prayer team promised to keep quiet about your intercession."

John sat in an armchair facing Pastor Ron. "Our intercession riled demonic forces, and evil spirits can inspire people to do their bidding without any knowledge of why they are doing it."

"Do you think I'm stupid?" Pastor leaned forward and pounded the table with his fist. "We just happened to receive a warning against fighting the transgender agenda two days after your intercession opposed it!"

"Andy and I will ask if anyone on our team inadvertently mentioned our topic of intercession. Whatever we uncover won't diminish the depth of spiritual battles we face."

Pastor Ron leaned back in his chair. "I almost prefer fighting with demons than dealing with Mary or digging to the bottom of who leaked details of your prayer meeting."

John heard a knock, and Andy poked his head in the door.

"Come on in," Pastor said with decided resignation in his voice.

Andy sat in an armchair next to John and muttered to John. "I'm sorry for not responding to your calls. Mary made me promise not to talk with you until she had an opportunity to meet with everybody."

John clenched his jaw. Demons may have visited Mary, but she sure liked to run the show. John looked at Pastor Ron, and Pastor Ron seemed as irritated at Mary as he was.

Pastor Ron exhaled sharply. "We were just discussing who might have chatted around about the latest subject of intercession. Have any ideas?"

Andy shook his head and looked at John as though he might know.

Pastor Ron pointed to the patched window. "A friend of someone from your prayer team sent us a warning." Pastor shoved the note toward Andy so he could read it.

While Andy studied the note, Mary and Doug entered the office and sat opposite John and Andy. Doug scowled at John.

"Did the meeting start without us?" Mary asked.

Andy handed the note to Mary and Doug. Andy waited a few seconds, giving them time to read it. "Somebody wrapped this message around a rock and threw it through Pastor Ron's window this afternoon. Have any ideas who might have discussed our intercession against the transgender issue?"

"Don't blame me or Doug," Mary squawked.

"Nobody is blaming you." John waved his hands in front of his chest. "Perhaps when you talked with others on the prayer team, they might have mentioned discussing the problem with family members." John didn't doubt she could easily have sought to garner support for her stance by seeking allies.

"Uh, if blame should be assigned to someone, you are the first person I would look at." Mary glared at John. "Your out-of-body voyaging has left the door wide open for demons to march right in. I wouldn't doubt that the forces of evil that you stirred up could have pitched the rock through the window without the aid of a single human being."

John sat back in his chair. "I would agree with you on that."

"What more proof do you need, Paster Ron? Tell Andy to stop their spirit-body traveling."

Pastor Ron folded his hands and planted them on his desk. "Several things bother me, Mary, about this whole incident. First, you refused to accept Andy's word that he would handle the situation. Second, you are letting a nightmare, albeit one from the pit of hell, convince you to stop praying in a certain manner. Third, you come running to me to make Andy do what you want him to do."

Pastor Ron hesitated, looking back and forth between all four of them. "And fourth, I dislike receiving messages wrapped around rocks thrown through my window, and I get extremely irritated at the suggestion that demons did it without the aid of human hands. I want to know who broke their promise not to blab about the nature of the prayer team's intercession."

Doug leaned forward. "Pastor Ron, I never meant—"

Ron put his hand out like a stop sign. "It doesn't matter. You don't like the way Andy leads prayer. Stay away from the prayer meetings on Saturday. Understood?"

"But Pastor—"

"Stay away!" Pastor Ron turned to Andy. "Until you can tell me who blabbed, stop interceding about the transgender agenda. No, change that. You are in charge of the prayer topics but pray quietly and in an orderly fashion. Don't give people an excuse to talk about your prayer meetings. And for heaven's sake, stop your spirit-body traveling."

As John walked to his car after the meeting, he discussed with Andy what they should do next. Until they convinced Pastor to decide otherwise, Andy planned to halt the out-of-body experiences. John couldn't blame him for wanting to do that, but abandoning a tool the Holy Spirit gave them in the battle against the forces of wickedness couldn't happen at a worse time. The enemy would attack them with everything they had because of the threat spirit-body travels posed.

Andy asked him what he'd do. Though John wasn't sure what fasting accomplished, he planned to fight against the attacks of the devil with the weapons he still had available, which meant he'd fast and pray. He told Andy he wouldn't ask anyone on the prayer team to join him in spirit-body journeys. Pastor expected him to comply with his edict for the prayer team to cease, and unless God told him otherwise, he wouldn't go against Pastor's desires. John believed the forces of evil would overplay their hand at some point.

Ye are of God, little children, and have overcome them: because greater is he that is in you, than he that is in the world.
I John 4:4 KJV

Twenty-Eight

When Pastor Ron entered their kitchen at home, Francine turned from the stove and pointed her spatula at Ron. "We need to talk."

Ron fumed and leveled his gaze at her. When Fran got like this, she wouldn't settle for a vague answer. "What!" he barked.

"What is going on with the prayer team?" Francine took two steps towards him and wiggled the spatula in his face. "Mary calls me, practically in tears, and tells me demons attacked her in her sleep. Then I hear a rock with a message sails through your window. I call Leah, and she won't tell me anything. Are we facing another church split?"

Ron shoved the spatula aside. "Calm down!" Ron waited until she backed off. "Leah didn't talk to you about the prayer team because everybody on the team agreed not to discuss the matter with anyone. For that same reason, I can't discuss it with you either."

Francine put her fisted hands on her hips. "How do you expect me to deal with Mary? . . .Do you want me to do nothing while our church becomes total bedlam?"

"Really? Total bedlam! Fran, have a little faith in your husband here." Ron felt disgusted with the whole situation and didn't feel like discussing it. "Listen, I told Andy and John to stop what they were doing, so that should be the end of Mary's fears or panic attacks, or whatever they were."

After dinner and a brief game of Scrabble, Ron apologized to Francine for keeping her in the dark about the prayer team's situation.

He explained that somehow word got out that they had prayed against transgender activists. That angered people and stirred up some demons.

How fast that happened mystified Ron. Certainly, the best approach consisted of asking what Jesus would do if He faced the same thing. Undoubtedly, Jesus had more authority and would bind the demon, but He would treat people with compassion. Before Pastor Ron went to bed, he wrote out a rough draft of the message he planned to give on Sunday. He planned to deliver a balanced sermon permeated with compassion for sinners suffering from feeling trapped in a body they didn't identify with. Of course, he would condemn efforts by transgender activists who propagated confusion among children. After all, his church followed the Bible, not the dictates of modern culture that had messed up what it meant to be a man or a woman. God's word and science plainly taught what made a person a male or female. Certainly, one's feelings didn't determine their gender.

# # #

In the morning Pastor Ron walked into a chilly church office. He gritted his teeth as he stared at shards of glass hanging from a sectioned portion of the window frame. He shivered, but not from the cold air blowing through another broken window. An eerie feeling of being exposed hit him. He felt helpless. What could he do to stop this?

Amidst the pieces of glass, Pastor Ron picked up a rock with a message around it. He carefully unwrapped the paper as puffs of frosty vapor hung in the air from his heavy breathing. After gently placing the rock on his desk, he read the note:

"Culture may decide how gender is expressed, but in a free country, each person defines for themselves their gender. Don't inhibit our freedom."

He stood there with shaky hands and fought to control his anger which threatened to burst loose with foul language he'd later regret. He dialed the police to talk to a detective. When they put him on hold, he changed his mind about reporting the incident. He didn't want the bad publicity, so he hung up. A minute later, he picked up the rock from the desk and squeezed it until his wrist ached as he fought the urge to throw the rock back out the broken window. His office window faced the street, so he couldn't risk hitting a car. The rock clanged when it hit the bottom of his wastebasket.

Suzi would arrive in an hour. He had better get the mess picked up before then. Otherwise, he'd have to endure her fussing and stewing while he taped another piece of plywood in the window. Finding the duct tape and wood went quicker this time. Pastor Ron snickered. He had experience.

Pastor Ron cut the board with a utility knife and stuck it in the window. After he taped it to the frame. He compared the tape job on the window to the one right next to it and shrugged. Maybe our rock throwers meant to hit the already busted window and just missed. How do we know if he was even the same pissed-off jerk? Pastor Ron paused and thought about the second message. He felt the blood drain from his face. That messenger seemed to have read his sermon notes. A shiver went done his spine. That could only be explained by demonic activity.

Pastor Ron booted up his computer. Demons might have read his planned sermon, but evil spirits instructed a person to write the note and toss it through his window. A blistering letter to the editor should set the record straight. He knew right from wrong and how to speak the truth without merely ranting against those who opposed him.

He wrote the first line of the letter to the editor and reasoned the rock thrower must be a church member. A sermon from the pulpit would be much more appropriate. We didn't have to air our dirty laundry in front of the rest of the world.

Pastor Ron went back to his sermon notes. His heart rate had slowed. How could he have let his temper make him think so irrationally? He studied his notes. Genesis chapter one plainly stated God created them male and female. If people attended this church, they would believe the Bible. If they struggled with what God meant by male and female, he wanted to help them. He had to resist getting incensed about their intolerance of those who didn't agree with them. Their intolerance meant they failed to understand how God defined gender and how Jesus commanded us to walk in love. As a pastor, he should be an example of speaking the truth in love, of how to turn the other cheek, even when they throw another rock through the window.

An hour later, Suzi knocked on his door and asked about an event for teenagers next month. She looked at the newly patched portion of the window and turned to Pastor Ron. "What happened?"

"Our friend returned with a familiar message."

Suzi's jaw dropped.

"I believe our friend is likely a member of our congregation. Don't worry. I will attack the problem in this week's sermon."

After Suzi left his office, he stared at the document he was composing. If someone in his congregation listened to demons, he had better explain how Satan lied and deceived people. Pastor Ron Googled scientific information about what determined whether a person was male or female. By 4:00 PM he felt he had a well-rounded message and went home to practice its delivery.

Pastor Ron practiced the message twice and thought he knew it well enough that he would hardly need his notes while he spoke on Sunday. As usual, he practiced the sermon in front of Francine so she could offer her feedback. When she heard the message, she interrupted him three times to complain he sounded too supportive of the transgender movement.

He reminded her, "We hate the sin but love the sinner."

"Oh sure, are you going to start painting rapists and murders with such compassion?"

"What will you say if they repent?" Pastor Ron suggested.

"Do you even tell them they are sinners?"

"They are hurting individuals, and if they attend our church, they know they need help from Jesus." Pastor Ron looked at his notes. He should fight the demons that harassed a member of his church. "You are right, Fran. If someone listened to demons, their pastor had better expose the evil behind transgenderism."

Ron went to his laptop, rewrote his message, and then read the newspaper before going to bed. He planned to work on his message again in the morning. Fran seemed riled about the issue and would want to hear his revisions. She rarely fussed this much about his messages, but since Eileen's granddaughter struggled with gender confusion, he figured she had strong feelings about the matter because of her close friendship with Eileen.

In the middle of the night, Ron woke up startled. He heard Fran scream from the living room. He ran out and found her trembling with a broken Danish Mother's Day Plate in her hand.

"What happened, Fran?"

Fran's eyes widened as she stared at the plate. "It flew off the wall and broke!"

"Well, those things happen."

"No, you don't understand. The plate sailed over my head and crashed into the wall behind me."

"You must have been dreaming."

"No, I was wide awake."

Ron went over to turn the living room light on. He didn't want to wake Fran if she was sleepwalking, but he needed to straighten this out. He hated to think that demons had harassed his wife. Just as he reached for the light switch, another Mother's Day Plate flew off the wall and towards his head.

He ducked.

The plate crashed into the wall. Ron squatted and gawked at where it landed. He jumped up and turned the light on. "Who did that!"

Ron glanced around the room. Nobody was there except for Ron and Fran. Nobody except a demon. "In the name of Jesus, I command any demons in this room to leave, immediately."

Ron looked at Fran. Terror was etched across her face. He did not doubt that a demon had thrown that plate. But the demon had left now. He put out his arm for Fran to come to him.

She curled her head into his chest. "How could they do that? I mean enter the home of a believer."

Ron hugged her and put his chin on top of her head. "I'm sorry that happened to you. It looks like we have a spiritual battle on our hands."

The future of this nation depends on the Christian training of our youth.
George Washington

Chapter Twenty-Nine

John entered Pastor Ron's office Friday evening and found Pastor and Andy standing behind the pastor's desk, deep in conversation. They hardly acknowledged his presence. Andy had his hand on Pastor Ron's shoulder, comforting him with words of assurance that they had Christ's power to defeat the devil. Pastor's head bobbed and his eyelids fluttered. At the same time, his hand trembled while fidgeting with his tie. John had never seen his pastor so agitated before.

Andy motioned with his head for John to join him in praying for Pastor Ron. John walked next to them and placed his hand on Pastor Ron's other shoulder. As he stood there, John noticed that Pastor Ron clenched his jaw. Whatever bothered Pastor, he appeared determined to apply his faith to the problem. Andy explained they needed to pray against demonic attacks that Pastor Ron and Francine had experienced last night.

As Pastor Ron recounted the horrors he and Francine experienced, John sensed they should intercede for their church members instead of just influential people in the nation. He wasn't sure what to pray for Pastor Ron, so he hoped to hear from Andy on how to intercede. As he listened to Andy bind Satan from threatening the pastor and his wife, John felt certain specific demons needed to be bound, but he didn't know which ones. He yearned to use out-of-body experiences to discern which demons needed to be bound. Maybe now, Pastor would allow them to implement this tool.

When Andy paused in his prayer, John didn't know what he should say, so he just prayed what seemed logical to him. "Lord, we thank You for Your word which promises that You have given us victory over all the power of the enemy. In Jesus' name, we bind the spirits of fear and anger, and we command them to stay away from Pastor Ron's home and family."

John wanted to pray more but didn't know where or on whom he should focus. Silently, he asked God to change Pastor Ron's heart to allow him the freedom to use the spirit-body journeys if the Lord wanted it.

Andy hugged Pastor Ron, and Pastor Ron turned to John and hugged him fiercely. "Thank you for your prayers, guys. Pastors aren't supposed to get attacked by demons. I guess we must have stirred up a veritable hornet's nest."

Andy looked at his feet and shook his head. "I'm sorry for inciting demons to attack your home."

"No, you shouldn't apologize. Having the devil bother us must mean we have upset his plans." Pastor Ron squeezed John's shoulder. "I should apologize to you. If I had let you continue to observe the devil's schemes with the trans movement, maybe you would have ousted him from our neighborhood entirely."

Andy's eyes widened. "You're not afraid you'll receive more demonic attacks?"

"If truth be told, Francine and I may have taunted the enemy into harassing us. We both lit into those who cause gender confusion."

"Will you give us permission to resume our spirits-body journeys?" John asked, believing that the enemy had overplayed his hand sooner than he had expected.

Pastor Ron's jaw jutted up and out. "We need to hit the devil with everything we have.

# # #

After meeting with Pastor and Andy, John could hardly contain his excitement—Pastor had changed his mind about their spirit-body journeys. He could hardly wait to share the good news with Leah. When John entered their living room, he saw Leah sitting on the sofa, wiping tears from her eyes. Leah pointed to the hall leading to the bedrooms. "You have to talk with Rachael. Here's a note I received from school that explains our daughter's feelings."

John read the school counselor's note stating their son's new name and preferred pronouns. They were to call their daughter Ray, short for Raymond. John struggled to focus his gaze as he attempted to reread the note. This couldn't be happening. Where did she get this idea?

Rachael was playing a hand-held video game when John entered her bedroom. "Hey, Partner." John figured that was a safe greeting without acquiescing to her crazy notions. He waited a moment for her to pause her game to acknowledge his presence.

She kept playing without any sign she'd heard him.

He grabbed the game. "I'm talking to you. Does your new choice of gender include the right to ignore your father?"

She looked down without making eye contact. "What do you want?"

"Where did you get the idea that you're no longer a girl?"

"In school we learned that gender doesn't depend on what your parents think or on the appearance of your body."

"Your gender is whatever God says it is." John struggled to keep his voice calm.

"Exactly how do you know what God says it is? If God is in me, He should tell me, but He hasn't." Rachael paused and looked up. "I asked Montana's mom, and she asked the spirit to tell her. The spirit told her mom I liked math and playing baseball, and that was because I was really a boy. That made sense to me."

"Oh?" John sat stunned. This couldn't possibly be happening to his daughter.

Rachael continued. "I talked about it with the school counselor the next day, and she encouraged me to immediately transition to becoming a boy. She made appointments for me to see a psychologist and a doctor next week to get puberty blockers to make sure I become the gender God wants for me."

"Well, we want you to become all that God wants for you. Don't you think you should pray about it first with your pastor? That's why we have a pastor. Shall we make an appointment with Pastor Ron for next week, too?"

Rachael blinked several times. "Oh! Okay."

John kissed the top of her head. He didn't dare say anything further. His emotions threatened to override his mind. He walked into the home office, closed the door, and cried out to God. "Why Lord? How could this happen? Lord, this can't be! Not to my daughter!"

While he prayed, David knocked on his door. "Are you okay?"

John opened the door and motioned with his head for David to come and sit in the armchair. John took a deep breath once they both sat. "What do you know about your sister's thoughts on gender?"

"Lots of girls think they are boys now. Girls who think that are mostly rejects or rebels."

"Your sister has never been rebellious, and she isn't a reject. Have you or any of her friends tried to talk some sense into her?"

"I have, but she won't listen to me."

John grabbed the top of his head with both hands. "She won't listen to me, either, but she has always respected you. You've been her hero. Maybe you can say something that can get through to her."

"Her mind is made up."

If she persists in wanting to be a boy, at least protect her from being abused by any of the other boys."

"Dad, you can't expect me to rush in and play God with Rachael. You have got to wait on the Lord to do his work."

John gritted his teeth. "We can't just sit back and do nothing. She'll get hurt."

"Isn't it our part to pray? You are always in such a hurry to fix things for us. When we wait on God, He will guide our prayers and take care of her."

John leaned back in his chair and looked at the ceiling. His son spoke the truth, but that didn't make it any easier to swallow. David spat out words from a Sunday school lesson because that gave him an excuse to do nothing.

"Right, David, my job is to pray. That's a task for all of us. While we pray for your sister, we need to listen for the Lord to show us tangible ways we can help her. Okay?"

Dinner conversation that evening consisted of small talk separated by long spans of awkward silence. John's plan to seek Pastor Ron's help with Rachael did little to mollify Leah. After dinner, John and Leah went to their office and sought God earnestly for their daughter's deliverance from the deceptive agenda of the transgender activists. That night as John lay in bed trying to fall asleep, he continued to cry out to God. Had he been so focused on praying for others that he neglected his family?

# # #

On the following Saturday afternoon, Leah sat next to John in their office and announced she would rejoin him in interceding with the prayer team. John told her about Pastor Ron and Francine's demonic attack and explained why Pastor Ron changed his mind about spirit-body journeys. "When the enemy throws junk at you to scare you, that's the time to use all the available weapons for spiritual warfare"

Leah straightened her back and her eyes widened. "Gosh, poor Francine."

John extended his palm toward Leah, pleading for her to understand. "Francine and Pastor need our prayers, and we have to let the Holy Spirit guide our intercession, even if that means out-of-body experiences."

Leah frowned. "Isn't that like abandoning the fort to sneak into the enemy's camp when you're under attack?"

"If the enemy lobs bombs at your fort, you should hit the place that's launching the missiles."

"We can trust Jesus to handle the source," Leah spoke slowly, enunciating each word distinctly. "That's. His. job."

"If a shell wounds one of your kids, you take the best course of action to treat the kid and make sure nobody else gets hurt."

"Gumby, I don't want to pretend that out-of-body experiences will solve our current troubles."

John held up his hands to signal her to stop. "I am not asking you to travel with me out of your physical body. Just pray with us."

"Of course, I want to help our daughter, and I will do everything that any normal, sane person would do."

Leah didn't say anything more and neither did John. He settled for her coming to the prayer meeting, and he thanked God he didn't have to abandon spirit-body journeys. She wouldn't stop others from going on a trip, especially if God could use their journeys to deliver Rachael.

John and Leah arrived before Andy, so they set up the chairs for the meeting and waited for the team to arrive. John smiled as he considered a powerful deliverance for their daughter that would change Leah's attitude toward journeys in their spirit bodies. When Andy entered the room, he smiled at John, and John grinned back at him. Andy appeared ready to experience God supernaturally.

After the entire prayer team was seated, Andy explained the attack Pastor Ron and Francine received and their subsequent meeting in the Pastor's office. Neither John nor Leah said anything about Rachael's decision because they agreed to let the Holy Spirit direct the focus of prayer. Their daughter needed Spirit-guided prayer. Anything less than that would not prove helpful and could easily lead to gossip and strife.

After Janet listened to Pastor Ron's experience, she asked, "Should the prayer team stop using out-of-body travels."

Doug glanced at Mary and cleared his throat. "Pastor called and talked to us about it. He wants to let the Holy Spirit lead us into spirit traveling if the Lord desires that."

Janet frowned at John, opened her mouth for a second, and then shut it.

Andy looked at John. "John, will you open our time of intercession?"

"Sure, I will just thank and praise the Lord for His power and presence here. Then let us be quiet for at least ten minutes so we can hear how the Holy Spirit wants to direct us. If you have any trepidation about traveling in your spirit, you can relax. The Holy Spirit won't force you to do anything that will harm you." Because of Leah's experience, he resisted telling them the Holy Spirit wouldn't force them, period.

After John praised and thanked God, he resisted thoughts of doubt about the value of spirit-body journeys. The evil one had seduced Rachael, but that didn't mean they hadn't done damage to the enemy's camp. As the minutes passed, doubts assailed John because the devil wanted to thwart their plans. They waited quietly for twenty minutes until Mary groaned and curled up on the floor.

A minute later John groaned from an intense pulling within his inner being, and he fell to his knees. Shortly, John looked down at his body and over at Mary who floated above her body. "Hey, I didn't expect to see you leaving your body."

Mary wrinkled her nose. "I didn't want you to have *all* the fun. Besides, I wanted to check this thing out for myself. Doug and I couldn't find anything in the Bible that forbids this, and a few verses suggested that God might do something like this."

An instant later, the Spirit transported John and Mary's spirits to a conference room where executives sat around a table with sordid demons laughing and cajoling behind them.

A man at the head of the table, who appeared to be a CEO or boss of some kind, asked the others to find dependable sources for increased revenue. One man sitting towards the end of the table challenged the use of transgender surgery and hormone therapy on adolescents.

The leader scowled. "Chuck, you are sitting in for Scottie today, right?"

A fat demon jumped on the table and yelled. *Don't say anything, Chuck. You will lose your job if you do.*

Chuck took a deep breath. "We may make thousands in profits, but we could easily end up spending millions in lawsuits defending our policy."

You are stupid, Chuck! He knows that.

"Have you discussed this with the legal team, Chuck?"

A woman on the opposite side of the table leaned forward. "We have zero liability, sir. We are faithfully following all AAP guidelines."

Don't be a fool! The demon's face practically touched Chuck's nose.

Chuck's face turned red. "Some parents will likely sue us anyway, and gender transitioning could easily harm our reputation."

"Talk with me after the meeting, or better yet talk with Scottie," The man at the head of the table turned to someone on his right. "Let's review your figures."

A demon whispered to the man on the right. *Remind him that transition surgeries and hormone therapy produce lifelong customers. On top of that several drug companies are paying us big money to use their products.*

John pushed himself down to the demons to pull them away from Chuck when suddenly he found himself and Mary in a warehouse. The stench of raw sewage assaulted his nostrils, and an acrid smoke stung his eyes. Two men discussed plans to intimidate school board members who sought to change the transgender policy. Around them lurked four demons, inciting them to violence.

Don't let them ignore the pain their opposition causes.
Make them feel your emotional and physical pain. Throw rocks at their cars.
They need to know what rejection is. Threaten them on the phone.
Throw salt on their lawns.

The demons laughed. One of the men wrote down names, addresses and phone numbers of possible targets as a broad-shouldered, muscular demon spoke them out.

One tall, skinny demon slapped the backs of two large ones. *Well done, Violence and Intimidation.*

One of two large ones jabbed the skinny demon in the ribs. *Thanks, Contempt, you made our work easy.*

Hey, you guys wouldn't have gotten to square one without me.

Contempt scoffed, *Thank you, Fear, for laying the groundwork. Let's ssssee you terrorize some Right-Wing rednecks, some truly religious onessss that put their faith in our enemy. Ha! If you're so hot, see if you can make them afraid their preciousss daughters will get raped by trans boys in their school restrooms. Get them agitated so they attack transitioning teens on social media.*

You are just jealous, Fear replied. *My scheme of pitting rednecks against trans has enraged most of the trans population. The visceral response of trans subjects has already escalated the violence beyond our vilest dreams.*

Contempt sneered. *None of that would be possible without me*

John noticed Mary had a disgusted look on her face. "Don't worry Mary. Jesus disarmed the principalities and powers of these demons and made an example of them, triumphing over them on the cross."

Mary nodded. "Yep, Colossians 3:16."

"I don't know why the Spirit brought us here."

Mary said, "Maybe He wanted to show us these demons so we learned their names and became more effective in casting them out."

John gave her a thumbs up.

A moment later, everything went dark, and a hard floor caused John's shoulder to ache. He opened his eyes and realized he had returned to the church. Mary lay ten feet to his right. He heard several voices praying for the Holy Spirit to show them everything they would need to be well-equipped to wage spiritual warfare in their intercession. John sat up slowly and reached for the chair behind him. This trip left him dizzier than the previous one. Perhaps the heaviness of the things he learned impacted his soul more this time. "We need to intercede for our country and our church to be delivered from the demons that are reinforcing the transgender movement."

Mary sprang up and shouted, "Praise the Lord, for He has defeated the power of the enemy!"

John jerked his head around and gawked at Mary. How did she get so energized when he felt enervated?

"Praise God! Sing praises to Him! Make a joyful noise unto Him!" Mary jumped up and down, waving her hands in the air. "Come on, people, our shouts of praise will defeat the power of the enemy!"

John figured Mary had the right idea. Psalm 22:3 told us God inhabited the praise of His people. When God appeared on the scene, the enemy's defenses were defeated, those held in bondage were freed.

After an anointed time of praise and worship of God, Mary and John led out in prayer, binding the spirits of fear, contempt, violence, and intimidation. They didn't finish interceding until almost midnight. John could hardly believe it was that late. He wanted to tell Pastor Ron what they learned before he delivered his Sunday message, but he decided to call Pastor Ron before he left for church in the morning because Pastor was likely in bed.

"You have only one way to convince others, listen to them."
George Washington

Chapter Thirty

In the morning, John woke with a start. The Holy Spirit never guided them to pray for their daughter last night. He had to believe that the demons they had bound and the prayers they had prayed made a difference in Rachael's life.

John looked over at the clock on his dresser. The alarm failed to wake him, and he had just an hour before the service started. Leah had risen without waking him. Pastor Ron always arrived at church an hour before the service started, and now he couldn't call him because Pastor Ron hated to be disturbed before the service. Pastor Ron would not be receptive to what he had to say if he interrupted his preparations for the service.

"Leah, are you ready for church?" John yelled as he yanked on his shirt.

Leah bustled into the room with her makeup on and dressed for church. "Good, I was just about to wake you. I turned off the alarm so you could sleep a little longer."

"What!"

"I woke up early to pray for Rachael. After I cried out to the Lord for over an hour, I felt God say that she would return to her senses soon. Then a peace washed over me. My soul felt so calm that I didn't have a care in the world. Anyway, we came in late last night, so I thought you could use a little extra sleep."

Of course, she didn't realize he needed to call Pastor before the church service. John sighed. If he hadn't been so tired, he would have told her he wanted to wake up early. John tried Pastor Ron's cell phone. No answer. He would have to catch him in his office before the service started.

As he drove to church, John explained to Leah the urgency he felt for speaking with Pastor before the service started. The demons used fear and contempt to inflame people, they used hyper-religious Christians to denigrate transgender people. Their fear—whether fear of transgender people, fear of parents losing authority over their children, or fear of losing the culture wars—would ignite rage in the transgender population. Their rage would cause violence against they deemed transphobic, which would increase hatred and fear among conservative Christians, rednecks, and the general population. Mutual misunderstandings would abound. God wanted our church to lead the way in bringing truth, love, and reconciliation.

John arrived outside Pastor's office and looked at his watch—only four minutes before the service started. Pastor always said he'd be open to last-minute changes to the service. John knocked and stuck his head in the office. "You have a minute?"

Pastor Ron scowled.

"Just felt I should share the guidance we received last night at the prayer meeting." John waited a few seconds for Pastor Ron to permit him to speak.

"Go ahead, John, spit it out!"

"The Bible says we have been given a ministry of reconciliation, and I believe the devil wants Christians to do just the opposite of that. He wants us to trash talk transgender people to exacerbate tensions and drive them further from the truth and love found in Christ."

Pastor Ron planted both hands on his desk and stood. "Sin is sin, John. God wants us to reconcile sinners to Himself, not capitulate to sinners. Sinners have to repent before they can be reconciled."

"Yes, but the Bible commands us to speak the truth in love."

Pastor pointed to the door. "That's enough. Leave!"

# # #

John sat by himself in the back during the service so he could pray over the congregation as Pastor gave the sermon.

Pastor Ron began the message with Psalm 5:5, "The Lord hates evildoers." Pastor paused and seemed to stare at John. "Yes, I know that's Old Testament, and Christ brought the ministry of grace. Liberal Christians try to shame us for lacking love and tolerance for sinners such as those caught in transgender lies. Is it loving to let sinners continue in their sin, to wallow in their muck and confusion and spend an eternity in Hell?"

John closed his eyes. He debated whether to leave so he'd be freer to intercede. Pastor's sermon seemed headed toward exacerbating fear and contempt in our congregation, exactly what Mary and he had seen demons promoting last night.

When Pastor honed in on the "dangers" the trans activist threatened their children with, his voice swung from high-pitched tremors to grave, ominous warnings. Pastor used his oratory skills to maximum effect.

The devil's schemes appeared to be succeeding, so John hurried to the pastor's office to intercede. Nobody would be there now, and the office offered the perfect sanctuary. Once John entered the office and closed the door, he prayed in Jesus' name and bound the spirits that their spirit-body traveling revealed the previous night. He didn't feel his prayers accomplished much, but he continued to intercede. Persistence often brought success; however, he figured he didn't battle against evil spirits. He battled people who had determined their perception was accurate and nothing would convince them otherwise, not even God.

Twenty minutes after the service ended, John stopped praying. Though he prayed as best as he could, he felt he had wasted his time. He looked at his watch and sighed. Leah probably wondered what happened to him. He stood to leave just as Pastor Ron entered.

Pastor Ron's eyebrows narrowed. "What do you want?" he demanded.

"The Spirit moved me to pray while you preached, and your office seemed like a good place to do it."

"You should have been listening to my message so you would know how to pray."

"The tone of your sermon is what made me intercede."

Pastor Ron's face flushed. "What is that supposed to mean?"

"Did you hear what I said before the service? Your message hardly promoted reconciliation between God and sinner. More likely it fostered fear and animosity in the hearts of church members."

"Is that what your spirit travels taught you last night?" Pastor Ron's growl scarcely concealed his anger.

"A lot of good it did," lamented John.

"On that, then, we can agree. I don't want to hear anything about what you learned from your visions. Understand?"

"Yeah," John replied and said nothing further. He felt like Pastor Ron had changed his mind again about their journeys in their spirit bodies, but he hoped the Holy Spirit would continue to guide the prayer team to wherever He wanted them. He'd avoid telling Pastor what they heard and saw.

John found Leah waiting for him next to their car, chatting with Mary. As soon as John approached, Leah raised her brows for a second. John figured she'd pepper him with questions, none of which he cared to answer.

Leah waited until John started the car to ask him where he went and whether Pastor Ron had found him. Their children sat in the back seat, so John hinted with eyes that he couldn't tell her in front of them. Besides, he felt too frustrated to explain the damage the sermon had likely caused. He had only one piece of good news to tell her— Pastor Ron had not reneged on permitting them to reconnoiter in the spirit. In the future he hoped Pastor would believe in the value of spirit-body travels if not their necessity, but that didn't appear to be likely to happen any time soon. John hoped to submit to their pastor, but ultimately, he had to obey God.

# # #

On Tuesday at 8:00 AM, John met Andy on Aurora Bluff and gave him a long hug. The polyester shell of their coats crackled in the frigid air as they signaled the end of their embrace by simultaneously slapping each other on the back. Without any wind, the outdoors felt invigorating instead of bitter cold like many January mornings. Though sunrise occurred progressively earlier till June, he hoped their later meeting time would become permanent.

Minus a breeze, white puffs of vapor hung above where they exhaled and spoke, making where they stood feel like the best place in the world to talk to God. They thanked God for His sovereignty over their town and nation, and then they walked to the overlook where they interceded for people living in the East End of Bluffview briefly. When nobody prayed for a moment, Andy looked at John, and John pointed with his forehead toward their cars.

They hopped in John's car to continue praying, sheltered from the cold.

"I wanted to talk with you about Sunday's worship service," John said after he turned on the car.

Andy gave him a knowing look. "Rough message from Pastor on Sunday. He kind of flew in the face of what we prayed against."

John fumed. "God placed me in this church, but how can I submit to its pastor when he runs off in the flesh?"

"God will work it out. Let me deal with Pastor Ron."

John squeezed the steering with both hands. "What am I supposed to do if the Holy Spirit takes us in the spirit to learn the enemy's strategies?"

"We intercede in light of where Holy Spirit takes us, but I reckon the real issue lies in knowing how to pray. Just because we discover a problem, we can't jump the gun and pray whatever way we think is best."

John looked at Andy to see what he meant. "We have to hear from the Holy Spirit so we pray according to the will of God."

Andy nudged John's arm. "That means learning to wait with our spiritual ears open, listening for Holy Spirit to tell us how to pray."

"Yeah, of course."

"Do we know what it means to wait? You're an investment advisor. You, of all people, should know the importance of being patient."

"Ha!" John laughed at the irony. How did he—with his impulsive nature—end up working in an Edward Jones office? John closed his eyes. Too much hinged on them interceding with the use of journeys in the spirit. "I want to be in submission to our pastor, but our intercession is vital.

"We have to trust God to deal with Pastor Ron's heart."

Behold, to obey is better than sacrifice
I Samuel 15:22b NKJV

Chapter Thirty-One

When John arrived home from Aurora Bluff, he realized he and Andy never prayed for Rachael. After praying for his daughter himself, John spent much of his free time Tuesday interceding for Pastor Ron and Bluffview Evangelical Free. He waited for the Holy Spirit to send him somewhere to reveal more of the enemy's strategies. By evening, he thought maybe he had been doing something wrong. Nothing happened even though he believed that the Lord wanted to use spirit traveling to show him how to best tear down the enemy's strongholds.

He asked God why the Holy Spirit wouldn't take him anywhere. After listening for a minute, he felt led to read from Job chapter 38, "Who is this who darkens counsel by words without knowledge?"

John lay out face down. "Lord, have mercy on me for being so presumptuous."

Then the Holy Spirit comforted him with words not audible yet quite clear. He erred not because he lacked practical knowledge, but because he failed to listen and learn from the Holy Spirit on how to pray. He should not expect to travel in his spirit alone. In the future, the Spirit would only take John's spirit on a journey if another person agreed to go with him. He needed another person to confirm what he heard and saw. John puzzled over what the Holy Spirit meant. How could he listen better?

Thursday evening, John discovered Rachael refused to see Pastor Ron to ask for his advice or his prayers because she thought him too harsh toward transgender people. Nothing John or Leah could say could get her to change her mind. He even asked David if he would reason with Rachael. He also had no success.

He knew he shouldn't press Rachael too hard on seeing Pastor for prayer. Pastor Ron often came across as harsh. With everything his daughter experienced, she had to feel terrible. If she would not listen to them, all they could do was pray.

On Friday morning after John met with two of his clients, he focused on praying for someone to join him in spirit-body travels. He had to get to the root of what his daughter fought and the problems at church.

At noon, Pastor Ron called him. "John, I need to talk with you. Can you come to the church?" Pastor sounded angry.

When John arrived twenty minutes later, Andy was already there. John figured Pastor Ron must have asked Andy to come in on his lunch break. That couldn't be good.

Andy cast John a worried frown. Pastor Ron appeared to be as agitated as he had been when he and Francine experienced demonic attacks. Pastor Ron glowered behind his desk while Andy and he sat in armchairs facing him.

"Do you have any idea why I called you and Andy to come here?"

In prayer over the past two days, John had received impressions of what might happen, but he knew better than to say anything. Andy likewise said nothing.

"Last night we received an anonymous phone call, screaming curses at us. Two nights before that someone left a message on our car, scratched with a sharp object through the paint. 'Transphobic bigots deserve a painful death.' Then this morning I stepped outside and slipped on the sidewalk. Overnight, someone had poured buckets of water on the concrete, turning the walk into an ice rink.

"Any clue who might have done that or any of the harassment we've received? Francine is almost at the point of hysteria. She had nightmares both last night and the previous night." Pastor Ron leaned forward and exhaled sharply. "Hasn't God revealed that to you as you gad about without your physical body?"

John waited to reply until Pastor Ron had blown off a little more steam.

Andy took a deep breath. "The Spirit revealed plenty that we are supposed to intercede for. We don't tell the Spirit what he must show us. We leave that up to Him."

"Leave. That. Up to. Him," Pastor Ron repeated back in a mocking sing-song tone. "How inconvenient! What about you, John? Why is your feckless intercession causing me more grief than grace?"

John met Pastor Ron's glare with a gaze that he hoped revealed the infinite compassion and grace found in Jesus. Pastor Ron's continued glare told him that anger or fear controlled Pastor's emotions. John shot up a quick, silent prayer for help from the Holy Spirit. He struggled to understand what Pastor's current opinion of their journeys was. "I have been praying without doing any spirit traveling for the last two days. Apparently, that hasn't been very effective."

"What!" Pastor Ron slapped the desktop with the palm of his hand. "Are you telling me now you don't want to travel in your spirit body, so you don't know anything?"

"Would it do any good?"

"You tell *me*, John!"

"How am I supposed to know whether prayer would be more effective if I could travel in the spirit?" John avoided reminding Pastor that he said to not talk about what they learned from journeys in the spirit body.

"Are you crazy? Our troubles all started with your visions."

John extended his hands, facing out toward Pastor Ron. "Whoa! I tried to warn you how the evil spirits planned to use fear and contempt to create problems. When I pointed out that we've been given a ministry of reconciliation, you got mad."

"Don't quote Scripture at me. The devil quoted Scripture at Jesus in the wilderness. I don't imagine Jesus liked it any better than I do."

"Are you saying I'm imitating the devil?" John struggled to not get mad at Pastor Ron's accusation. "Perhaps you want me to leave the church if I'm in league with Satan."

"Calm down, John. I'm just saying your visions seem to be more like a tool of the devil than an instrument of God."

John glanced at Andy. His eyes appeared to be examining the floor, and John realized Andy would offer him little or no support for continuing their spirit travels. John took a deep breath. "Useful tools need to be grasped by the possessor of the tool and handled appropriately. Jesus said that to whom much is given, much is required."

Pastor leaned back in his chair. "Are you trying to tell me you just need to learn how to use your spirit voyages properly?"

"No!" John stated a bit louder than he intended, so he paused to dial down his ire. "I'm not the one who is using the tool improperly. You are."

Pastor Ron sprang forward on his chair. "You blame me? Now I have heard everything."

"I am sorry I came to you at the last minute, but I did give you what we learned from our spirit-body journey on Sunday before the church service. The Spirit warned you, and you ignored Him."

"We're not going over this again," Pastor Ron barked. "You are to stay away from spirit voyages."

John leaned back in his chair, grappling with Pastor's changing opinion on their intercession. "Do you want us to pray against the demons who are harassing you?"

"People are attacking me. Not demons. Deceived, gender-confused people who heard my message on Sunday and couldn't stand to hear the truth."

"No demonic activity there," John mumbled to himself.

"What did you say?" Pastor Ron demanded.

Andy glanced at John and shifted forward in his chair. "Of course, people attacked you, but they might be listening to demons. We will pray against the forces that deceive God's people, and we won't travel in the Spirit to do it."

"Good! Pray that next Sunday's sermon clears everyone's mind of the deceptive evil that transgender beliefs promote." Pastor squinted at John. "No more going somewhere without your physical bodies. Is that understood?"

Andy looked at John. "We understand."

John looked up at the ceiling and exhaled sharply. "Yes." He wanted to add that Pastor Ron had the slippery sidewalk and the hysterical wife, but he had a daughter who imagined she was a boy. Pastor wasn't the only one under attack. If they wanted to defeat the devil, they needed to listen to the Holy Spirit, but John didn't say anything more.

#   #   #

John stood next to his car as he talked with Andy after leaving Pastor's office. Because of the pastor's prohibition, the battle against the problems facing Pastor Ron had become a Hindenburg ready to burst into flames. Andy made his position clear. The prayer team should not participate in future out-of-body experiences. Andy planned to call everybody on the team and ask them to follow Pastor's directive on the matter.

John didn't feel Andy or Pastor Ron could tell God what to do. That seemed arrogant. If the Holy Spirit took one of them out of their body, why should they stop it? However, none of the intercessors would go against Pastor's wishes, and he would obey his pastor as well. Besides, even if John desired to go, he had nobody to accompany him.

John drove home contemplating his alternatives. He had one appointment late in the afternoon at his downtown office, so he had lunch with Leah and discussed his longing to travel in his spirit body. John asked her whether she would travel in her spirit body with him if Pastor changed his mind. Leah encouraged him to follow their pastor's directive and made plain her desire to distance herself from out-of-body experiences. Praying at Edward Jones before his appointment, he begged the Holy Spirit again for permission to travel alone, and he received a resounding, "No."

After his appointment John received a text message from Andy, informing him that the prayer team would meet on Thursday evenings from now on. Pastor Ron changed the day to earlier in the week so he would have time to react to what they prayed. John texted Andy back: "Does Pastor feel our prayers would have a positive impact?"

Andy didn't respond to John's text message.

For those who live according to the flesh set their minds on the things of the flesh, but those who live according to the Spirit, the things of the Spirit.
                                                         Romans 8:5 NKJV

Chapter Thirty-Two

John arrived for the prayer meeting Thursday evening ready to intercede for the church and the nation according to Pastor's instructions. Moving the prayer meeting to Thursdays frustrated John. If Pastor had moved the day two weeks earlier, John might have been able to convince Pastor Ron to change the tone of his sermon. Pastor Ron likely changed the day now to keep tabs on them, and on John in particular.

At the start of the prayer meeting, Andy reviewed the latest attacks that Pastor Ron had experienced for those who hadn't heard about them. When he finished his explanations and responses to their questions, he led them in prayer for protection and guidance for Pastor and his wife. Several others added their prayers to what Andy prayed. John remained silent.

When they finished praying for the pastor, John received an impression from the Holy Spirit that they should pray for their country and the war in Ukraine. John shared his impression with Andy, and Andy asked Mary to lead out in praying for Ukraine. John sensed Andy didn't trust him to avoid spirit traveling, but that didn't bother him. He planned to pray just what seemed reasonable.

Mary prayed for several minutes. Then several others prayed. After about five minutes of silence, Mary moaned and crumpled on the floor. John's eyes widened.

Andy glared at John, and John jiggled his head in denial. How could he be responsible for what someone else did?

Andy knelt next to Mary and tried to get her up.

John prayed silently. "Lord, what are You doing here? I don't want to get into trouble. Show me how to pray for the people of Ukraine. Hundreds of thousands of people have died, been wounded, and lost their homes. Comfort those who are grieving. Bring peace to the country."

John felt a deep pulling in his inner being. Then he tumbled onto the floor and blacked out. A moment later, he floated in the air and looked down on his body. Mary's body lay on the floor, but her spirit had already traveled somewhere.

Andy rushed over to John's body and shook it. "No you don't. You can't leave your body here."

Leah stood and walked next to Andy. "What are you going to do?"

Andy pulled out his cell phone. "I'm going to call Pastor Ron. Let him handle this."

Leah put her hand on his phone. "Why? What good will it do? Pastor can't put their spirits back in their bodies."

"At least, he won't blame me."

"Think of the whole team." Leah paused and looked at the others. "If Pastor closes down the prayer team, you will hinder the team from doing their job."

Andy glanced at the others.

"Bluffview Evangelical Free and our nation will suffer as a result," Leah added. "We should pray as we wait for Mary and John to return, and when they return, we ask the Lord what to do next."

"That's a decision for Pastor to make, not me." Andy pressed the icon for Pastor's cell phone.

"Thank you for trying, Sweetheart," John shouted. She couldn't hear him, so he'd be sure to give her a thank-you hug when he returned. John figured the Spirit kept him lingering here a little longer to witness Leah's support. "Okay, Holy Spirit, please take me to where Mary is."

An instant later John hovered in a dark cavern next to Mary.

"Thank heavens you're here," Mary said. "These demons are reminiscing about past skullduggeries they implemented. You can help me remember any details that they brag about."

A demon with a nose like a turkey boasted: *The whole groundwork for the Ukrainian war began with me. I convinced President H.W. Bush in 1992 to promise Yeltsin that the US wouldn't push for NATO membership in countries adjacent to Russia. Many times I convinced leaders and diplomats to assure Russia that NATO wouldn't expand toward her. Five times I aggravated Russia by maneuvering NATO to expand toward her. Then, the crowning splendor of my wickedness came when I convinced the US President to ignore his advisors and suggest NATO membership to Ukraine.*

A gaunt demon snorted, and his coal-like eyes glowed an ominous red. *I'm the one who made it all happen at this time in history, a time when a nuclear holocaust could sweep the remainder of humanity into the fires of hell. Ha! I maneuvered corrupt Ukrainians into power to accept bribes. Men who didn't care about the loss of lives or destruction of businesses and homes. In Turkey in April of 2022, I persuaded leaders of the United Kingdom to sabotage peace between Russia and Ukraine. Ho! But the master is pleased with me.*

A grotesquely obese demon waved them off like pesky flies. *Big deal. That's evil, but without me the US never would have entered the fray. My maneuvers allowed mainline media to squelch the truth that Putin had no intention to invade NATO countries. I hid the corruption in Ukraine and made their leaders appear noble, innocent, and deserving of protection. Oh, but my most wicked suppression of the truth has been the complete omission of the fact that if America neuters Russia, their nuclear arsenal will be available to every terrorist group in the world. With America's track record in Afghanistan, Iraq, and Libya, terrorists and malcontents will have as many weapons of mass destruction as their hearts desire.*

Nuclear radiation will end the current civilization and bring in new dark ages! Oh. . . how deliciously wicked will that be!

A hooded demon whined, *I don't get it! None of what any of you did would have amounted to anything without my dirty deeds smothering news about Zelensky canceling elections, closing churches, and siphoning off billions of dollars meant for aid. Master compliments Corruption and doesn't say one word to me.*

Okay, Half-Truths, the master has good reason for not giving you a thumbs up. Plenty of independent media outlets have leaked the truth. What about the Twitter fiasco? RFK Jr. still has a shot at blowing your work to smithereens.

Oh, I've done a number on Kennedy. Most of America doesn't even know he is running for President. Even those who do aren't aware of his strategy for dismantling Big Pharma's control over the healthcare industry or his plan to sever the military industrial complex's connection to the CIA and US foreign policy. Ha! I have so flooded the news with half-truths that most Americans have given up on the two major party candidates, and many have stopped following the election entirely.

John leaned in closer. He wanted to hear what the demons planned for Kennedy. He feared Biden had refused to give Kennedy Secret Service protection because the CIA would out him. Before he could hear anything else, the Spirit zipped him and Mary to an office lunchroom where two aides chatted in hushed tones.

"Julie, this is a crazy world we live in. That's all I can say."

"Yeah, I became a Democrat because I hated war. My father died in Iraq, a senseless war that Bush dumped on the

American people. Republicans used to be the party of the Hawks. Now both parties are. The only ones for pulling out of Ukraine are the ultra-conservative Republicans."

"There's a reason for that."

"Okay, Linus, lay your astute insight on me."

"Money. Follow the money. You've seen the military-industrial lobbyists hang around Senator Swain's office.

"I've seen them around Senator Bradly's that's for sure. But that doesn't explain why members of both houses of Congress on both sides of the aisle embrace defending a Ukrainian border and neglect our own border."

"Bill Peterson surprised me when he supported expanding the national debt with the Stop Gap Funding so he could send more weapons there."

"Oh, I get that. Republicans are all about wars, but neither the Democrats nor the Republicans mention that Social Security is due to run out of money in about six years."

John looked at Mary. "That fries me. The politicians vote for war so they can stay in power. Lobbyists help fund their reelections, and during a war, people hate to change leadership in the midstream."

"I wonder which Representative or Senator those two work for?" Mary asked.

"Does it make any difference? I sounds like whether they're Republican or Democrat they are all about seeking power for themselves so they remain in office."

"If you label them all as power grabbers, you will only incite hatred or fear instead of solving the problem," Mary said. "Many from both sides of the aisle enter politics because they seek to help our nation."

Her comment bothered him. The last thing he wanted to do would be to stir up fear or contempt. That would only aggravate the current polarization and short-circuit his prayer. But certain measures needed to be addressed. "Uh, you heard them mention Bradly's name."

Before John could express his thoughts, everything went dark, and he felt the floor on his hip. When he opened his eyes, Mary sat a few feet away, rubbing her neck. Both his hip and his rib felt okay, a marked improvement over previous journeys. John looked around at the rest of the prayer team.

"You returned quickly," Carl said after he helped John stand. "Did your travels seem short to you as well?"

"Quick, but informative."

Andy handed Mary the cell phone that fell out of her pocket as she rose from the floor. When Mary turned and held out her hand to receive her phone, Andy said to her, "I thought we agreed to cease traveling in our spirit bodies."

"I didn't ask God to take me on a journey in the spirit. I just asked God to show me how to pray."

Andy scowled at her. "You could have told the Holy Spirit that you didn't want to go."

Andy turned to John. "I don't suppose you thought to tell the Holy Spirit that He shouldn't take you anywhere because you wanted to be *submissive* to your pastor." Andy's disgust was evident by the ominous way he emphasized the word *submissive*.

John shook his head. Though he'd been out traveling for only a short period, his mind struggled to get oriented. "What am I supposed to do? If the Holy Spirit wants to take me somewhere, tell Him, 'Don't do that?'"

"I've heard the Holy Spirit is a Gentleman, and He won't force you to do anything or go anywhere against your will."

"Where does it say that in Scripture?" John snapped back. "If the Holy Spirit badgers my conscience like a nagging housewife, my love for God will cause me to submit to Him instead of to man."

"Tell that to Pastor Ron!" Andy said.

"You be the judge of whether I should obey you rather than God!"

"I won't have to judge. I called Pastor while you were out of your bodies. He will be here any minute, and you can lay your case before him." Andy turned and stepped toward his chair.

John grabbed his shoulder to turn him around "You can tell him I didn't do anything to try to make this happen. Mary went down, or up, before I did."

Andy stuck his right palm ten inches from John's face. "Save your breath for Pastor. I'm not coming to your defense." Andy shook his head. "The Holy Spirit is a nagging housewife, huh? Good luck with Pastor on that one."

John turned to Mary and pleaded with his eyes for her to defend what happened.

Mary said, "Andy you saw what took place here, but our spirits went to—"

"Save it!" Andy snapped. "I heard Pastor Ron's pickup truck enter the parking lot. He'll be in here shortly."

Pastor Ron entered the prayer room two minutes later. Nobody said anything for several seconds. Pastor Ron glared at John. "What's this I hear about you leaving your body again?"

"We didn't intend to journey in our spirits," Mary said.

Pastor Ron glanced at Mary, then stared at John. "On top of rebelling against my explicit instructions, you persuaded Mary to join you."

"The Holy Spirit didn't take us to report on the transgender agenda," John said hoping to appease his ire.

"Oh?"

John hesitated to say anything.

"Is that supposed to make your journey acceptable?"

"Not in your eyes, I guess." Feeling vulnerable, John held his hands out sideways, hoping to catch raindrops of mercy. "But God didn't send us where you didn't want us to go."

"I didn't want you traveling. Anywhere. Period."

"You don't even want to know where the Holy Spirit sent us?"

"No!"

John backed off and grabbed his Bible to leave. Pastor was furious, and he had no hope of reasoning with him in that state. John looked at Leah and pointed with his nose at the door. Leah stood and walked toward him.

Pastor's nostrils flared, and his face turned red. "John, I think it best you find another church to attend."

"Don't worry," John said, "Leah and I will not pollute your flock any longer."

Nobody said anything as John and Leah walked to the door. The room sizzled with tension. When John opened the door, he turned and spoke to Pastor Ron. "You realize that the Holy Spirit didn't show us things the enemy planned with the trans movement because you wouldn't heed the warnings He gave you. Now you won't hear God as He tries to warn us about disaster in Ukraine."

"Leave!" Pastor Ron growled with a low, menacing tone of voice. "And don't come back!"

> *We the people are the rightful masters of both Congress and the courts, not to overthrow the Constitution but to overthrow the men who pervert the Constitution.*
> Abraham Lincoln

Chapter Thirty-Three

John argued with Leah as they drove home from the disastrous prayer meeting. He knew he shouldn't discuss what happened while their emotions skewed their ability to reason objectively. Pastor Ron didn't make him mad. He forgave his pastor. His frustration sprang from his inability to intercede with the rest of the intercessors over the visions he had just received.

Leah refused to join him in prayer over the Ukrainian war. She sputtered furiously over leaving the church because she was sure none of her friends would speak to her now. His antics caused Pastor to throw them out of the church. No amount of reasoning on his part could convince her otherwise. When he suggested they pray together, she refused and acted like he shouldn't ask God to bring reconciliation. He wanted to stay in Bluffview Evangelic Free as much as she did. He would miss his church friends as much as she did hers. After they returned home, John received the silent treatment.

In the morning her attitude hadn't changed. He figured, though, in a couple of days, she'd be willing to pray with him. If Mary or Francine called to maintain their friendship, the likelihood of her now praying with him would increase tenfold. After breakfast John went to their office to take part in a webinar. When the webinar ended, he kneeled by the guest bed and prayed for Pastor Ron and Leah. He had prayed only a few minutes when Mary phoned to talk with Leah. John considered her call an answer to prayer. The call had to bless Leah's heart and should have relieved Leah's angst about losing all her friends.

Though he planned to pray for Leah, Pastor Ron, and the church, he sensed the Lord wanted him to pray against the demonic activity in the Ukrainian War. He asked the Lord to take him in the spirit so he could learn how to focus his prayers better. The Holy Spirit reminded him He already had received insight into the demonic activity there. More importantly, he had to understand more about intercession before he journeyed in his spirit alone.

John asked the Lord what he needed to learn, but what he heard from the Holy Spirit was restrictions, which made little sense to him. God wanted him to wait and be still. People were dying in Ukraine and Russia. Love demanded he do something. When John begged the Holy Spirit to speak to him about Ukraine, he didn't receive any guidance, so he prayed for Rachael. After all, she was closest to his heart. Then it dawned on him. The needs of his neighbors, his former church, and his country had to come after his daughter. That had to explain why God hadn't spoken further on the other issues.

For about twenty minutes, John interceded for Rachael. He prayed in Jesus' name that the spirits of deception, confusion, and rebellion would be bound over his daughter. Though he didn't know what other evil spirits had lied to Rachael, he named every kind of wickedness he could think of. Then he prayed for Rachael's friends and teachers. He asked God to send mature Christians across her path who would speak the truth to her.

John paused and was searching for what to pray next when Leah entered their office.

"Mary wants you to call her when you're done praying." Leah didn't smile, but she seemed mollified.

John grinned. Mary's call seemed like an answer of sorts. "Thanks, Sweetheart."

He continued to intercede for Rachael, and several issues came to his attention that he thought should be addressed. When he started to pray about those things, he sensed the Holy Spirit say God would take care of Rachael, so he called Mary.

"I am so glad you are willing to talk with me," John said after Mary answered the phone.

"I want you to know that am willing to talk with you but not to pray," Mary stated emphatically. "Pastor forbids voyages in our spirits, and I plan to submit to his leadership and to Doug on this."

"Okay, will you pray separately over what we saw?"

"Not if it means leaving my body."

John believed the Spirit wouldn't be taking her anywhere separate from her body. He wouldn't be taken anywhere either. He'd have to settle for praying over what they already knew to pray for, and he would have to take that information and wait on the Holy Spirit to show him how best to intercede. After Mary disconnected from their conversation, John returned to interceding over the War.

John's ire rose as he recalled Congressman Hartwood accepting money from lobbyists and bending to their wishes to vote for billions of dollars more on weapons for Ukraine. He grew even madder when he considered the lies of omission that Jack Wilson leveraged through his control of the press. John paced as he interceded for the hearts of Wilson and Congressman Hartwood.

After pleading with God to stop them from completing their schemes, he remembered how the President refused to follow the custom of ordering Secret Service protection for RFK Jr. Before John could pray, he had to stifle the anger that rose in him against the injustice of not giving Kennedy protection.

They had assassinated two Kennedys. Wasn't that enough? People had questioned whether the CIA had been involved in JFK's assassination, but John felt certain. Corruption in the CIA had undoubtedly become worse since the early 1960s. John fought to keep his hands and forearms from shaking as he considered the CIA guilty of most of the schemes they'd been accused of in Central America and Africa. John believed they'd love to take out RFK Jr. too. He interceded passionately for RFK Jr. and bound and rebuked the devil and the people the devil had influenced.

By bedtime, his outrage at the injustices and corruption he saw remained undiminished. He interceded for several minutes without any sense he had obtained the results he desired, but he felt too agitated to continue praying. His thoughts raced, keeping him awake. Around 1:00 AM he crawled into bed exhausted. He lifted the situation up to the Lord again, but he didn't feel his prayers accomplished much.

In the morning John read his Bible as usual, but he struggled to intercede. The Holy Spirit didn't show him how to pray. Because his hatred of what corrupt people did had aroused his flesh, he fought a losing battle against his emotions and failed to pray in the Spirit. The media protected politicians who received improper favors from lobbyists, and thousands died or suffered needlessly. He begged the

Spirit to help him pray. He didn't ask for spirit journeys, just inspiration to intercede. John received nothing from the Spirit, so he opened his Bible. When he thought he heard the Spirit say Psalm 37, he looked there excitedly. God had finally spoken. He had forgotten what that Psalm said and the first few verses stunned him:

> Do not fret because of evildoers,
> Nor be envious of the workers of iniquity.
> For they shall soon be cut down like the grass,
> And wither as the green herb.
> Trust in the Lord, and do good;
> Dwell in the land, and feed on His faithfulness.
> Delight yourself also in the Lord,
> And He shall give you the desires of your heart.[9]

John didn't think that God wanted him to apply those verses to the situation the Spirit revealed on Thursday night, so he read on:

> Rest in the Lord, and wait patiently for Him;
> Do not fret because of him who prospers in his way,
> Because of the man who brings wicked schemes to pass.
> Cease from anger, and forsake wrath;
> Do not fret—*it* only *causes* harm.[10]

This had to be the devil's attempt to prevent him from praying. If Satan used Scripture against Jesus in the wilderness, the evil one could have done the same thing here, couldn't he? John slammed his Bible shut. He hated the thought of misapplying Scriptures."

John went to bed mad, and in the morning he woke up mad and drove to the Edward Jones office mad. His temper threatened to ruin his ability to deal with clients. He was mad at the devil, mad at corrupt politicians, mad at Pastor Ron for squelching the Holy Spirit, and mad at Pastor Ron for kicking him off the prayer team. John paced back and forth in their office and sought God for a breakthrough in prayer.

When he stopped pacing, his conscience told him he could be angry, but he shouldn't have let the sun go down on his anger. He recalled Bible verses that said he should have no anxiety about anything, but he should give thanks in all things. Those exhortations

---

[9] Psalm 37:1-4 NKJV

[10] Ps 37:7-8 NKJV

jolted him. He realized he had let fleshly emotions control his mind. "Help me, Lord!"

Just as he said that, his cell phone rang. Mary called. This had to be another quick answer to prayer.

Mary sounded worried. "Are you okay?"

"I am now. What are your thoughts about what happened Thursday night?"

"I prayed for an hour as the Spirit guided me to intercede for US Senators and Representatives."

"An hour?" John tried to restrain his frustration because he hadn't been able to pray longer than ten minutes before his emotions took him elsewhere. "Congressman Hartwood and Senator Blackstone need to repent or better yet, be exposed and expelled. They maneuvered their chambers to spend billions of dollars that will cause the loss of countless lives."

"We don't know if those two did that."

John pulled the phone away from his ear and stared at it in disbelief. Had she actually said that? "Mary, you heard their aides talking as well as I did."

"We don't know whose aides they were or whether those Congressmen accepted any bribes."

"Those demons may have been bragging, but much of what they said had a ring of truth in it. Those men undoubtedly know the truth. They have access to records even if we don't."

"You're jumping to conclusions."

"Yeah, I add two plus two and conclude it equals four. Or in this case, it equals foul. "Didn't it bother you that the President failed to offer Secret Service protection to Kennedy? Without their protection, he's a sitting duck to be killed by any passing psycho that the CIA chooses to hire. We heard them brag about getting the CIA involved in plots in Ukraine, as well as in Central America and Africa."

"We don't know if that is true."

John seethed as he strained to control himself. Mary heard and saw the same things he did. How could she remain so nonchalant? "If you *really* don't know, ask God to show you."

"I'll talk to you tomorrow," Mary said and promptly hung up before he could answer.

John's phone stayed connected for a second or two longer than usual as he considered how to respond to her. The thought came to him that maybe the CIA or FBI had hacked into his or Mary's phone, but he shrugged it off. Why would they bother with him? Nobody on the prayer team would have blabbed out the conversations he and Mary had heard. Besides, conspiracy theorists abounded all across the nation, possibly for good reason, but the government hardly had time to chase even a tenth of them down.

John put his phone on his desk and paced back and forth in the office. "Lord, help me. There is nobody I can turn to, and my emotions are short-circuiting my ability to intercede."

Right after he prayed, a thought whispered to him. "Don't worry. I am with you. But beware of people listening into your phone conversations."

John stopped pacing. Did he hear that right? Was that God warning him or was the devil trying to scare him? John waited to hear more, but when he heard nothing else, he reckoned his imagination must have been playing tricks on him. For the next two hours, John alternated between checking his computer, yelling at the devil, and reading the Bible. At dinner, John told Leah about his phone conversation with Mary. Leah still refused to pray with him.

Socialism will triumph by first capturing the culture via infiltration of schools, universities, churches, and the media by transforming the consciousness of society.

Antonio Gramsci
Founding member of the Communist Party of Italy

Chapter Thirty-Four

John decided he could stick closer to Scripture if he didn't fret over evil schemes or let the sun go down on his anger. He recited the appropriate Bible verses repeatedly to himself and gave God thanks before he went to bed.

When he picked up the morning paper from the steps to his front porch, he noticed a thick layer of frost on his windshield. He recently installed a remote starter to warm the car on mornings with subzero temperatures. He didn't feel like scraping the windshield, so he headed inside and flicked on the remote starter to remove the frost while he read the front page. Perhaps remote starting wasn't necessary, but he bought the remote for his convenience.

A moment later, he heard a loud whoosh. He checked outside. Flames engulfed the hood of his car.

John dashed to the kitchen and grabbed a fire extinguisher. He yelled to Leah, "Call the fire department!"

He ran outside and sprayed the top of the hood. Flames continued to pour from the front end of the car. He pushed unlock on his key and pulled on the door handle.

The door wouldn't budge.

He pushed unlock again. He pulled the handle with all of his might. Nothing!

"John," Leah screamed. "Get away from the car! It could explode any minute!"

John saw flames licking their way toward the gas tank and hurried back to the house. When he reached Leah, the entire car exploded into flames. He looked in disbelief.

They both stood there staring, dumbfounded at the demise of their car. When they heard sirens from the approaching fire trucks, John said, "I guess they're too late to save our car."

Leah turned and pounded his chest with her fist. "What were you doing, putting yourself in danger like that?"

"I wanted to open the hood so I could use the extinguisher on the engine."

"Didn't you stop to think how dangerous that was?"

John exhaled sharply. If he hadn't used the remote starter, he would have been in the car, and he would have been able to open the hood to use the fire extinguisher on the flames. He seethed at the damage to his car. His inability to open the door bothered him. Then another thought struck him—what would have happened if he'd been stuck behind the driver's wheel when the car burst into flames? Would he have been able to open the door?

After the fire department extinguished the last flames, John explained to them what had happened. They didn't know why a new car like his would suddenly burst into flames. Their chief recommended John report it to the manufacturer for any recalls that might be needed.

Later, as he read the newspaper, he remembered the feeling that someone might have hacked into his phone and been eavesdropping on his conversation with Mary. He thought about the people manipulated by the devil, possibly those in the CIA, who would want to harm him. John shuddered and rejected the idea.

Mary called in the afternoon. "Wow, I heard about your scare with the car."

"I reacted pretty foolishly. Would have ended up in the hospital if Leah hadn't yelled at me to back away."

"What caused it?"

"Can't say," John replied. He considered telling her his thoughts about the CIA but decided against spreading foolish conspiracy theories.

"After you challenged me yesterday about the CIA, I Googled information about the CIA's clandestine involvement in various foreign plots," Mary said. "Most articles labeled reports of CIA subversion as conspiracy theories. Coupled with what we heard those demons brag about, I am thinking you might be at least partially right about the CIA."

"Does that mean you are coming around to my way of thinking?"

"Maybe. Here's the scary part, John. I had the uncanny feeling that someone listened to our conversation yesterday."

"I did too. Hang up and drive over here so we can talk in person."

"I'll have to wait until Doug comes home at 5:00. He has the car."

"Okay, see you at 5:30?" John had no other choice but to wait. His car was toast, and Leah needed her car for errands. Besides, even if he decided to ride his bicycle to Mary's, talking with her would be difficult because of the constant interruptions from her toddlers. He just hoped Doug stayed home to watch the kids when Mary came over.

# # #

Mary's car pulled into John's driveway at 5:45 PM. John watched as her entire family, including Doug, piled out of the car and walked or toddled to the front door. He hoped Doug planned to give him a stern lecture against spirit voyages and then leave with the children.

Doug didn't give him a lecture, but instead, he stayed. While Mary and Leah tended to the children, Doug asked John about his car and his worries about possible sabotage. The real reason Doug came was to make sure John didn't persuade Mary to travel in the spirit. He assured Doug that he wouldn't do that. Nevertheless, Doug insisted that he stay to monitor the situation. Mary could talk with him, but he wouldn't allow any praying.

Once Mary occupied her oldest child with his toys, she sat down with her youngest on her lap. John described some research he did on the Internet—the assassinations that the CIA perpetrated, the coverup by members of Congress, the potential for abuse the Patriot Act offered in allowing the FBI to monitor private citizens, government invasions of homes of individuals who opposed government policies,

CIA manipulating elections through smearing a Presidential candidate, and the censorship of social media.

John didn't think Mary agreed with all that he said, but Doug did. Doug knew about some things the CIA did and expressed concern for Mary's safety if she spent time over at John and Leah's. Doug hated how government policies stole basic freedoms and destroyed the traditional family, so he relented and came along with her. When they prepared to return home, Doug promised to pray for the nation at home with Mary. John and Leah agreed to pray too.

Mary and Leah planned to write to their US Senators and Representative. John and Doug figured they should write letters to the editor. The four promised to search for political candidates with integrity who would uphold family values, safeguard freedoms of religion and speech, and prevent CIA abuses and wars instigated by corrupt men in league with the military industrial complex.

After Mary and Doug left, John looked on his computer for suitable candidates to support. Later in the week, John talked with Doug and Mary about candidates for the school board and city hall. Their oldest child, Chad, was in first grade, and Mary felt her son's teacher had been promoting gender confusion that didn't align with their faith. Because of her concern, she planned to attend the next school board meeting to seek a remedy for the issue. Doug said that he would go to support her. John said that he'd join them so he could give the school board a piece of his mind, too.

# # #

After the school board had concluded old business, they opened the meeting to any new business. Mary had submitted a request to the board to discuss the topic of gender education. When they appeared ready to move on without bringing up gender education, Mary stood next to the microphone and asked to be heard.

"I sent a request in two weeks ago for the board to address the curriculum that is being taught to first-grade students," Mary said.

"I am sorry, but we choose course materials for fall in June," the school superintendent said. "We'll discuss the materials then."

"The current curriculum is jamming gender confusion into my son's mind *now*! And I want it stopped now."

"Sit down!" a man yelled. "We don't need some transphobic mom telling us how to educate children."

A woman behind Mary said, "Let her speak!"

"I don't like having my daughter share toilets with trans girls," the man beside her said.

"Can't we show some compassion for the trans students?" a woman said.

John jumped up and stood next to Mary, and Mary put her mouth almost touching the microphone. "Excuse me, my friend John Greenberg would like to say something." Then she pushed the mike toward him.

"Thank you, Mary. For me, the issue isn't just about the curriculum because the trans agenda extends beyond the classroom. My daughter received advice from the school counselor who encouraged her to transition to a different gender. On top of that, she made appointments for my child with a psychologist and a doctor to start hormone treatments.

"Transgenderism is a belief system, which makes it a religion, and propagating religion in our public schools violates our Constitutional rights. I am a Christian, and I am not allowed to promote my religion in public schools. The transgender activist shouldn't be able to spread their religion either."

"Sit down, you transphobic bigot!"

"You Christians are all a bunch of intolerant morons!"

"Christians have rights, too!" a man behind John yelled.

A man six feet from the mike shouted obscenities at John and Mary. Doug pulled Mary away from the man. People from both sides of the argument shouted at each other. John could feel his neck and ears warm as blood rushed to his face. Instead of presenting their reasons logically, everybody simply vented their prejudices at whomever they deemed pigheaded and wrong.

The convener of the meeting shouted for everyone to be quiet.

A man to John's right pushed Doug. John jumped to Doug's defense. Another man shoved John. Someone else tried to protect John, and soon, fighting broke out all over the auditorium.

"The meeting is adjourned," the convener announced.

The police arrived right as the fighting subsided. John calmly left without being apprehended or dragged from the meeting. John saw nothing positive about what happened. Those who disagreed with him reacted more vehemently than he had imagined. He wanted to discuss things openly and honestly, but no one would listen to him. Nobody could hear anybody. In the middle school and high school, Rachael and David faced an even heavier indoctrination from the transgender agenda than Mary's children did. Their beliefs hit his adolescent children at a very vulnerable stage of their development.

      John thought back to when he went through puberty. What a horrible time he had trying to figure out if he had what it took to be a man. He thanked God he hadn't had someone there to add to his confusion. He boiled inside at the people who added to the confusing mess his children had to wrestle with.

      Mary and Doug left at the same time as John. Later, they discussed what happened with both John and Leah. Mary explained that she understood why people there shouted her down, calling her transphobic. While that frustrated her, she saw through their accusations. Her accusers resorted to name calling to avoid debating the issue. They used character assassination and intimidation to force their belief system on everyone else.

      John shrugged off the unfair treatment he had received at the meeting, but he struggled to muzzle his anger over the injustice done to the families of all those who had similar beliefs. Several days later, John realized his biggest mistake consisted of not praying earnestly over the school board meeting. He had heard of the FBI raiding the homes of people who protested at school board meetings in Virginia. He knew most of the people at the school board meeting. None of them would ask for FBI agents to harass him.

Occupants of public offices love power and are prone to abuse it.
George Washington

Chapter Thirty-Five

On the following Tuesday, John stayed up late researching on his computer while he waited for Leah to come home. This was Leah's night out with the girls; however, she usually came home by 10:00 PM. An hour later, when she hadn't arrived, John called her cell phone. Leah apologized for being late, but Mary and Eileen had gotten into arguments with her and Francine over journeys in the spirit body.

"Tears have been shed, Scriptures examined, apologies made, and differences between conflicting beliefs resolved. I'll be coming home soon," Leah promised.

John wondered what conclusions they came to. Leah's report would have to wait until tomorrow morning. He planned to be fast asleep before she came home. John had heard sniffling in the background when Leah answered the phone. He reckoned Leah wouldn't get home for another hour.

John fell asleep shortly after he crawled into bed. The next thing he became aware of was shouting in the hallway outside his bedroom.

FBI! . . .FBI!" tense voices yelled.

John sprang out of bed.

A sharp bang on his bedroom door. The door slammed open against the wall.

A blinding light flashed in his eyes. "Freeze! Hands on your head!"

"Now!"

John staggered back and put his hands up to shield his eyes from the light.

"Hands on top of your head! Now!" screamed an urgent voice. Trembling, John put his hands on his head.

"On your knees!"

John's heart raced. He used the side of his bed against his thigh and then his hip and ribs to lower himself to his knees.

A second man in SWAT gear entered the bedroom.

"Hands behind your back!" he yelled.

John placed his hands on his backside, and the side of his head fell against the bed. Hard metal clamped both wrists together.

A third man searched through his closet and the drawers of their dresser.

Another man in SWAT gear entered the bedroom. "The first floor and basement are cleared. Two teenagers are cuffed and being placed in the custody of the social worker out front."

"On your feet!"

John stumbled, and the second man grabbed John's shoulder and kept him from falling. Then he pushed John out the door and into the hall. He staggered down the hallway to the living room.

"This way!" a man yelled.

When he came to the living room, a man shoved him onto the sofa. "Where is your wife?" he yelled.

"Why are you shouting at me? Why are you here?" John asked, beginning to feel indignant about being treated like a drug dealer.

A woman searched through the bookshelves and entertainment center.

The man didn't answer John. A minute later, another man shouted, "The whole house is clear."

"You have the wrong place," John said. "Do you have a search warrant for my property? I demand to know—"

"Stand and shut up!" the first man yelled.

A second man unlocked his handcuffs and tossed his trousers and jacket at him. "Put these on."

As soon as he finished pulling his coat and pants over his pajamas, they cuffed him again and shoved him toward the front door. A man in SWAT gear held the door open.

John stumbled again and landed partially on his side with his face hitting the door jamb. "Ow!"

"On your feet!" a man yelled.

John staggered outside. Several SWAT cars were parked in the street. A van was parked in the driveway with men and women in SWAT gear, manning spotlights and talking on phones. A man held a rear side door open. Neighbors peeked out windows or stood on lawns across the street.

When John stopped by the open van door, he saw his next-door neighbors Janet and Willy gawking at him from the side of their front porch. Next to them with horror etched on her face stood Leah.

He received a shove that propelled him face-first into the seat. With his hands cuffed behind him, John struggled to sit up to communicate some kind of reassurance to his wife. By the time he positioned his face next to the back window, Leah was out of view.

"Sit back!" commanded a man sitting next to him.

"Sit back? What do you mean, sit back?" A surge of rage shot through John. "You have no right to bark at me. You idiot! I'm not some kind of drug dealer!"

Crack! A riot baton smacked John on the side of his head. "Shut up! You're John Greenberg, aren't ya?"

John scrunched down and placed his head next to the van's side door with his back to his assailant.

The man swung again at John and hit his back.

"You broke up the school board meeting last week, right?" He took another swing at John and clipped the back of John's head and sputtered, "You're no better than those J6, fascist insurrectionists."

"You are going to hear from my lawyers. If you don't have your body cams on, you are all going to be in big trouble—"

"Guess again, buddy. FBI don't need body cams." He swung at John's head.

John ducked as he swung. "That's crazy!" John pushed his rear end against the man to put more distance between the man's nightstick and his head.

"I'll show you crazy." The man grabbed John's shoulders and slammed him up against the door. When the man grasped his club, John ducked and twisted his body to protect his head.

The man grabbed John's shoulders again and pulled upward.

John gasped for breath. "That doesn't give you a right to beat me. We were at the school board meeting exercising our rights as citizens with freedom of speech."

"When we are done with you, you and your kind will think twice about exercising freedom of speech."

"Hey! That's enough," a man in the front passenger seat said. "We can *communicate* with him better when we've got him in a place where people can't see us."

John didn't like the way he emphasized the word *communicate*. He shuddered as he thought of what they might have in mind. He hoped Leah called an experienced lawyer who would get out of bed and arrive before they beat him senseless. Another thought struck him. How would a lawyer know where they took him? The odds of John experiencing more pain look grim.

John calculated that more than an hour passed before they stopped, which meant they had likely taken him to Minneapolis or St. Paul. They shoved him into a room, uncuffed him, and told him to change into the orange jumpsuit they had laid on a chair.

John didn't see any of the men who arrested him. The man who watched him dress didn't look any friendlier than the man in the back seat of the SWAT vehicle. As soon as John finished dressing, they put handcuffs on him again. John demanded to see a lawyer. They ignored him and acted as though he hadn't spoken.

After they took mug shots and fingerprints, they put him in a holding cell and informed him they would be back shortly. Right after they left, two large men came to "question" him. Their fists and clubs did most of the talking. Five minutes later, they brought him to an interrogation room. For the next hour, they threatened him with more "communication" from men in the holding cell if he didn't sign confessions to plotting to interfere with the government's duty to defend the nation.

#   #   #

Leah gasped when she turned the corner two blocks down the street from her home. Lights lit up half the block around her house. A SWAT car blocked the way at the corner, keeping traffic clear for the last 250 feet before their raid. Leah parked her car and ran across front lawns and down the sidewalk toward where they lived. SWAT Vehicles parked in her driveway and on the street in front of her home. Men, wearing what looked like bullet-proof vests, stood blocking the sidewalk and keeping people away. They all faced toward the front door. Leah froze as she gawked at what grabbed everybody's attention.

John fell against the doorjamb of their front door and struggled to get back up.

From somewhere outside of her stunned mind she heard Janet call to her. "Over here, quick!"

Janet motioned vigorously with one hand for Leah to join her on their front porch next to Willy. Leah ran up onto her neighbor's porch and watched, horrified, as the SWAT team shoved her husband into a van. Several neighbors took pictures, their cell phones flashing.

"Where are they taking him?" Leah muttered in disbelief.

"Let's find out," Willy said. "I'll follow them in my car."

"Where are Rachael and David?"

"They brought them out a few minutes ago and put them in another car," Janet said. "They left just before John came out."

Leah put her hands on top of her head. "My poor kids! They must be terrorized. We have to find out where they took them."

Willy hopped into his car while Janet helped Leah collect her thoughts. Janet suggested two lawyers she knew who could get John out on bail. Micheal Brauer, the second lawyer they called, agreed to help and told her to text him when they learned where they took John and Leah's children.

An hour later, Willy informed them they took John to a Hennepin County building in Minneapolis. Janet texted Brauer with the location, but she figured he wouldn't do anything to help until normal business hours later that morning.

Three hours later, Janet received a call from Brauer and handed her phone to Leah. Leah learned Brauer had arrived at the federal building ninety minutes after she had texted him. That was the only good news she received. Brauer could not arrange bail because they suspected John of plotting to overthrow the government. Because they suspected him of sedition, Brauer's hands were tied. The children would be in the custody of Hill County social services in the morning. He told Leah not to worry about her children. He thought he'd have no trouble getting them put into custody of their grandparents. From people Brauer knew in the federal building, he learned the FBI also planned to apprehend Leah and Mary, but they couldn't find them.

Janet called Mary to discover what had happened and warn her if necessary. Her phone went right to voice mail. Leah had last seen

Mary at Francine's home, getting ready to drive home. Mary lived fifteen minutes in the opposite direction of Leah's home from Francine's. The longer distance helped explain why she had escaped arrest and likely had not even seen her children arrested. Otherwise, she would have thrown herself into the middle of the raid and tried to rescue her family.

Leah decided to call Mary's neighbors and realized she had left her phone at Francine's home. Consequently, she used Janet's phone again. She learned from the neighbors that SWAT vehicles had descended on Mary's home as well. Mary wasn't there, but the SWAT team arrested Doug and their children. The Leah called Francine and listened to Francine frantically describe last night's events.

Mary had arrived at Francine's home, distressed about finding her house vacant and her family gone. They discussed various alternatives and called the police. That was when they learned FBI agents came and arrested Doug and their children. Mary turned herself in to the authorities after she contacted a lawyer and learned how best to free her family.

Leah tried to gather her thoughts as she talked with Francine. She recalled John mentioning that he thought either Mary's phone or his phone and had been hacked. If the FBI had hacked her phone, they would be able to locate her by tracking her phone.

Leah asked Francine to pray that God would guide her and disconnected from the call. She thanked Janet for all her help, and she praised God that she had forgotten her cell phone at Francine's home. She drove to Eileen's home to hide and told Eileen everything that had happened.

"The FBI is sure to look for you here." Eileen wrinkled her brow. "I have a friend who lives in Suckerville. She is single, and I'm sure she would let you hide there."

Leah felt jittery after a night of getting hit like a ping-pong ball batted about by players on steroids. Eileen had to go to work but called Janet and asked her for help. Leah's mind went numb as she overheard Eileen talk to Janet in the background of her jumbled thoughts.

"Can you meet Janet at Joe's Minnoco in ten minutes?" Eileen asked.

Leah shook her head to bring herself back into the present. "Yeah, sure." Both she and Janet liked the mechanic there. He wouldn't report her to the FBI.

By the time Leah arrived at Joe's garage, Janet was already there. Leah hopped out of her car, and Janet gave her a long hug. Janet's voice sounded shaky. "What a nightmare! I never should have let you leave my place alone. I talked to Joe, and he said you could leave your car here if you have mechanical work that needs to be done."

"Why would I do that?" Leah asked

"Because I am driving you to Suckerville. They have the police and everybody else looking for your car."

"I'll be stuck there then."

"I'm staying with you. That's the least I can do."

Leah felt like crying. "Are you sure?"

Janet grabbed and hugged her.

Leah clung to her friend for several minutes as she broke down and sobbed. When she stopped, she went inside the station and told Joe to check her brakes and change her oil and filter. She thought to pay him in advance because she didn't know how soon she would be returning to get her car. Just before she put her credit card into the device to pay for the work, she remembered the FBI could trace her purchase if she charged it. "Just a minute, Joe. Let me see if Janet has the cash or will let me use her credit card."

Leah trotted to Janet's car and rapped on the driver's side window. "Janet, I want to pay Joe ahead of time for the services, but I don't want to use my credit card. The FBI will trace the charge and be hot on my trail. Do you have any cash I can borrow?"

Janet handed Leah her husband's credit card. After Leah paid for the work, she parked her car in the garage and asked the mechanic to keep the car inside as much as possible. Thirty minutes later they arrived in Suckerville at the home of Stacy Peterson. Stacy's home was a typical ranch style house in a neighborhood of similar homes. The sidewalks were shoveled, and evergreen bushes decorated the front of Stacy's creme-colored home. Nothing about the outside of the house made the home stick out from the neighbors, which helped make it an ideal place to hide.

Eileen had informed Stacy what had happened, so Stacy parked her car at the curb and left the garage door open for them. Janet drove her car right into the open stall in the garage. They had no idea what to do next. Stacy welcomed them with a smile, and they filled Stacy in on the details that Eileen missed. Stacy expressed sympathy for their plight and assured them they could stay there as long as necessary. The basement was carpeted and had a large bedroom with two beds and a full bathroom. Because the neighbors knew Stacy worked evenings, Leah and Janet decided to stay in the basement with the curtains pulled and the lights off on the main floor to prevent curious neighbors from investigating. Stacy's shift started at 3:30 PM, so once Leah and Janet were situated in the basement, they prayed with Stacy before she dashed off to work.

As a Catholic, Stacy said that she didn't feel comfortable with the extemporaneous praying Janet and Leah did. She wouldn't pray with them anymore, but she encouraged them to pray as much as they wanted by themselves. She hated the government's attempt to control the lives of ordinary citizens and expressed gratitude for the opportunity to hide and feed them.

My brethren, count it all joy when you fall into various trials.
James 1:2 NKJV

Chapter Thirty-Six

When they shoved John back into the holding cell, he called out to God. "Lord, do You still have me in the palm of Your hands? I know You must. Are my children safe? Have mercy on Rachael. She's been tricked by the devil and doesn't mean to rebel against Your will for her life. Just let me know if they are all right." When John finished praying for Rachael, an unexplainable peace came over him. Joy flooded his heart as he used the cot in the cell to let himself down onto his knees. "Thank You, Holy Spirit, for Your comfort. 'Where can I go from Your Spirit? Or where can I flee from Your presence? If I ascend into heaven, You are there, If I make my bed in hell, behold, You are there.'[11] God, You are indeed in control of my life." John covered his face with his hands, hardly noticing aches from his facial wounds. God's assurance of His presence continued to fill him with peace and joy.

John believed joy would provide him strength and help him pray with sufficient faith to defeat the powers of darkness, which appeared to have the upper hand in this present material world. "Lord, take me in my spirit to the source of this darkness that put me here."

John thought for sure that God would have him leave his hurting body on the floor of the cell and take his spirit body somewhere to reveal how he could best pray. After thirty minutes, nothing happened. God said nothing. He knew the Holy Spirit wanted him to pray, but he didn't know what to pray. Certainly, God wanted to show

---

[11] Psalm 139:7-8 NKJV

him what prayers to pray. He couldn't comprehend what prevented him from hearing from the Lord.

Thoughts came to John about the oppression, intimidation, and censorship in operation during his arrest, and he assumed the Holy Spirit put those ideas in his mind. Therefore, John prayed vehemently against the spirit of oppression. His thoughts wandered as he recalled how intimidated he felt, and then he imagined what Leah must have been thinking when she witnessed him being shoved into the back seat of a government vehicle.

John soon fell asleep.

He awoke with a start. Why hadn't he prayed with intensity? Instead of the Holy Spirit transporting his spirit to the source of the spiritual stronghold that put him in jail, his body ached from lying on the floor and his head throbbed from the beating he received at the hands of an FBI agent. This couldn't be happening, not here in America!

Last night, peace washed over him. This morning, he felt nothing but pain and frustration as he knelt on the floor. John called out from the depths of his soul, "Lord, why aren't you speaking to me or showing me how to pray?"

John placed his forehead on the floor and mulled over why God chose not to speak with him. Just as he gave up trying to find an explanation, he heard the Holy Spirit clearly, in a voice almost audible.

Because you lack sufficient spiritual maturity, I will not take you on voyages in your spirit body alone. Continue to trust me. Others will go, and they will join with Me in intercession.

What did the Holy Spirit mean? Was he too proud? He could deal with that quickly. "Lord, I put my pride on the cross with You. Have your way in my life. I surrender all to You." After John prayed that, he realized saying a simple prayer wouldn't accomplish what he desired instantly. Dealing with pride involved a lifelong process, but he wanted to start immediately.

John sat on the cot and sang praises to God with his whole heart. The Holy Spirit had assured him that other Christians would pray for him. He didn't know how their intercession would free him, but America was still a land where Christians prayed boldly and believed in miracles. With God's grace and friends praying, he could be walking out of his cell in a few hours. That thought buoyed his spirits, and he praised God and sang even louder. The Apostle Paul and Silas sang praises in prison, and the prison experienced an earthquake that shook the doors of the jail off their hinges. Maybe God would do that same thing now.

John sang at the top of his lungs. A man in a cell farther down yelled for him to shut up. A guard came to investigate the reason for the disturbance. John continued to sing at maximum volume. This couldn't be just his emotions that aroused him. God had to be the source of this joy.

"Shut up!" the guard yelled.

"Praise the Lord Almighty!" John said and started to sing the doxology. "Praise God from whom all blessings flow—"

"I said, 'Shut up!'"

"Praise Him, all creatures here below—"

"Put your hands between these bars!"

John stuck his hands between the bars, and the guard handcuffed his hands to the bars.

While the guard unlocked the cell, John sang, "Praise Him above, ye heav'nly host—"

John didn't finish the doxology. Instead, he ducked and grunted as the guard beat his arms and shoulders. After a few blows, the guard left the cell and let John collapse to the floor when he unlocked the handcuffs.

John crawled back to his cot where he pulled himself up to a sitting position. That didn't look like the earthquake he had envisioned. Where was God in all this? A few hours later, they brought him to an interrogation room and drilled him with questions about plots to overthrow the government.

The more he denied it, the more they threatened him. They wanted to know where Leah was. John laughed. That gave John the only good news he had received since they woke him out of a sound sleep in his bedroom. Leah had escaped and remained hidden from these goons. He could only hope that she prayed and received guidance from the Lord about what to do. He had to believe that included hiring a smart attorney and broadcasting his plight to any media outlet that could avoid government censorship.

The FBI thug who beat him the night of his arrest compared John to Jan 6 demonstrators. They hadn't charged him with anything yet, but he figured they kept him under the same outrageous pretense. That offered the only explanation he could think of for how they could neglect to offer him his right to have an attorney, to be read his Miranda rights, and to be held without bail or charged with any crime.

One week after being arrested, John changed tactics. He pretended he wanted to help them find insurrectionists but didn't know their plans. If he could convince the interrogators of his sincerity, they would have to believe that they had arrested him by mistake. Likewise, he talked to them about his faith in democracy, America, and the Constitution, so he could make them understand he would never overthrow the government. In spurts, he asked them about their faith and what they believed about the Constitution. He cautiously challenged their beliefs in God and justice. His interrogators grew increasingly irritated at his attempts to prick their consciences. After two weeks of his revised strategy, they left him in his cell and didn't bother him anymore.

You will keep him in perfect peace,
Whose mind is stayed on You,
Because he trusts in You.
Isaiah 26:3 NKJV

Chapter Thirty-Seven

When Stacy left for work at Bluffview Shoe Company, Janet and Leah went into the basement and prayed for guidance. Janet didn't like the idea of traveling in her spirit, and Leah assured her she didn't like it either. They sought the Lord about practical matters and told God they didn't want to leave their physical bodies. They both felt confident that He would not send them traveling abroad against their will.

With Stacy's help and the Lord's guidance, they withdrew several thousand dollars from Leah and Janet's bank accounts to pay for an attorney and several weeks of groceries. They spent the second afternoon cleaning Stacy's garage so she could park her car inside easily. They knew Stacy planned to travel to Rochester to buy groceries, and when she returned, they wanted her to drive the car into the garage before she unloaded the groceries. That way neighbors would be less likely to learn Stacy had guests.

After cleaning the garage, they made up a work list of things they could do to help Stacy. Though the list looked nice on paper, they both realized they had to find more to do, and most of all, they needed to become stronger in prayer. Stacy wholeheartedly agreed to their plan to keep neighbors from learning she had guests. She informed Leah and Janet about what happened to Mary. Mary had turned herself in to the authorities less than a day after the raid, but she was freed immediately along with the rest of her family. Several witnesses vouched for her innocence in obstructing a school board meeting, and a judge ruled that in the absence of any charges they could not be detained. Though Stacy joined Leah and Janet in thanking God for the judge's ruling, she said that she would leave the rest of the praying to Leah and Janet.

Since Stacy was uncomfortable praying aloud, Janet and Leah did most of their prayer time while she was at work every afternoon. The first few prayer sessions felt like watching an hourglass drain of sand. Leah and Janet came to identical conclusions at the same time. They could no longer depend on prayers that sprang from their minds. If John was going to get freed, they had to have the Holy Spirit more involved in the way they prayed. When they asked the Lord about that, the Holy Spirit reminded them they were the ones who put the limitations on the way He would operate in their prayers.

Leah collapsed on the floor when she sensed what the Lord wanted. Nothing she could say or do would help her circumvent traveling in her spirit, for she knew she could not abandon John. If she didn't do everything within her power to help, she'd never forgive herself. She kept hearing the words of Jesus, "To whom much is given, much is expected." On top of that, she kept hearing John's reminder that if she wanted to find joy in the life Jesus had for her, she would have to stop trying to please other people. For Leah, that meant letting go of trying to please all her girlfriends. It also meant not putting Pastor Ron's opinion ahead of what God told her to do.

Leah rose from the floor and knelt to pray. "Lord, I am scared to leave my body, especially without John, and I don't want to lose my friends. But I put Your will and my husband's welfare before what my friends want and before what I fear. Holy Spirit, You can show me how to pray in whatever way You think is best."

After surrendering her fears to God, Leah shared with Janet what she had told the Lord.

"Okay then," Janet said. Her worried expression showed it wasn't so okay.

Leah put her hand on Janet's hands, which were folded on her lap. "Nothing has changed for you. The Lord hasn't suddenly revoked your free will."

Janet smiled. "You don't mind traveling in your spirit body alone?"

"I kind of do, but I have surrendered my likes and dislikes to Jesus."

"Do you think the Holy Spirit will send your spirit somewhere?"

Leah shrugged. "I know He won't send me somewhere if I don't want to go, but I want to go if that's what John needs. If Pastor Ron or Francine get mad at me, they will just have to understand. I have to join the Apostle Paul in saying that the love of Christ controls me, not to mention that my love for my husband has to overrule any allegiance I owe Pastor or friends."

Janet knitted her brow and stole a sideways glance at Leah.

"Do you want to quit praying with me if you see my body lying on the floor?" Leah asked.

"No, but I might leave the room until you come back. Having a lifeless body lying there is a bit disconcerting."

Leah nodded. "I understand." She didn't blame her for feeling that way. She felt the same way when she saw limp bodies lying there. Besides, she thought the possibility of her spirit traveling was very unlikely because she doubted the Holy Spirit would send her if she didn't like it.

After praying for an hour, an intense pulling within Leah caused her to double over and crumple to the floor. Everything went dark and the next thing she saw was her body lying on the floor and her spirit floating in the air.

Leah noticed Janet's prayers intensify. "Lord, will You call Janet to come with me?"

Janet knelt on the floor, holding her stomach. A few seconds later, she lay on the floor, and her spirit floated next to Leah. "Whoa!"

"Are you all right?" Leah asked.

"I am glad you were out here before I arrived. Floating around like this spooks me out."

"I am sorry if you felt pressured to join me," Leah said. "What comes next is even scarier."

An instant later, they appeared in a large room with three men who glowered over a large square table filled with a roadmap.

Janet recoiled in horror. "What are those grotesque creatures leaning over those men?"

"Demons," Leah said.

Janet turned and faced Leah. "Let's get out of here," she whispered.

"Don't worry. Neither the men nor the demons can see or hear us. The Holy Spirit brought us here to teach us something."

A heavy-set man with rolled-up sleeves pointed to a location on the map. "We found Leah's car here, at Joe's Minnoco, an hour ago. The mechanic says Leah left the car there for him to work on two weeks ago. She rode off with another woman in a white, compact sedan. The mechanic doesn't remember the make or model of that car, doesn't even remember what the other woman looked like."

Another man with a full head of gray hair shook his head. "No sense in continuing the all-points containment search. She could have walked all the way to Canada or Mexico by now."

"We know she doesn't have her passport, so she's not going to be in Mexico or Canada," a third man said.

"Good grief, I didn't say she'd be *in* Mexico or Canada, but if you've looked at the condition of our borders, I don't imagine the lack of a passport would slow her down much."

A demon spoke in the ear of the heavyset man. *"Don't give up so easily. Think about the information the mechanic gave you. Which way did he say the woman's car turned?"*

The heavyset man pointed to the map again. "The mechanic said they turned left out of his gas station. If they wanted to head north, east, or west, they most likely would have turned right. We calculated the chances of them going south were the greatest, so we put a tight lid on both Interstate Highway 35 and Minnesota 58."

"A lot of good it did," the gray-haired man said. "Irritated thousands of people. Alarmed half of the state. Pundits accusing the FBI of creating a police state."

No, no. A demon shouted at him. *Don't give up.*

"I've got this feeling they are still in Bluffview. If we listen in on conversations their friends are having, they'll turn up. Very soon."

Yes, yes, another demon said. *Monitor the calls of their friends, of everyone in her church. Get as much dirt on them as you can. When they pretend they don't know her whereabouts, threaten them with complete humiliation from anything that embarrasses them—whether real or suggested by association.*

"Our boss answers to the President," the gray-haired man said. "He has already embarrassed the President with our search of cars on the Interstate. Why make matters worse?"

"Nobody will notice us tapping more phone calls of different people. The boss doesn't even need to know. If we scoop up a little poop about Leah's friends, they'll hardly feel inclined to squawk about their phone being tapped and risk having their crap hit the fan."

The Holy Spirit transported Leah and Janet to a dark room filled with demonic spirits who were cowering in front of an enormous, darkly clad demon who sat on a throne, his eyes pulsed with an ominous, red glow.

"Can they see us?" Janet's voice trembled.

Leah answered, "No, don't worry." She saw a transparent gold bubble around her and Janet that she'd never seen before.

"Do you see the bubble around us?" Leah asked. "I feel such an amazing sense of God's protection and peace."

"Yes! Thank You, Holy Spirit," Janet said.

The enormous demon growled at a pitch almost too low for their ears to hear. *Among us here, I sense contemptuous opposition to our kingdom.*

"Well, maybe they can't hear or see us," Leah said, "but the monster on the throne must sense our presence."

No, no, no. All the smaller demons cried and made a ruckus. *We'd never disobey you or switch our allegiance to the enemy.*

Hmmm. . . The demon on the throne growled with contempt at those in front of him. *Lust, Perversion, Pornography, and Shame—step forward.*

The four slid forward, snarling, chortling, and grinning slyly. They bowed low when they reached the throne.

I want all four of you to ply your wares on the likes of Willy Anderson. He has the potential to disrupt my plans, but with his wife gone he should be vulnerable. Bring Sloth, Passivity, and Witchcraft with you. Use their devices to overcome any resistance the enemy might bring to oppose you.

Three demons appeared next to the four.

Seduce, trap, and humiliate Willy Anderson.

Yes, Master! the seven said in unison.

"Don't fail me!

The seven disappeared instantly.
"No," Janet cried. "That's not fair! We have to pray for Willy."
Leah and Janet returned to their bodies. They understood who they were up against and quickly prayed for their own protection and for them to remain hidden from the FBI. Then they concentrated on interceding for Willy. Leah knew Jesus asked demons their names so he could cast them out. Now the Holy Spirit saved them the trouble of asking. They knew exactly which evil spirits they needed to bind and cast out. Since the Holy Spirit had shown them the demons involved, they prayed with fervency and faith. They cast out Lust, Perversion, Pornography, Shame, Sloth, Passivity, and Witchcraft one at a time.

They determined not to quit until the Spirit told them they had accomplished the task. After two hours of intercession, they sensed they could praise the Lord for Willy's deliverance and could start interceding for John.

*But You, O Lord, are a shield for me, My
glory and the One who lifts up my head.*
Psalm 3:3 NKJV

Chapter Thirty-Eight

Willy booted up his computer and checked his email. A coupon for spicy chicken delights appeared as the subject of one of his emails. For the last few weeks, he routinely deleted emails from questionable sources.

Janet hadn't been around to cook dinner for him, and though his sons enjoyed frozen pizza and hot dogs, he'd grown to despise them. Chicken struck him as a good idea. When he clicked on the chicken delivery link, a naked lady begged him to taste her chicken delights.

Willy stared at her seductive body and swallowed hard. His pulse spiked immediately.

What are you doing? Delete that immediately. A solemn voice spoke to him in a manner he couldn't ignore.

He shuddered and quickly hit the delete button. He'd been set free from that addiction, and he wasn't going back.

That close relapse back into his addiction bothered him. Willy had kept quiet about his wife's hiding with Leah for two weeks. Janet left a note apologizing for leaving without letting him know where she was going. She hoped he'd understand, but she had to help her friend who was in desperate need.

He understood why Janet did what she did. Like Janet, he had watched the spectacle the FBI put on to intimidate anybody who'd challenge the government's right to monitor citizens for the sake of "everyone's safety." Though he hated the lies perpetrated by the federal government, fanatical Christians had to share part of the blame for

John's arrest and Janet running off with Leah. He had been patient long enough. In the morning Willy planned to talk with the pastor.

# # #

On Wednesday Ray hopped the bus after school without David because he stayed late for gymnastics practice. He would take the activities bus. The boys' basketball coach wouldn't let her try out because he said the deadline to sign up had passed. That was a bogus excuse for not letting a trans boy try out. She tolerated riding without David when she took her the bus to her real home. From now on, she was stuck riding by herself on a new bus because she lived with her grandparents. The idiots on this bus irritated her. They usually just made obscene gestures or ignored her, but occasionally they mocked her by asking embarrassing questions.

"How ya doing, dude?" a cocky senior called to her as he got on the bus. "Or is that dudette this week?"

"Hey, don't make fun of her," a nerdy senior said. "Her parents are dope dealers. Haven't you heard?"

"No, they're insurrectionists," a girl said, "and her preferred pronoun is *he*."

"Uh, how do you suppose they raise money to overthrow the government."

A boy in front of the nerdy senior turned around and swatted him with his stocking cap. The nerd grabbed the cap and flung it away, sending to Ray's seat. Two boys raced to the cap and wrestled. Ray pushed them away.

The bigger of the two boys shouted. "Whoa! He hit me!" He turned and stuck out his chin at Ray. "Come on, you want to fight? You want to prove that you are a man now?"

"Sit down, Steve," one of the senior girls said.

"Why? She wants to be a guy now. She can fight like a guy."

The bus monitor jumped up and stood tall next to Steve. "You lay a hand on her, and you or your parents will be driving you to school for the rest of the school year."

"He hit me first! Make her or her parents drive to school."

"Yeah, yeah," the monitor said as she pointed to a vacant seat toward the back of the bus. "And Ray's preferred pronoun is *he*."

"I've got your number, Ray," Steve yelled. "We'll see if you've got what it takes to be a guy."

"Shut up, Steve," a girl yelled.

"You better watch it," the nerd said. "Ray's parents might be part of a drug cartel and they'll come after you with AK-47s."

"Is that right, Ray?" the cocky senior shouted from the back of the bus. "Should we be scared of retaliation?"

A large senior pushed Tim, a scrawny sophomore, out of his seat, and the sophomore had to sit with Ray.

Three of the guys poked fun at Tim for keeping a big space between him and Ray: "Hey Tim, why are you sitting so far from Ray? Are you transphobic?"

"No, he's homophobic! Timmy, you don't have to be afraid of sitting next to a guy. Sit a little closer! If you sit any farther away, you'll fall off the seat."

"He's transphobic, not homophobic. Don't be afraid of Ray, he's a guy now."

"You're both wrong! Tim is gay, and he is pissed at Ray for snubbing him."

"Is that right, Ray? Did you snub Tim?"

"Ray! He asked you a question!"

"Ray, what did you do to snub Tim?"

"Tim! Ray isn't talking to us. Tell us what he did!"

"Hey, lay off them! They obviously had a lover's quarrel."

When Tim rose to leave the bus, he swung at Ray with his cap as he gathered books sitting between them.

When Ray left the bus, she swung her backpack over her shoulder, and she kept the visor of her baseball cap down, covering her face to hide her tears.

Once in her bedroom at her grandparents' place, Ray called Pastor Ron's home phone. Francine answered. Ray breathed a sigh of relief when she heard her voice. Pastor Ron took such a harsh view of transgender people. That was why she had canceled the appointment that her dad made for her when she first contemplated transitioning. Besides being a good friend of Mom, Francine was very understanding.

When Francine heard her cry for her mom's help, she expressed her sympathy for what Ray experienced and offered to pray for her. Ray mostly wanted to know if she could somehow talk to her mom or dad. Francine told her to come over to her home, and she would pray for her and her mom.

After Ray arrived at Francine's home, she prayed with Francine, and she learned that her mom and Janet were likely at Stacy's house, a friend of Francine's in Suckerville. Then Francine let her know she planned to meet Stacy tomorrow afternoon, and she asked if Ray wanted to go with her to talk with Stacy.

The following afternoon, Ray skipped two classes and walked to Francine's home. Francine drove with Ray to the Bluffview Shoe, where Francine talked first with Stacy privately. Afterward, Ray talked with Stacy alone and arranged a ride with to see her mom after Stacy finished her shift at Midnight. Francine agreed to call Grandma to assure her that Ray would be in a safe place for a few days.

Ray waited at Burger King until 11:30 PM, and then she walked the back streets to Bluffview Shoe so nobody would see her and discover her plan to meet Mom. While Ray waited for Stacy, she leaned against the side of a building near Stacy's car and gazed at the clear, winter sky. Myriad sources of city lights—predominately the floodlights of the parking lot next to where she stood—dimmed the comforting light reflected from an almost full moon. Ray thought of times when she sat with Mom and Dad, studying the night sky. "God, if You are out there, make it possible for me to be with my mom and dad again."

Stacy came out to her car shortly after midnight, and on the drive to her house, she laid down the house rules. Ray hadn't asked Stacy to stay for any length of time, but if Stacy was fine with visit that lasted several days, that would be wonderful.

# # #

When Leah saw her daughter, she couldn't hold back the tears. She hugged Ray and kissed her face repeatedly. "I missed you and worried so much about what happened to you," Leah cried as tears continued to flow.

Ray cried as she slumped into her mother's embrace. "You have no idea how much I missed you, Mom."

After Leah fussed over Ray for several minutes, she held Ray out at arm's length to examine her. "Stacy said that Grandpa and Grandma Greenberg had temporary custody of you." Leah took a deep breath, shaking off her disgust at Ray's decision to transition her gender. "Are you getting along with them okay?"

Ray shrugged. "Yeah, I suppose."

"How are things at school?"

Ray looked down at the floor to her left.

Leah grabbed both shoulders and gave them a gentle shake to coax her daughter to look up into her eyes. "Ray? What's happening at school?"

Ray's lower lip and jaw quivered. "Mom, the boys at school are so mean to me. Some boys make fun of me for changing my gender! Others laugh at me for still being a girl. The worst are the ones who dare me to be a boy and challenge me to fight them."

"Oh Sweetie, that's terrible!" Leah pulled her in and caressed her head, searching for comforting words.

Her daughter shook as she sobbed. "Mom, will you forgive me for being so stupid and rebellious?"

Leah pulled back so Ray could see her face. " Of course, I forgive you. I am sure your dad will too, but he is in jail and not allowed to have any visitors. I am sorry life is messed up right now."

"It's all my fault. If I hadn't agitated Dad with my transitioning, he wouldn't have felt compelled to protest at the school board meeting."

"Do you still think you want to be a boy?"

"I am not a boy, I don't want to be a boy, and I don't want to be a man. I chose to transition for all the wrong reasons. Montana said I would be her boyfriend, and we could date and do all the cool stuff couples do. Then, when she tried to make out with me, she made fun of how I kissed. She dumped me. Didn't want anything to do with me. In the lunchroom she ignored me, and later, I heard she made up lies about me. Where does she get off doing that?"

"Wow, that must really hurt."

"I lost my best friend. At least, I thought she was my best friend." Rachael's lower lip trembled.

Leah hugged her daughter. "I am sorry, sweetie."

Rachael clung to her mother and sniffled. "You think Dad will forgive me?"

"I am sure he will. You know what else he'd likely tell you?"

Rachael's head quivered next to her mother's chest.

Leah kissed the top of Rachael's head. "He'd say you have a Friend who has never left you nor forsaken you, and He longs to be your Best Friend again."

"Yeah, he would remind me that Jesus hadn't forgotten me." Rachael wiped her eyes. "How could I have believed all those lies and been so easily deceived?"

When Rachael stopped sniffling, Leah asked, "Would you like to make things right with Jesus?"

Rachael drew in an unsteady breath and whimpered, "Yes!"

"Jesus already knows you are sorry for ignoring Him, but you can ask Him to forgive you. He *will* forgive you and will cleanse you from all unrighteousness."

"Oh, Jesus, I am so sorry for not listening to You and for rebelling against You and my parents. What can I do to make things right?"

Leah stroked Rachael's hair. "You already have, Rachael. He's forgiven you and removed your sins as far as the east is from the west."

Rachael looked up and pleaded with her eyes. "Can I stay with you?"

"Your father is in jail, and I am hiding from the FBI and living in someone else's home. You need to be with your grandparents for now so you can go to school."

"Mom, I don't want to be in school. Stacy expects me to stay at her home. I belong here with you." Large tears welled up in Rachael's eyes, wearing away at Leah's resolve.

"Ray, I'm a fugitive from the law. What happens when the FBI discovers our hiding place?"

Rachael shook her head vigorously. "I'm Rachael, not Ray. I am your daughter, and I belong with you. If FBI agents grab you like they did Dad, the worst that can happen is that I end up back with Grandma."

Leah pulled Rachael back into her bosom. "We'll see how it goes."

Leah rested her chin on top of Rachael's head. How good it felt to hold her, to have her daughter back as Rachael. Perhaps, if an ample number of days passed, Rachael's return to school as a girl would be smoother.

Confess your faults one to another, and pray one for another, that ye may be healed.
James 5:16 KJV

Chapter Thirty-Nine

Ron's phone rang at 10 AM. It was Suzi, telling him that Janet's husband, Willy, wanted to speak with him. She didn't need to tell him that. He couldn't help but hear Willy's booming voice through the closed door.

"Hello, Willy." Pastor Ron scooted around his desk to shake Willy's hand firmly. "Good to see you again. It's been a while since—"

"It's been a while since I've seen my wife. Where is she?"

"I didn't know she had left you. I'm sorry to hear that. Sit down, sit down." Pastor Ron motioned toward a padded armchair, and he sat in the one opposite to it.

Willy sat but leaned forward. "She didn't leave me because she's mad at me. She's helping Leah hide and hiding along with her."

"Oh." Pastor Ron frowned. Francine thought Janet helped Leah hide, but he had hoped that wasn't true. Now he had to pray that Janet didn't backslide into John's heretical visions.

Willy appeared ready to explode. "Are you going to tell me you know nothing about Janet or Leah hiding?"

"Settle down. I'm as upset as you are about what the government has done to a member of my church." Pastor Ron paused. Willy seemed too riled to reason with. Honesty and transparency might disarm his hostility. "Francine told me yesterday that she hadn't been able to reach Janet for a week. That was the first hint I had that Janet might be with Leah. Neither one has communicated with me."

"My wife is off with John's wife, and there's no telling the demons those two might conjure up under the influence of John's deception. You are their pastor, and I hold you responsible for allowing John to perpetrate that crazy vision of his."

Ron hung his head down. He worried about the demons John stirred up, too. To hear about it from a wayward member of his flock stung. Why didn't the prayer team repent with tears at their pastor's rebuke? Instead, he had to hear an accurate assessment of John's visions from this backslider. "Listen, Willy, I feel the same way, but it's easier to criticize than find solutions. Maybe this whole incident can be turned around for the good. It might drive us together, to become more unified."

Willy's lips curled. "I came here for answers, not pie in the sky."

Pastor Ron rose from his armchair and walked behind his desk to sit on his swivel chair. "You want your wife back, safe and sound. So do I. If you have any ideas on how to bring her back, I'm all ears."

"So there's not a single. Blessed. Thing. You are going to do." Willy stood and gazed at Pastor Ron.

Pastor Ron held his gaze as he stood. "I will ask around. I will tell people to pray. I will exhort them to be unified. I will start by inviting you to join us."

Willy waved Pastor Ron off and stalked out of his office.

Pastor Ron clenched his jaw. He didn't blame Willy for being upset. What he told Willy, he planned to put into action, starting with the prayer team. On Wednesday he called Andy to set a time they could meet before the Thursday prayer meeting.

# # #

Thirty minutes before the prayer meeting, Pastor Ron met with Andy in his office. After a perfunctory prayer to cover their discussion, Pastor Ron described his meeting with Willy.

Andy gripped the armrests of his chair. "So, you feel the prayer team needs to unify by repenting with sorrow in their hearts for allowing John to lead them astray."

Pastor Ron studied Andy's expression. Andy didn't appear to say that because he agreed or as a restatement of facts. No, he seemed to be challenging his pastor's discernment of what had occurred. "We agree, don't we? John brought all his troubles on himself because he dipped his soul into things that Christians should avoid."

Andy frowned at him. "I submitted to your authority as my pastor, but I did not agree with your assessment. John submitted to you as well. A lot of good his submission did for him!"

"You don't blame me for his run-in with the law, do you?" Pastor Ron felt his face flush as he fought to control his anger.

"His submission to your edict left him without a powerful weapon to defeat the schemes of the evil one."

"His experiences put him smack dab into the middle of the enemy's camp."

Andy paused and held Pastor Ron's gaze. "When I look at what motivated John and what motivates your discernment, I can easily see the difference. John operated out of respect for your position as the pastor and his passion for intercession. You seemed to have been moved more by fear and a desire for control."

Ron pounded his desk with his fist. "So you have no sorrow for fighting me on my instructions to the prayer team?"

"Like John, I submitted to your leadership out of respect. I will continue to stay as the leader of the prayer team—if you allow it—because Christ has put His love in my heart for our church and for you."

With the prayer meeting due to begin in less than ten minutes, Pastor Ron realized he'd have to accept Andy's concession for what it was.

# # #

When Pastor Ron arrived home after the prayer meeting, he asked Francine about any further news she might have heard about Leah or Janet. She mentioned Eileen heard rumors that Stacy deposited cash into her account that matched an amount that Leah had withdrawn. Francine said she figured Stacy had received the money to help Janet and Leah hide. The hesitant way Fran responded to his inquiries about Leah and Janet made Ron suspect she knew more than she told him.

Ron drove to Stacy's home the following afternoon to talk with Stacy and investigate what she knew about where Janet and Leah might be hiding. He pulled up to the curb in front of Stacy's neighbors and waited because he thought Stacy would return from work in a couple of hours. After waiting less than ten minutes, Stacy's garage opened, and a car drove out. Janet's car sat in the stall next to the car that had just left. Pastor Ron had his answer, and he didn't need to tip Janet and Leah off by talking to Stacy. Leah had to be hiding there, and Pastor Ron would do his part, something that any law-abiding citizen would do. He would report them to the authorities to bring justice and truth to those who rebelled against governmental authority.

Pastor Ron called the non-emergency number for the police. He informed the operator he had a tip on where some fugitives might be hiding. The operator said an FBI agent would return his call shortly.

While he waited, he decided to drive home. Janet and Leah had been at Stacy's for two weeks now, and they weren't going anywhere. He asked Francine to ride down with him to Suckerville so she could extract Janet before the FBI raided Stacy's home.

"No!" Francine said. "What about Leah? Why would you protect Janet but not Leah?"

The answer seemed obvious to Pastor Ron. John and Leah were heretics. Four hundred years earlier, they would have burned them at the stake. "John and Leah have brought this on themselves. Janet is just an innocent bystander who's been seduced by their deception."

Francine stuck her chin out at him and glared. "Oh, that makes perfect sense. If all three have accepted what you have labeled as a deception, what's the difference?" Francine straightened and put her hands on her hips. "You know what the difference between you and them is? They walked in love toward you and toward one another. They submitted to your requests even though they doubted your discernment on the matter."

"Look, Francine, I have a responsibility as a pastor to make sure the sheep in my flock don't stray from the straight and narrow path. Love dictates I go after the one who strays and bring them back into the fold."

"What! Are you saying the other two have strayed so far from God's will that they are no longer part of the flock?"

Ron stared at her openly. She would never understand that they had chosen to leave the church. Janet rejected their heresy but was dragged into it unwillingly. Pastor Ron exhaled sharply. "Will you go with me to help me bring back the one who strayed?"

"No! I will stay here and pray you recall Christ's last words to the Apostle Peter, 'Do you love me more than these? . . .Feed my sheep.' Jesus wasn't referring to clubbing people over the head with your interpretation of doctrine. He meant for Peter to tend His sheep with love. Jesus wants love to motivate you, Ron. Is that what motivates you?"

Ron drove back to Stacy's home. Francine's comments rankled him, but he had to do the right thing. The book of Romans commands us to obey those in authority. Jesus set an example himself by obeying an evil Roman empire. For Fran to needle him about the submission and love of other people seemed unfair. Yesterday, Andy said the same thing. Neither one understood the right thing, the thing he had to do.

The Lord is merciful and gracious, slow to anger,
and plenteous in mercy.
Psalm 103:8 KJV

Chapter Forty

Ron called the FBI number the agent gave him. He told the FBI the home was difficult to find, and he'd meet them at the gas station on Highway 58 in Suckerville. They were testy about not getting the address of the home, but he insisted they meet at the station.

He didn't tell them the real reason. He wanted to talk Janet into leaving Leah so they would just arrest Leah. After all, that was the loving thing for a pastor to do.

Ron arrived at Stacy's home thirty minutes before he agreed to meet the FBI at the gas station which was four minutes away. When nobody answered the doorbell, he hurried to the back door of the attached garage. He breathed a sigh of relief when it opened. The door from the garage to the house opened easily as well.

He said a quiet hello as he entered. Both ladies expressed shock but joy when they saw him. Then Pastor Ron saw Ray, but he didn't say anything to her. She was a reprobate just like her parents, and she deserved to have the hand of the government bringing the full weight of the law on her.

Ron hugged them stiffly. "I may not be the answer to your prayers that you imagined."

Leah and Janet glanced at each other and then directed their gaze at him.

"John and Leah have brought the wrath of the federal government on themselves. I can't be held responsible for that. I tried to guide and correct them. I don't know. I must have failed. But that doesn't mean I can't rescue you, Janet, from the government's administration of justice."

"What are you talking about? Justice!" Janet raised her voice, registering her protest. "I saw the SWAT teams make a mockery of justice. They swarmed John and Leah's home. They accused them of insurrection to justify the circus they orchestrated in front of their neighbors."

Pastor Ron studied Leah's countenance. "They must know something, or they wouldn't have arrested John."

Janet glared at Pastor Ron. "Really, Pastor?" She exclaimed in disbelief. "They didn't have anything on John. They couldn't find any stashes of weapons, so they claimed they found large amounts of Fentanyl and accused him of selling drugs to raise cash to buy weapons. Do you believe John and Leah are drug dealers?"

Pastor Ron shrugged. "I don't know. The FBI had reasons for what they did, and they know your whereabouts. The second I leave here, the FBI is set to swoop in here to arrest Leah and whoever is with her. I will inform them that Janet is innocent. Janet, are you coming with me or not?"

"I am not!"

"Why? What am I to tell your husband and the rest of the church?"

"Tell them that the love of Christ compels me to stay with my friend. Christ will be with us wherever they might take us."

"I don't understand. What about love for your church and your pastor?"

Janet pointed with her outstretched arm toward the door. "Leave. Go ahead. Let the FBI know that the coast is clear for them to swoop in here. I will pray that Jesus will show you what His love looks like. Maybe He'll show you that love means suffering the scorn of religious people and abusive government leaders. That's what Jesus did. He suffered scorn from religious and government leaders.

Pastor Ron left but sat in his car deliberating his next steps. Janet's words stung. She reiterated the same reasons that Fran had. They were both right. He knew he failed miserably in the love department. He loved his wife, and he loved his ministry and the church as a whole. However, when it came to loving individuals other than his wife, there were probably many ways he sold them out for the larger picture. He always used his responsibility as pastor as an excuse for ignoring the personal needs of a person right in front of his nose. How many times had he read the story of the Good Samaritan and felt convicted that he was like the Pharisee who couldn't be bothered with the suffering victim on the side of the road?

Pastor Ron glanced at his watch. The FBI expected to meet him in five minutes. If he didn't take them to Leah, they would throw him in jail instead. Pastor Ron closed his eyes. "Lord, I have taken my eyes off of you and focused on my desires for the church. I want to walk in the kind of love that Janet demonstrated. Help me get out of this mess I've gotten myself into without hurting those I love and bringing shame to your church."

Pastor Ron looked at his watch again. They'd be waiting for him by the time he got there. He had to go and bear the consequences of his self-centeredness. When he turned on the ignition, he remembered that the Smiths lived in a hard-to-find cul-de-sac close by. They happened to be on vacation this week.

By the time Pastor Ron met the FBI, he had the perfect excuse for why Leah wasn't there. He told the FBI he had heard rumors that the Smiths had let Leah hide there. He had scolded the church member who told him about the rumor, and that person heard him call the FBI. He never imagined in his wildest dreams that the individual would rebel against not only the government but against the will of his pastor.

The excuse didn't turn out to be as perfect as he had hoped. The agent in charge accused him of trying to embarrass the FBI and of complicity with the insurrectionists. Since it was his word against the agent's, they didn't bring Pastor Ron for questioning.

When Pastor Ron returned home, he told Francine what he did and why. She seemed pleased, and she said she prayed the love of Christ that she knew dwelt in his heart would rule in his decision. When Pastor Ron mentioned going to Leah to let her know what he did, she insisted he not go down to talk with them. Leah and Janet would figure out what happened. Fran would catch Stacy before she started her shift at the Shoe to fill her in on the details so they all could rest at ease.

\#   \#   \#

Stacy told Francine she'd pass the good news on to Janet and Leah. She also shared with Francine the intercession they had experienced for Willy. Though she didn't know the details of what they prayed, she suggested Francine ask Pastor if Willy had any spiritual breakthroughs recently, especially in the area of spiritual strongholds that Willy might be fighting.

After Fran told her husband about the intercession the two ladies did, Ron figured they had used John's vision to do their spiritual warfare. He had to talk to Willy. If Willy confirmed that he had experienced deliverance in the last couple of days, Pastor Ron realized he needed to repent for his hardness of heart toward John, Leah, and the rest of the prayer team.

On the following afternoon, Pastor Ron waited at Willy's home for him to return from work. When Willy arrived, Pastor Ron mentioned he wanted to talk to him about a personal matter, Willy scowled but invited Pastor Ron into his home.

"Willy, I don't know where to begin. This may sound crazy because I have to ask you something, and I am not even sure what I am asking. I've been told that two individuals recently prayed for your deliverance, and I am unaware of what kind of deliverance you needed or if you even needed deliverance. That sounds crazy. I'm sorry for bothering you."

Tears welled up in Willy's eyes. "Unbelievable. A few days ago, I opened an email from the pit of hell. A seductive woman beckoned me with her naked legs. I heard a voice interrupt the impulses she tried to stimulate, and the voice told me to delete that email immediately. Pastor, I had been addicted to porn for years. Nearly destroyed my marriage. John prayed for me, and I got free from it. John's intercession saved my marriage. That's part of the reason I'm glad Janet helped Leah. I just got a little impatient with things."

"You say John saved your marriage because you think his prayers freed you from your addiction to porn?"

"Yeah, I don't like talking about it. I'm glad John kept a lid on it too. He kind of irritated me at first with his claims of seeing visions of me watching porn. Said he traveled in his spirit body and watched me do it. Man! That freaked me out. He helped me kick my addiction for good, though. You could kind of say that was the ultimate type of accountability." Willy looked at the floor and appeared embarrassed.

Ron didn't know how to respond to that. He had been so wrong in his judgment of John, Leah, and the rest of the prayer team. They had walked in sacrificial love, and he had failed miserably. He needed to get it right. Pastor Ron noticed Willy's embarrassment. "Hey, Willy, we're all sinners. Your testimony just convicted me of a terrible sin."

"Yeah?"

"Perhaps, even worse than that porn."

When Pastor Ron called Andy that evening, he asked if Andy could call what remained of the prayer team for a special prayer meeting on Saturday. He wanted to ask their forgiveness for judging their methods of intercession. If the Holy Spirit wanted to lead them in this manner, who was he to interfere? In fact, he wanted to join them in prayer. Their type of intercession worked.

Who shall separate us from the love of Christ? Shall tribulation, or distress, or persecution, or famine, or nakedness, or peril, or sword? Nay, in all these things we are more than conquerors through him that loved us. For I am persuaded, that neither death, nor life, nor angels, nor principalities, nor powers, nor things present, nor things to come, Nor height, nor depth, nor any other creature, shall be able to separate us from the love of God, which is in Christ Jesus our Lord.
Romans 8:35, 37-39 KJV

Chapter Forty-One

On Saturday, the remaining prayer team—Doug, Mary, Carl, Andy, and Eileen—graciously accepted Pastor's request that they forgive him for his blindness, judgmental attitude, and failure to walk in love. They also invited Pastor Ron to join them as they prayed for John's freedom.

Andy opened their time of intercession by thanking God for His presence and restoring unity to their church. After leading the team in singing the Doxology, Andy encouraged everyone to wait quietly for the Holy Spirit to lead them. Two minutes later, Eileen and Andy groaned and landed on the floor.

Pastor Ron gawked at their bodies lying on the floor and reminded himself that God was in this. God works in mysterious ways. Even when Jesus healed people in the Bible, bystanders occasionally said that the person was dead just before they rose up healed. Pastor Ron noticed the rest of the team appeared to be praying quietly to themselves. He trusted Andy would lead the group, but he didn't know how long they'd have to wait or what to do next. Though he was their pastor, he couldn't be the leader here.

He looked at Carl, hoping for some guidance. Carl encouraged Pastor Ron to join him, Doug, and Mary in praying for Eileen and

Andy while they traveled in their spirit bodies. After they prayed for twenty minutes, Andy and Eileen's bodies gently stirred, and Carl and Mary helped them up.

When Eileen and Andy settled in their chairs, they shared how the tentacles of the military industrial complex were responsible for John's arrest. The Holy Spirit told them to pray against the spirits of tyranny, totalitarianism, greed, destruction, cruelty, and deception. They thought other spiritual strongholds needed to be torn down, but the Holy Spirit indicated He wanted them to focus first on those six.

#　　　#　　　#

For the first two weeks of his detention without a cellmate, John praised God by confessing Psalms 23, 46, and 103 over his life. He thanked God for urging him to memorize those Scriptures years ago. For the next two weeks, he centered his thoughts on verses from Romans chapter eight to bolster his faith in God's love and power to intercede on his behalf. The first sixteen verses of chapter eight grounded him in a life that depended on the work of the Holy Spirit. With the next eleven verses, the Holy Spirit had instructed him on a new way of interceding. These Scriptures encouraged him greatly to embrace the spiritual battle he faced. With the last twelve verses, he felt inspired to claim the victory that God's love and sovereignty provided.

Shortly after switching his focus to the verses in Romans eight, John thought the evil one had been defeated. He fell to his knees and raised his hands. "Thank you, Lord, for Your light which is brighter than the darkness. Hallelujah! You said whom You set free is free indeed, and You have given us authority over all the power of the enemy. You promised that if we say to the mountain: 'Be moved into the heart of the sea' and do not doubt in our hearts, the mountain would obey."

John jumped up from his knees and pushed on the door to his cell. "In the name of Jesus, I command these doors to open. I speak to the hearts of the people who have imprisoned me. Because You, Lord, have written steadfast love and faithfulness on the tablet of my heart, I have favor with them and will have outstanding success,[12] and they will release me this very hour."

---

[12] Proverbs 3:3-4, Paraphrased by D. Henry Roome

John stepped back from the door and raised his hands to praise the Lord. "Glory to the King of the Universe! Nothing is too difficult for You. If You supernaturally rescued Peter from prison two thousand years ago, You can do it again for me. Praise the Lord! You are the same yesterday, today, and forever.[13] Your word exhorts me to call upon You, and You will answer me. You will be with me in trouble. You will deliver me and honor me.[14] So, Lord, I am calling for You to deliver me out of this jail. I am standing on the promises in your word. You said Your word shall not go forth void but shall accomplish that which you please."[15]

John sang praises to the Lord as loud as he could, singing his favorite songs from church. His voice had grown hoarse when a guard opened the door and two guards entered his cell. John quieted as he waited to see if the guard would beat him like the last time he sang praises loudly. They put cuffs on him and marched him to an interrogation room.

While he walked, he kept quiet for fear they might beat him. Inwardly, he rejoiced. Just like he prayed, they had opened the door, and they would soon set him free. The room where they brought him did not look like the setting he imagined for announcing his release. That didn't phase him. If they didn't apologize for abusing him, he wouldn't complain. Jesus said to turn the other cheek. John had prayed for his captors, and he would continue to love them.

They sat him in a dimly lit room in front of a small table. Across from him sat two grim-faced men who were probably upset that they had to release him. He could scarcely contain his joy.

"What are you so happy about?" the taller of the two men asked.

"You are going to have to set me free," John replied. "You may not be happy about it, but God will forgive you for the evil you meant to do to me."

"Shut up, you idiot!" the stockier of the two said. "You're not going anywhere."

"You don't know my friend Jesus. At His word he can send a legion of angels to set me free."

---

[13] Hebrews 13:8

[14] Psalm 91:15

[15] Isaiah 55:11

The taller one stood and slapped the table with his hand. "Are your insurrectionist friends planning to spring you?"

"How many times do I have to tell you? I am not an insurrectionist. You might say I'm a resurrectionist because the Bible says I have been united with Jesus in a death like his, that I might be united with him in a resurrection like his. Christ's resurrection power is going to free me."

Why are we listening to him?" the stocky man said.

What are your resurrectionist friends, then, planning to do to undermine the government?"

"We just want to free you from demonic influences. Jesus can set you free. You can know true freedom by turning over your life to Jesus. If you confess your sins, God is faithful and just to forgive you of your sins and cleanse you from all unrighteousness."[16]

"Enough of the religious talk. If you won't tell us what your friends plan, tell us why you are opposing the laws of duly elected government officials."

"I don't oppose duly elected officials, nor laws that are passed by representatives of the people. I submit to bureaucrats and mandates whenever they reflect the will of the people and don't violate God's will."

"We're wasting our time with this J6 Trumper."

"I don't support Trump. There's a better candidate running."

"Are you a member of QAnon?"

John shook his head.

"Come on! Why else do you keep talking about demons controlling government officials?"

"The love of Christ compels me to declare the truth to you. God loves you and wants to set you free from the works of the devil."

"Did God tell you to oppose what the school administration advocated at the board meeting? Are you frustrated because Biden and Trump appear to be the only likely candidates for President?"

"Biden and Trump aren't the only viable alternatives." John grew tired of talking with these goons. Did they think they could elicit a confession right before they released him?

"Oh? Is QAnon fielding a candidate for President?"

"How would I know?" John sighed. He wanted to give these guys one last piece of advice before he pointedly asked them if they

---

[16] I John 1:9 (Author's paraphrase)

planned to release him now. "If you paid attention to the polls, you'd know that RFK Jr. has occasionally been ahead of both candidates. The majority of Americans are tired of the polarization and bickering from people at the extreme ends of the political spectrum. They are ready for someone who doesn't have a hidden agenda and truly cares for the people."

The taller man shoved a paper in front of John. "Are you ready to sign this yet?"

John perused the document. "Nope! No last-minute confession. You can give me back my clothes and let me out of here."

"I told you we were wasting our time. Send this idiot back to his cell."

"Yeah, yeah, give me back my clothes."

The stocky man signaled someone at the door, and two guards entered and put handcuffs on him. John frowned. Were these guys continuing to play like they didn't plan to release him so they could eke out a last-minute confession? God had answered the first part of his prayer and opened his cell door. Certainly, He wouldn't tease John with some kind of mirage.

When the door slammed shut to his cell, he realized how warped his perception of the interview had been. The stocky man had been right. Everything he had said sounded like the rantings of a deranged fool.

John looked heavenward and cried out to the Lord. "God, why didn't You answer my prayer? You won't take me traveling in my spirit body, so I have confessed your word over my needs and have believed you would send angels to perform Your will for my life. Psalm 103 says that angels will obey the voice of Your word. You have sent the Holy Spirit to use me in supernatural ways, so I did not doubt my deliverance would happen. Have I missed something here?"

John kneeled and waited for the Lord to speak to him. He heard nothing, but he had nowhere to go. No matter how long it would take, he would rest in confidence because he knew God wanted to communicate with him. After waiting for over an hour, John felt like talking to God, but he stuffed the urge and continued to concentrate on listening to the Lord for several hours. He focused on God's written word and emptying himself of his own thoughts. As he meditated on several verses in Proverbs, he realized how much pride had motivated him. What a fool he had been!

You have been worse than just a fool. You are a man who is wise in his own eyes. There is more hope for a fool than for you.

[Examine your attitude. Your supernatural experiences have aroused pride in you. Don't mistake pride for confident trust in My power.]

Your pride is an offensive stench in the nostrils of God. That is the real reason He will no longer take your spirit body traveling.

John wept. "Lord, forgive me! Without You, I don't have a hope."

You are hopeless.

[The God of hope will fill you with all joy and peace in believing, so that by the power of the Holy Spirit you may abound in hope,][17]

John raised his voice and prayed, "Lord, when I interceded for others and prayed for myself, I quoted Your word because I believed You were faithful to Your promises."

[Quoting Scriptures and having Bible knowledge can stifle your requests when you allow pride to pervert your heart and misdirect your petitions.]

You are wasting your time trying to make God do something.

"Lord, fill me with Your love so the God kind of love moves me to intercede for others."

Your love is pitiful.

---

[17] Romans 15:13 paraphrase by D. Henry Roome

[Your love is growing. Through patience, you will possess your soul, and you will receive your heart's desire to bring glory to Me.]

"Lord, I trust You to break through the darkness surrounding me."

You will show me the path of life;
In Your presence is fullness of joy;
At Your right hand are pleasures forevermore.
Psalm 16:11 NKJV

Chapter Forty-Two

A week later, the prayer team received their first breakthrough. The government permitted John to have an attorney meet with him, and the attorney comforted John with family news. His parents were taking care of David and Rachael was hiding with her mom. The prayer team —which now included Willy, Carl, Eileen, Andy, Doug, Mary, Pastor Ron, and Francine—continued to intercede for John, and they received another answer to their prayers. Some mainstream media outlets carried stories about John's detention in jail on doubtful charges of insurrection.

The recent news coverage helped make Michael Brauer, his attorney, more available to John and move the legal process forward for either his release or for official charges to be made. Before his second meeting with Michael, John learned more about what happened with the prayer team, and he received much better treatment from his guards. John learned that Doug and Mary had been arrested but had been released because several witnesses testified the couple hadn't been involved in the fighting at the school board meeting.

When John entered the visitor room for his second meeting with his lawyer, he saw a very somber-faced Michael sitting at a plain wooden table. The guard standing at the exit reminded John that no privacy existed anywhere in jail. John greeted Michael and sat across from him. Michael smiled and pulled an envelope out of his briefcase and handed it to John. "You will want to read this right away. It is from your wife."

John bit his inward-folded lips to hold back tears as he read Leah's letter.

Dear Gumby,

I love you more than words could ever tell. Our sudden separation has made the loss of your faithful encouragement and support hard to bear. I miss you for many reasons, as does everyone. Janet, Rachael, and I are praying for you and that your release from jail will be as soon.

Please forgive me for bucking you on your desire to teach me to intercede and get information through spirit-body voyages. The Lord taught me through the sacrificial love of Janet that I had not loved you as I should. Ultimately, the Holy Spirit brought me to a place where I had to face my obligation to love you and put your needs before my friends' opinions and reactions.

God answered your prayers in awesome ways. Rachael now prefers to be called Rachael. God's Spirit has taken Janet and me to unpleasant places in our spirit bodies. We learned of several demonic strongholds that we needed to demolish. As a result, I believe God answered our prayers, and you have freer access to your attorney and can read the letter you are now holding.

While we hid from the FBI, I received word that Pastor Ron endorsed your method of intercession and joined the prayer team. This all happened because the Lord revealed how your spirit-body journeys delivered Willy. Pastor Ron realized the error of his ways when he heard Willy's testimony and learned the extent of your submission to him. He confessed to us his deep sorrow for resisting the Holy Spirit and your efforts to do what God wanted to do. He begs your forgiveness, as do I.

Love,
Leah

John bowed his head and thanked God for His faithfulness. The Lord had worked all things together for good by providing people and orchestrating circumstances to bring about transformation in Rachael's and Leah's hearts. John looked again at the place in the letter where Leah described God moving in her heart. Then he tilted his head back and closed his eyes. Amazing! He had asked the Lord to move supernaturally in defeating the forces of evil. Though he had been impatient, God had been busy working, waiting to reveal the answers to his prayers until he had learned something about patience. He never would have understood about waiting on God if he hadn't been locked up in jail. Yes, he could thank the Lord for his confinement.

John looked up at Michael shuffling papers. "Thank you for the letter, and for all your efforts to get me out of here."

"Well, don't thank me yet. We have a long way to go before we get you out of here. I have been in contact with your pastor, who has devised a rather circuitous route to communicate with Leah. She has managed to find a way to travel to Rochester, and she has called me from there. I have talked with her three times. She's eager to find out how you are doing. If you write her a note, I can get it to her."

Micheal handed John a pen and a legal-length pad of paper. "We've got some options we need to discuss first. You'll be able to write her a long letter or a brief note, as time permits."

"What are my options?"

"The government wants to charge you with insurrection, obstruction of an official government function, assault, and disorderly conduct. All of it, bogus, but they are willing to offer you plea bargains if you plead guilty. Of course, I would recommend turning them down. Your other options include suing them for undue use of force or police brutality, unlawful detainment and invasion of privacy, loss of income due to unlawful detainment, and emotional and psychological injuries from the aforementioned. I have petitioned to have an independent doctor examine your wounds. I need you to sign these agreements and petitions to the court." Michael handed John several forms.

John examined the documents. "Do you want me to sign all of these?"

"You can sign all of them or just the ones that are your top priorities, but I will only use the ones you request me to pursue. What are your priorities? Shall I work on compromises to get you released as soon as possible?"

John scribbled his signature on the forms in front of him. "I am willing to be patient so the corruption responsible for putting me here is exposed, but my family needs me at home. See what you can do to get me out of here quickly without giving the government a free pass on what they did." John chewed on his lower lip. He especially longed to pray with others instead of by himself. While isolated in Jail, he learned to appreciate the value of listening to what the Holy Spirit would show others when rejoining the prayer team.

"I imagine you are eager to see them." Michael raised his brows as he collected the forms John had signed.

John closed his eyes and sighed. "I can see myself hugging my wife and kids right now."

Michael grimaced. "I wish I could reassure you with positive news that you'll be out of here shortly."

John ran his hands through his hair. If God wanted him to wait in jail longer, he knew the Lord would use the time to impart truths to him about God. "I have to let God do His thing. My part is to pray. With God, nothing is impossible."

Michael tapped the pen and notepad in front of John. "Keep this note short. I'm supposed to be out of here in four minutes."

John wanted to thank and encourage everyone, so he wrote the message for Leah, the prayer team, and their pastor:

Dear Leah, Pastor Ron, and prayer team,

> I love you all. Of course, I forgive any misunderstanding or shortcomings. I am doing well now. Thank you for your prayers. Don't forget to pray for the Presidential elections. Recently, I felt the Spirit say that if we didn't elect the right President, we could expect disaster in America. We need a President who will extricate our nation from the war in Ukraine and endless wars throughout the world, dismantle Big Pharma's control over healthcare, and replace spiritual ideologies and pseudoscientific fabrications with compassion and common sense. In my opinion, only RFK Jr. will accomplish that. I also believe he would push legislation that helps the working class instead of the rich, advocate to provide healthcare for everyone, make honest moves to preserve our environment, and restore unity to the nation. Tell David and Rachael that God is faithful to answer their prayers, and I will see you soon.
>
> Love,
> John

John handed his attorney the note and thanked him for his help. Immediately, a guard escorted John back to his cell. Once in his cell, he thanked and praised God for the miraculous work He had done in everyone's life. When he stopped praising the Lord, he sat quietly on his cot. "Lord, have I learned enough patience?"

[What I have begun in you, I will keep on perfecting until we see each other face to face.]

John laughed. "Okay, Lord, I am willing to be patient, but please don't make Leah and the kids suffer for it."

[Your family won't suffer. They will join you in praying. Your patience will be tested in the Presidential elections. The military industrial complex is a formidable foe in the fight to end the war in Ukraine. Likewise, Big Pharma is fueled by greed that will make fixing the healthcare problems more than you can handle in your own strength. Search for other prayer teams and join them in interceding for the nation.]

"Will you continue to use spirit-body journeys?"

[As you wait patiently in faith, the Lord God Almighty will work miracles on behalf of His people. It is through faith and patience that you inherit My promises.]

John buried his face in his hands. God longed for him to be patient and persevere. His Heavenly Father had been patient with him, and now God had provided the way for him to learn patience and perseverance. He couldn't go alone on spirit-body journeys because he had to slow down to learn patience. Knowledge of the enemy's plan just made him rush into intercession too soon. Hurried intercession often meant he prayed out of his own reasoning instead of the Lord's desires.

John looked heavenward again and took a deep breath. "Wow, Lord, You slowed me down in jail to make me learn patience so I could grow in my knowledge of You. That was what You desired most of all, for me to know You and Your tender care for me."

Shortly, a wave of peace swept over John, and he prayed that Leah, David, and Rachael would not have to wait too long to be reunited with him. He left the political problems in God's hands for the moment.

# # #

Three weeks after John's second meeting with Michael, several uncensored media outlets put pressure on the government to allow Leah to stay out of jail if she turned herself in. Once an agreement was reached for her, Michael made arrangements with the judge in charge of John's case for John to do video chats with Leah and his entire family. John also received newspapers so he could enjoy keeping abreast of the news.

Some polls had Kennedy increasing his margin over the other candidates. John believed people saw the lies, selfishness, and divisiveness of the other two candidates. When he considered the possibility of a President who didn't ignore justice to make political points, he fell to his knees and prayed. Though the Holy Spirit didn't show him how to pray, he believed patience would make his faith effective and produce miraculous results.

A month later, a whistle-blower released information to Congress that implicated the FBI in numerous attempts to intimidate people and repress freedom of speech. One of those attempts included planting fentanyl at John's home on the night of his arrest. The administration and the FBI categorically denied the allegations but dropped the charges of sedition against John and Leah.

John embraced a teary-eyed Leah as he exited the jail. He listened intently on the drive home while she described her experiences hiding and the lessons she learned from out-of-body journeys. If he had been released two months earlier, he might have been tempted to interrupt her. He longed now, with everything that was within him, to listen patiently.

When they turned the corner onto their block, John saw numerous cars lining the street. Members of their church stood milling about on their lawn, and a long banner hung across their porch. "Welcome Home John!"

John inched into his driveway to avoid running over people who pounded on his hood and roof, creating a thunderous sound inside. When he stepped out of his car, a teary-eyed Rachael ran into his arms.

"Hey, Partner!" John lifted his daughter off the ground and swung her back and forth. "Oh! God is good!"

"Dad, I am so sorry for the grief I caused you. Will you ever—"

"Hush, that's been forgiven long ago. The Heavenly Father has removed that from you as far as the east is from the west. But we can talk later about where I may have failed you, huh?"

Rachael planted a firm kiss on John's cheek and slid back down onto the driveway. John kissed her forehead before releasing her. Then he gazed at David and grinned. Though David hadn't grown taller in five months, the way he carried himself made him appear to have matured several years.

"During my absence, you've been the man in our family, huh?" John grabbed and squeezed David's right hand and forearm with both hands.

David replied, but the crowd noise grew too loud for John to understand his words. The massive ruckus jangled his nerves and disoriented him. Nothing, however, could lessen the joy he felt at the moment.

"I'm proud of you!" John shouted.

Carl stood on the steps to their porch and shouted above the crowd noise, "God, who has begun a good work here, is faithful to bring it to completion."

The crowd erupted into cheers. Andy and Pastor Ron gave him long embraces. Over the hallelujahs and whistles of dozens of church members and neighbors, John heard Andy and Pastor Ron declare their gratitude to God for answering their hours of intercession for his release from prison. John tried to communicate his gratitude for their prayers, but he doubted they heard what he said. After a few minutes of failing to understand each other, John signaled for the crowd to quiet down. When the noise level lessened, John thanked everyone for their support and prayers, but they still didn't seem to hear him above the hubbub.

Andy stood on the porch and whistled with ear-piercing volume, grabbing everyone's attention. "I can tell my good friend John is exhausted, and more than anything, his heart longs to reconnect with his family. You can see him in church in a few days and around in the neighborhood."

Andy looked over at John, and John nodded, grateful for his friend's thoughtfulness.

John turned to Pastor Ron. "Where did all these people come from?"

Pastor Ron patted John's shoulder. "Between your notoriety and the effectiveness of our new way of interceding, our church has doubled in size."

"Really?"

Andy slapped Pastor's back. "The work God has done in Pastor's heart and his preaching has transformed our church."

"Incredible," John said as he scanned the crowd still milling about on their lawn.

Mary and Doug, along with Carl, Eileen, Janet, and Willy, took turns shaking John's hand or hugging him.

Leah stood tip-toe on the porch. "Thank you, everyone, for this surprise homecoming welcome! John's prison life wasn't easy. I know he will appreciate having space to recover his strength, and we will be grateful for some privacy to make up for the time we lost loving on him."

Thirty minutes later, John settled on their living room sofa between Rachael and Leah. John held Leah's hand while Rachael leaned her head on his shoulder. John wanted to close his eyes and inhale their contentment, but he could tell David wanted to say something.

David sat on the edge of the recliner rocker seat and leaned toward him. "Dad, our whole church is fired up about what God is going to do in the upcoming Presidential elections. Not everyone knows about your type of intercession, but they know that God is guiding and supernaturally answering our prayers. I want to join you in demolishing what the Democratic and Republican parties are plotting."

"Have you heard from the Lord that's what we should do?"

"Of course, that's what He wants us to do."

John raised his eyebrows at David and smiled. "Do you remember when you told me we shouldn't rush in and play God with your sister? You said I needed to wait until I heard from the Lord. When He guides our prayers, we'll see Him do miracles."

"Oh yeah, I guess I got ahead of the Holy Spirit."

John nodded. "My culture or my likes and dislikes have often deceived me into thinking I had the perfect way to pray, and I figured anybody who believed differently had to be wrong. Knowledge of what caused a situation wasn't enough. I needed to wait on the Holy Spirit to show me how to pray."

Leah cocked her head to one side. "You must have learned plenty about waiting on the Holy Spirit while in jail."

John pressed his lips together for a minute. "Well, I am thankful my time in jail taught me patience. I also learned that in many cases knowledge of what caused certain problems wasn't necessary."

"Does that mean everything we learned traveling without our bodies wasn't vital to our intercession? I could have avoided those out-of-body experiences?"

"No, no, they were necessary, but I realized it was more important to have God's heart and understanding concerning what we saw. Our minds are swayed too much by our culture and our preconceived notions. We need God's perspective to pray and accomplish what is best for us. As I grow more intimate with the Lord, I doubt I will require journeys in my spirit body."

Leah nudged John's arm with her elbow. "Does that mean you are ready to pray for our nation now?"

Discussion Questions

1. John wanted to be compassionate to transgender people but lacked a thorough understanding of their problems. How do you feel about the issue? How can you show love and still boldly speak the truth?
2. Patience, humility, love, prayer, and spiritual warfare are some of the key spiritual motifs presented in *Journeys into Suprafuge*. What are the themes you saw? Which ones spoke to you the most?
3. How did John's attitude toward prayer change from the beginning of the novel to the end? What motivates you to pray? When do you see answers to prayer most often?
4. Do strange supernatural phenomena cause strife in your church or family? How can you best deal with it?
5. When you pray, how do you deal with your lack of knowledge of the subject for which you are interceding?
6. How do you motivate yourself to pray? Does it help to pray with a group of people or do you shy away from praying together with others? Why or why not?
7. Do you find your daily routines keep you too busy to intercede for others?
8. John struggled to care about Willy when Willy shunned him. Do you have to work to find sufficient love for people or situations that you long to pray for?
9. In the end, John was overwhelmed by God's love when he learned that God felt having John know Him better was more important than just receiving answers to prayers. Have you ever felt God didn't answer your prayer because He wanted you to learn something? Has unanswered prayer caused you to seek God more?
10. Do you lack patience and endurance when praying? What could you do to motivate yourself to be patient and endure until you receive God's answer? What Bible verses do you use to bolster your faith?
11. Which character in *Journeys into Suprafuge* do you relate to most? In what way do you relate to them?
12. Leah had to overcome her fear of demons, the supernatural, and losing her friends. Pastor Ron had to release his control over

people and his ministry. What are your major obstacles to praying? How can you overcome them?
13. Do you feel inspired to pray for our elected officials? How vulnerable do you feel politicians are to demonic influences? Does that motivate you to pray more?
14. The author imagined demons affecting our healthcare system, the war in Ukraine, the transgender movement, and RFK Jr.'s Presidential campaign. How do you feel the evil one has affected these or similar situations?
15. Are you well-informed about the issues facing our nation? How can you learn more about issues?
16. Did you notice the Holy Spirit in the story was often called *Holy Spirit* without the article, *the*? Does your relationship with the Holy Spirit feel intimate enough that you could just say, "Holy Spirit, how do you feel about this or that?"

About the Author

D. Henry Roome loves to write fictional stories that deal with contemporary issues from a Christian perspective. God has been leading him to learn more about prayer and how to hear and follow guidance from the Holy Spirit. Mr. Roome has on occasion wept as the Spirit moved him to pray. However, if he has ever moaned during intercession, it has never led him to travel with his spirit body detached from his physical body. Even if spirit-body journeys were possible, he doubts whether he would want to do it or would advise anybody else to do it. Mr. Roome graduated from the University of Minnesota in 1972 with a BA in History. In 1995 he graduated from Normandale Community College's nursing program and worked as an RN from 1995 to 2012. In between those times and since then, he has worked as a missionary in Mozambique, Brazil, and Spain. In 2000 he married and three years later began writing fiction. Since 2012 he has focused on missionary work, writing, and working with the local church.

For comments or questions, contact D. Henry Roome at Dhenryroomeauthor@writing2inspire.com. To learn more about the author's writings, go to writing2inspire.com.

Milton Keynes UK
Ingram Content Group UK Ltd.
UKHW012252110624
443988UK00006B/359